D0329536

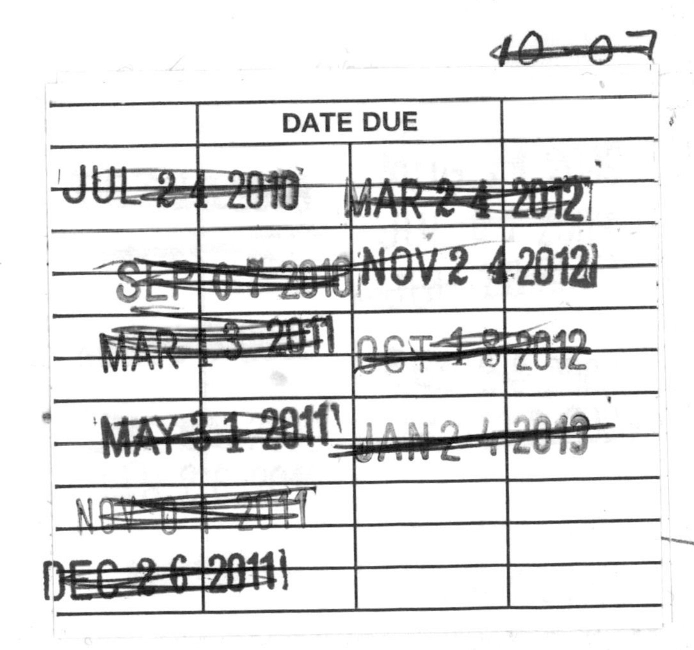
DATE DUE
JUL 2 4 2010
MAR 2 4 2012
SEP 0 7 2010
NOV 2 4 2012
MAR 1 3 2011
OCT 1 8 2012
MAY 3 1 2011
JAN 2 4 2013
NOV 0 1 2011
DEC 2 6 2011

To my sweetie,
who's lived for years with obnoxious cats, large dogs, and overflowing piles of books in our North Georgia cabin.

Acknowledgements

Many thanks go to Maureen and Nancy for their enthusiasm and wisdom, and to the Renaissance Faire Research Team - Shannon, Christina, Graham and Jack, who endured turkey legs, jousting, sunburn and wench kisses galore, to Summer for the vet help, and to my fab editors Andrew Karre and Rhiannon Ross, who read, reread and made great and valued suggestions, and to my awesome agent Richard Curtis (you're the best!), and all the supportive and creative folks who dwell at the teenlitauthors Yahoo group.

GILLIAN SUMMERS

The Tree Shepherd's Daughter

THE FAIRE FOLK TRILOGY

flux™
Woodbury, Minnesota

10.07
9.95

First Edition
First Printing, 2007

Book design by Steffani Sawyer
Cover design by Kevin R. Brown
Cover illustration by Derek Lea
Editing by Rhiannon Ross

Flux, an imprint of Llewellyn Publications

Library of Congress Cataloging-in-Publication Data
Summers, Gillian.
The Tree Shepherd's Daughter / Gillian Summers.—1st ed.
p. cm.—(Faire Folk Trilogy ; 1)
ISBN: 978-0-7387-1081-5
[1. Magic—Fiction. 2. Fairs—Fiction. 3. Fathers and daughters—Fiction. 4. Elves—Fiction. 5. Moving, Household—Fiction. 6. Death—Fiction.] I. Title.
PZ7.S953987Tre 2007
[Fic]—dc22

2007015339

This is a work of fiction. Names, characters, places, and incidents are either the product of the author's imagination or are used fictitiously, and any resemblance to actual persons, living or dead, business establishments, events, or locales is entirely coincidental. Cover models used for illustrative purposes only and may not endorse or represent the book's subject.

Flux
A Division of Llewellyn Worldwide, Ltd.
2143 Wooddale Drive, Dept. 978-0-7387-1081-5
Woodbury, MN 55125-2989, U.S.A.
www.fluxnow.com

Printed in the United States of America

one

Trees. Keelie Heartwood didn't think her life could be more depressing than it already was, but the sight of the green forest before her made her feel gray inside. She could already feel the tingling of her allergic reaction. Wood of any kind made her feel sick, but living trees were the worst.

She stepped forward, slipping a little, and a ghastly smell greeted her. She looked down. She'd stepped inside a circle of rotten and decaying mushrooms. "Gross!"

Thunder boomed in the dark clouds that hung from the overcast sky, promising more rain. More bad news for her white Skechers. Lately all her news had been bad.

The black mud on the wide, winding, tree-lined path sucked at the shoes, staining them as she struggled to keep up with Ms. Talbot's fast pace. The woman was her mother's attorney, and Keelie hated her almost as much as she already hated Colorado. Behind her, the taxi that had dropped them off spun its wheels on loose gravel, then skidded onto the paved road and sped away. Keelie didn't look back in case her longing to return to California showed on her face. She'd sworn to herself she wouldn't cry, but the tears pushed at her throat, trying to rise. Maybe it was the trees. There were too many trees, and her tingling was turning into full-blown jitters.

Heart thumping, she hitched her heavy leather messenger bag higher on her shoulder, not wanting to risk ruining her few remaining clothes. The airline had misplaced her luggage, another black mark against her miserable day, her miserable life.

The enticing scent of roasting meat wafted by, cutting through the wet, earthy smell that covered everything like a moldy blanket. Her stomach growled. The only thing she'd eaten all day was the tiny bag of peanuts and miniature pretzels tossed at her by the flight attendant on the plane from L.A. Too bad she'd been too depressed to accept Ms. Talbot's offer to buy her an Au Bon Pain sandwich at LAX.

At least it wasn't raining any more, though it looked and sounded as if it could start again any second. Dark clouds like spongy cannonballs hung low over the evergreens. Ahead, the trees thinned, revealing two tall, ancient-looking yellow stone towers on either side of oversized wooden gates with black iron hinges. The doorway was flanked by giant topiary lions. One stood on its leafy haunches, its paw on a huge wooden shield that read, "Welcome to the High Mountain Renaissance Festival." The other crouched as if ready to spring.

Framed by the tall trees of the forest, it looked like a leftover set from *The Lord of the Rings*.

Fake, she thought. Everything here was fake, except for the trees. Her fingertips tingled from all the living wood around her. She'd never been in such a big forest. Any minute now she'd break out in hives.

People milled around a ticket kiosk, some regrouping, ready to leave, others digging through wallets and purses for the admission fee. Beside the kiosk, a big painted map of the fairground showed the place was enormous, with lots of streets, even a lake. And a depressing amount of forest. Forget lunch. She was feeling nauseous.

Ahead, Ms. Talbot bypassed the ticket booth and disappeared through the gates, intent on her objective. Keelie was abandoned to make her way on her own. So what else was new? Her mom had been a busy woman, too. Keelie was used to fending for herself. She was going to be sixteen, not six.

Two big security guards in movie armor ran after Ms. Talbot. "Hey miss, stop. You have to buy a ticket."

Keelie smiled, pleased that the lawyer was caught. Served her right.

Keelie flashed a fake smile at the ticket taker, smoothing her hair behind her ears. She'd wait right here for the taxi that would take them to the airport as soon as La Talbot got booted out on her can.

The ticket taker's eyes widened and he bowed low. "You are most welcome, milady. Your father awaits within. Welcome to the High Mountain Renaissance Faire." He handed her a small map and brochure.

Keelie stared at the papers in her hand. Was the man psychic?

"Keelie, get a move on." Talbot was waving her in. The two guards were walking back to the ticket booth, one of them counting money.

Keelie groaned, her elation short-lived. She approached the lions. No one stopped her. A movement at the corner of her eye made her turn. Had the lion shrugged? She could have sworn she saw a green ripple run through its body. Impossible. Must have been a gust of wind.

A flicker to her right. The tasseled tail of the crouching lion had twitched, as if it was ready to jump off its stone planter and leap into the woods. The costumed man at the doorway glanced at her and waved her through. He hadn't noticed the movement, and either she was expected or this place was totally lax about letting people in.

She shivered as she passed under the banner and through the tall gate. It was like a noisy fortress. A raucous prison. Primal drumbeats kept time for clashing trumpets, fiddles, and bagpipes in a dizzying mix that these poor idiots seemed to enjoy.

Despite the friendly greeting on the lion's shield, there would be no welcome for her. She certainly didn't want to be here.

She glanced at her watch. Two hours into her new life and already her shoes were ruined, her luggage was lost, her back hurt, and she'd probably wrecked her manicure. Not to mention the skin-crawling, nauseous feeling she got from the woods. And she was seeing things.

She wanted—no, needed—a hot bath and a massage. Back in the day, Mom would call TJ at the Beautiful Dreamer day spa and make an appointment for side-by-side hot stone massages. Keelie wished she could take the next plane back to California and civilization. Back to Mom.

Mom, who would say, "Okay, babe. Let's talk it over," whenever she'd seen or felt something strange, something inexplicable. The older she got, the more of those talks they'd had. Mom always made her feel normal again.

Except there was no Mom anymore. She inhaled, finding it hard to breathe. The pines pressed in all around, and she felt as if they were murmuring to her. Claustrophobia wasn't far behind, but where could she run where there weren't any trees?

"Hurry along, Keelie," Ms. Talbot's voice came from somewhere ahead. "I've got to get back on the road in thirty minutes, or I'll miss my return flight."

Ms. Talbot, who also worked at Mom's law firm, had apparently drawn the short straw, and it was obvious she wasn't thrilled about it. Keelie imagined how the meeting had gone. "Take the kid to Colorado?" Talbot would have said. "Can't we just drop her off at the airport?"

But no, that would have been too easy, and she was already labeled a flight risk, after the incident the first weekend. A potential runaway who had to be escorted like a baby. It was infuriating, even if it was true.

Irritated, Keelie blinked back the tears that threatened to return.

"Suck it up," she muttered. "Show no fear." She didn't want to be all weepy when she saw her father for the first time since she was a toddler. Her bio dad, she reminded herself.

The mud made slurping noises against her feet as she struggled to follow the lawyer's prim, dark blue suit. She was so not dressed for this. Neither of them were.

The visitors who streamed toward the entryway looked tired, but laughingly retold their favorite parts of their day. Keelie rolled her eyes as they passed. If they'd all lived through the same events, why retell them? Did they all suffer from short-term memory loss?

Ms. Talbot moved upstream through the human river, effortlessly sidestepping to avoid colliding with the tourists. How did she do it? Her high heels should have sunk into the mud, but she moved as efficiently as if the rustic path was the polished granite floor of Talbot, Talbot, and Turner's L.A. office.

Keelie moved faster, determined not to stop. No whining, she told herself. Ms. Talbot paused at a jewelry booth and talked to the clerk behind the counter. She pointed toward Keelie and brandished a folder. Keelie knew its tidy white label read, "Keliel Heartwood," project number whatever in Ms. Talbot's busy life.

The pinch-faced clerk behind the counter, plump and tightly corseted in her medieval costume, shook her head.

"Don't know, ma'am," she said. Her enormous bosom

looked as if it was about to burst out of her bodice, like cantaloupes in bondage. She looked over at Keelie, frowning.

An ancient relic of a man, his weird medieval outfit covered by a disgustingly greasy leather apron, tapped Ms. Talbot's shoulder.

Keelie hid a smile as the attorney stifled a shriek.

"She means the woodcarver," the old man told the clerk, speaking with an outrageously fake British accent. He turned to Keelie. "So you're one of them? We heard you'd be coming. Ye be wanting to go down the way a bit, miss. Heartwood's in the two-story wood building, next to the jousting. Isn't that right, Tania?" He cocked an overgrown eyebrow at the big-bosomed clerk.

Jousting. Keelie shook her head. Too much. And what did he mean that she was one of them? She wasn't one of anything in this place. She pretended to look at the necklaces and charms on display. A box of polished stones caught her eye.

"How much are these?"

"Just two dollars, dearie." The word was affectionate, but the woman's tone was cold.

Keelie pulled two crisp bills from her bag and laid them on the counter, careful not to touch the wood. Ms. Talbot called her name from farther up the dirt road. Keelie ignored her. She examined the rocks in the box and pulled out a white-veined pink oval. "I'll take this pink one. What is it?"

"Rose quartz." The dollars had vanished. "Go on, that woman's calling for you. And thanks for the business. This is the second straight week of bad weather. One more like it and we'll all be in the Muck and Mire Show."

Keelie took it, afraid the woman might start a laying on of hands and chanting to the rain gods. Thunder boomed again, causing Tania the melon smuggler to scrunch her face with worry.

"Good thing it's near closing time," she said. "Looks like another devil of a storm brewing."

Wind gusts made the colorful banners overhead snap and stretch against their ropes. The breeze smelled sharply of ozone—rain was definitely near. Keelie hooked her leather bag back on her shoulders, then glanced down at her white sweater set and light blue linen capri pants and muttered, "I shouldn't make fun of La Talbot. I am so overdressed for Never Never Land."

Across the wide dirt path, a family guffawed as they stumbled out of a tent marked "Magic Maze," bumping into each other dizzily. Keelie hated them for being happy, for being together. The mother glanced at them as they passed, eyebrows raised as she eyed Ms. Talbot's suit. Keelie figured their clothing made them as remarkable as the jesters, stilt walkers, and medieval peasants that swarmed the grounds. Her stomach rumbled, again. "Ms. Talbot, can we—"

The lawyer was gone. Keelie looked around. No blue suit anywhere.

A crash sounded behind her. A shelf of jewelry stands had fallen. Necklaces were pouring onto the muddy ground.

"My stuff!" Tania scrabbled around, gathering them up. "This Faire is cursed."

"Hush, girl. Don't let management hear you say that." The old man had lost his accent.

The place was packed with visitors, not all heading toward the exits, and it was hard to go in a straight line. She thought she saw a glimpse of the blue suit, but then she was surrounded as a crowd of faux peasants, cheering and singing, came down the path from the crest of the hill.

One huge man, wearing a red coat lined with fake fur and trimmed with dozens of jingling silver bells, yelled out in a megaphone voice, "Make way for the king and queen."

The peasant-dressed crowd that surrounded Keelie shouted, "Huzzah, huzzah."

She tried to push her way out, holding her breath. It was humid and hot, and several of the peasants were carrying authenticity a bit too far. Her nose detected that some of them had a serious need to get reacquainted with using modern-day deodorant.

A flash of blue flitted through the trees on the other side of the path. Ms. Talbot.

Keelie shoved her way clear, then saw the attorney waving her folder in a man's face. The man wore a jester's hat and multicolored patched silk pants. And stilts. He leaned over from the waist, trying to read the papers Ms. Talbot waved. A black-haired goth girl stepped up, dressed in a form-fitting black gown with long, flowing sleeves pushed back to show tight undersleeves that buttoned from her elbows to her wrist. She spoke to Ms. Talbot and pointed toward a clearing on the other side of the hill, then turned and melted into the milling throng. The man on stilts yelled, "Long live the King and his new Queen."

"Yeah, whatever," Keelie said. Long live the King and his new Queen. Well, she hoped so. Long lives to them. She wondered what had happened to the old Queen. Probably came to her senses and fled this loony bin.

Keelie blinked back the tears that seemed to hit her by surprise every once in a while, even though Laurie's mom, Elizabeth, told her she was taking it very well. Yeah, well, that meant she could fake being okay when in public, and she wasn't about to quit now. She blinked fast to get rid of the wetness without having to wipe at her eyes and give herself away.

Through blurred vision she saw another flash of dark blue. She pushed through the jostling crowd, ignoring the curious looks she got from several of them. She suddenly realized she wasn't queasy any more. She looked down at the smooth pink rock in her hand. Whatever works. She tucked it in her pocket.

At the other side of the mob was a throng of people watching a man with a bird with a leather hood on its head. Falconry. Okay, now this was interesting. She'd studied medieval history in eighth grade at Baywood Academy and had done a report on falconry.

Up close, she could see the big falcon also had long leather ribbons tied around its legs. Jesses, she remembered.

Poor birds. They were prisoners, too. Just like Mom had said, the people here were a bunch of childlike dorks who wanted to live in the Middle Ages. They were totally out of touch with reality. Who'd want to relive a time when there was no sanitation and people walked around with scented pomander balls held up to their noses to cover the stench of unwashed bodies?

Mom had warned her about these Renaissance folks. And about her father, who had done the medieval version of running away to join the circus.

An owl hooted next to Keelie and she saw that there were more of them in the enclosure, along with hawks and falcons.

There had been a stuffed owl in Mr. Stein's biology lab at Baywood Academy, but it had looked bald and moth-eaten. The white owl on its stand swiveled its head to follow her, yellow eyes huge and unblinking, feathers fluffy and soft. Keelie wished she could touch it.

A man in a puffy-sleeved white shirt and soft, black knee-high boots walked into the center of the circle, a hawk on his gloved hand. Despite the bird's size, the man held it as if it didn't weigh much. "Can anyone tell me why this bird's eyes are covered?" His voice was loud, and he was faking an English accent, too. Voices offered answers.

Keelie looked at the bird, its wings fluttering. It shifted its weight from foot to foot, as if impatient.

"Hello. Interested in the birds?" The voice made her turn quickly. She hadn't heard anyone come up. The woman wore her hair boy-short and was dressed in a feminine version of the falconer's outfit, with a big poet's shirt and tall boots. She nodded at the owl Keelie had admired.

"This is Moon. She's a snowy owl," the woman said. "She bites, so don't get too near."

"She's beautiful," Keelie said. Her voice sounded grumpy to her own ears. She didn't want to be here, and she hadn't planned to live in the Colorado woods with a bunch of hippie weirdos, but she wasn't a liar. The birds were incredible.

The sound of running feet made them both look up.

"I need more bait," a man said breathlessly, sweat dripping down his sun-reddened face, following the tributaries formed by the wrinkles around his eyes.

"Ariel is in the tree." He pointed up toward the tops of the tall pines around the clearing.

Keelie looked up into the wind-tossed tree tops, not sure what she was looking for. A climbing woman? Branches swayed and needled boughs fluttered wildly in the wind, but near a fork in the trunk of a large tree she saw the still outline of a large bird. Ariel, she bet. She wanted to tell her to fly free. Keelie would escape, if she could. If she had wings, she would fly home.

Or maybe she'd fly back to the past and cherish each day with her mom. She'd tell Mom not to take the flight back from San Francisco to L.A. She'd tell her not to trust the commuter plane.

Her chest hurt. She took a deep breath. No crying. No more. "Fly free and never look back," she whispered.

"Keelie, keep up. I'm running out of time," Ms. Talbot said. She was standing about twenty feet away and, for the first time, looked a little cross. A thin dribble of mud stained one of her stockings.

The bird handler looked Ms. Talbot up and down, then bit her lip, as if trying to keep in whatever she was going to say.

"Can you tell me where I can find Mr. Zekeliel Heartwood? This is his daughter. I promised to deliver her in person, and it's getting late. I have to catch a flight back to California." Ms. Talbot's smile seemed insincere.

The bird woman pointed to a leaning post in the crossroads, covered in haphazardly nailed street signs. "Follow Water Sprite Lane to Wood Row. He's on the left. Can't miss him." She turned to Keelie. "And you're his daughter. I'm ashamed of myself for not seeing it. You're the image of him." She grinned. "I'm Cameron. I'm a friend of your dad's."

A friend? She just bet. But despite her certainty that the Faire was full of geeks and weirdos, for some reason she felt herself warm to Cameron. She frowned and walked away quickly, then slowed as she realized that she didn't need to follow Ms. Talbot's blue suit. She knew the way. Cameron's directions were clear.

A few yards away the path split. The left side of the fork was marked "Wood Row." Just her luck. More wood. The right read, "To The Jousting Ring." She pulled the map out. Sure enough, a big oval was marked "Jousting." Interested, and not eager to see if Ms. Talbot succeeded in her quest, she took the right fork.

She jumped back as a big bird flew in front of her, swooping low over the path before arching into the trees. For a second she thought it would hit her. Was it the hawk? She looked up and saw a flash of bright red. Not the hawk. There was too much wildlife around here for her taste.

The jousting ring wasn't a ring at all. It looked like a sandy football field, with a grandstand on one side and a wooden wall across from it. People still milled around excitedly, and the stands were crammed full. Food vendors hawked steak on a stick and turkey legs.

"Get your food poisoning on a stick," Keelie muttered, keeping a tight grip on her bag. The place was full of pickpockets and thieves, according to Mom.

As she climbed the hilly road, she got a better look at what lay beyond and stopped, mouth open. Knights in armor galloped toward each other on giant horses, just like in the movies. For a moment, she wasn't at a twenty-first-century Renaissance Faire. She was there, in sixteenth-century England.

The horses were covered in brightly colored cloth that rippled with their movements, and the knights' armor looked real, although instead of being shiny, most of it looked sort of dented and used.

They held long wooden pole lances, and every time they passed each other one would try to knock the other down by hitting him with the pole, which made the crowd go wild. Bloodthirsty geeks—what a concept.

Behind her the birds cried out, their keening cries competing with the long trumpets blowing fanfares, yells from the crowd, and the clang of armor and swords, a confusion of sound that echoed and swirled through her body.

Her father was close by. This place was supposed to be her home now. How scary was that? She looked around at the cheering crowds and the costumed players. She didn't know anybody aside from Ms. Talbot. Even though she didn't like her, she was a part of her old life, and Keelie wanted to hold on to every little piece that was left.

When she was gone, Keelie'd be left alone in this lopsided fairy tale land. Well, not alone. She'd be with her father, and she'd heard enough about him to know that life was going to be less fairy tale and more nightmare.

She imagined what would happen if her friends ever learned that her father was no better than a gypsy, a man who made his living traveling between Renaissance Faires, going from show to show, hawking his wares to the public like some Wild West snake oil salesman. It sent shivers of embarrassment coursing through her.

When her friends asked about her dad, she told them he was in the government, working for the National Park Service in Alaska. It was too remote for him to come home. That would definitely be preferable to the truth. Alaska seemed very REI and outdoorsy, but this—this was not dealing with reality. She watched a woman go by, carrying garlands of flowers to sell as hair ornaments. She wore a laced-up bodice and a flowing skirt. It seemed to be a kind of uniform around here. Some wore their bodices tighter than others. Trailer-park tight.

Raindrops hit her, and Keelie touched her blunt-cut hair, smooth and shiny from her morning session with gel and a straightening iron. Now it was going to frizz and curl in every direction. She'd spent an hour on it for nothing.

The hawk screeched in the trees behind her. She'd thought she was like the hawk, tied up, blindfolded, and told what to do, but maybe the hawk was scared. Maybe it needed the safety of its handler's arm. Who knew? No one had asked the hawk what it wanted before it was captured and tamed. No one had asked Keelie before turning her life upside down.

Lugging the bag, she caught a whiff of a delicious green scent. Not a scary tree smell. More like the smell of a meadow in the morning, or so she imagined. Her allergies had kept them away from forests and parks. She followed the smell to a booth with a wooden sign that said "Herbs." By the doorway was a smaller sign: "Remedies for sore muscles and bad cooking." Was that a joke?

The shelves inside held baskets, bottles, and different kinds of soaps and lotions. A whole section was labeled "Herbal Remedies." That got her attention. She loved anything to do with medicine, although her mother would have dragged her out of here. She had scowled when Keelie mentioned volunteering at the hospital and told her to focus on her studies. She had, of course, meant her future law studies.

It made Keelie feel guilty to be in the shop, even if her mom was gone and couldn't tell her to leave it alone. Would it betray Mom's wishes if she just glimpsed the herbal tinctures and salves and sniffed a few? The open sample jars smelled wonderful.

The lady in charge wore a flowing purple gown laced in front with a silver leather cord. A snowy apron was pinned to her chest with straight pins and tied behind her waist in a bow. Her big, flowing sleeves almost dragged on the ground and were laced to her shoulders with more silver cord.

This was something Keelie could see herself wearing—if she were going to stay here, that was.

"Can I help you find something?"

Keelie lifted an intriguing pot. "What's this used for?"

"It's a form of liniment for sore knees."

"Keelie Heartwood, where are you?" The call from outside almost made her heart stop. She'd forgotten Ms. Talbot! It was as if her mom's voice had called out, reminding her that this wasn't her world. The herb woman seemed startled, too, and seemed about to speak.

Keelie didn't give her a chance. She stepped outside, looking up the hill toward the sound of Ms. Talbot's voice. She tripped on the lifted end of a flat gray paver and went down hard on her knees.

Her bag flew off her shoulder and hit the side of the stone, spilling her belongings down the hill. Keelie jumped up and ran, grabbing things up before anyone could get them. Her hairbrush, with leaves stuck in it; her extra panties, muddied; her journal, safe—thank goodness. With each thing she scooped up, the tears she'd fought earlier came closer to the surface. No amount of blinking would send them back. She brushed her arm across her face and reached for her clear plastic toiletry bag.

A hand reached it first, and Keelie followed it up as the person straightened. Knee-high laced boots, emerald green tights, a fancy tight black and gold jacket with a hawk embroidered on the chest, and a green and black satin cape.

What an outfit. And above it all, a handsome face like a California surfer, all blonde and sun-browned.

The boy smiled and handed her the bag. She took it from him, unable to say a word, hovering between extreme thrill and rock-bottom mortification.

"Here's your bag, Keelie Heartwood." The woman from the herb booth had picked up her leather bag. The stuff that hadn't rolled downhill poked out of it at crazy angles.

"Thanks." Keelie shoved her panties into it before the guy could see, then dropped in the rest of what she'd managed to gather.

"Did you get everything?" His voice was low and sweet.

"Yes. I mean, I don't know."

"Oi've got her mirra."

She turned. A massive man held her pocket mirror, the little blue plastic clamshell, pinched between two very grimy fingers. He was caked in mud, every inch of him, and behind him were three other grinning Mud Men.

The head mud guy held out her mirror. She reached for it, and he laughed and tossed it to one of his mud buddies. Keelie knew they meant it to be funny, but all she could think of was Christmas morning last year, when she'd found the mirror in the toe of the stocking her mom had fixed for her. Mirrors and lipstick. It was a tradition.

Tears ran down her cheeks, and she didn't wipe them away. Why didn't it rain? Why didn't it rain so that all these bozos with their stupid kiddie tricks would go inside and leave her alone? No one could see her tears if it was raining, and she felt as if she could cry all day and all night.

"Ho there, Blurp," the prince beside her called out. "Give the lady back her mirror, or I'll thrash ye with my sword."

Blurp, the mud guy, roared with laughter, then glanced at Keelie. Something crossed his face. Regret, maybe, although he was too coated in mud for her to tell. "Here, lad," he said, and tossed him the mirror.

The prince wiped it clean with his beautiful satin cloak and offered it to her, bowing from the waist.

Keelie nodded, but her nose was going to run if she said anything, and she couldn't come up with a smile.

A girl in a pink and gold hoopskirt picked her way through the mud, a golden harp cradled in her arms. She glanced scornfully at the mud guys, then frowned at Keelie and the prince. Long golden curls twisted down her back, like a fairy princess from a storybook.

"Lord Sean o' the Wood, the Queen awaits your pleasure," she said, eyeing Keelie up and down.

Lord Sean? How likely was that?

"Thank you, Lady Elia." He turned back to Keelie, looking embarrassed. "I have to go. I hope you found everything."

"I think so, thanks." Her voice seemed kind of choked, but at least she got the words out.

"Oh, you poor child," Lady Elia said, pouting.

Poor child? Where did this Elia person get off calling her a child? They seemed to be the same age. Keelie felt her eyes scrunch up with distrust. The airy-fairy princess pouted like someone who wanted to be admired. Keelie knew the type. Her long wavy hair and green eyes probably got her lots of attention.

"Did you have an accident?" the golden girl asked. "Shall we call security?" She twitched her skirt back as if Keelie might get mud on it. Keelie hated her already.

"No need," Lord Sean o' the Wood said. "She says she's fine. I think she is, too. Right, Keelie? I may call you Keelie, may I not?"

Had she just heard that? Keelie nodded dumbly, afraid to look at him, in case he didn't mean what she thought he did.

"Keelie Heartwood! Come up right now. I've found your father." Ms. Talbot's strident voice rang through the crowd. "You'll have time to play with your new friends later."

Play? Mortified, Keelie froze. The pink and gold girl folded her arms and stared at her, eyes narrowed.

Keelie was positive that Ms. Talbot's use of the word "friend" was premature.

Murmurs erupted around her. She thought she heard someone murmur "Heartwood."

She didn't wait to hear what they said. Dork! she thought. She was a dork for coming here, and a dork for mooning over the prince. Lord Sean. As if.

She whirled and ran up the hill, trying to outrun her humiliation. Slipping in the mud, she still moved fast enough to get all the way to the top without looking back. Her father was up there somewhere, and that was trouble enough.

two

Ms. Talbot stood at the top of the hill, a disbelieving look on her face as she watched Keelie approach. A small, smiling brown woman stood next to her, looking just like a gingerbread man's wife from a kid's picture book.

Keelie glanced down at her capris and realized she was smeared with mud. She stood, embarrassed, in front of the attorney.

"I'm Mrs. Butters, from the tea shop just beyond yon clearing," the little brown woman said. "When I saw you fall, I said to myself, *Mrs. Butters, we've got to get that poor girl something to clean off with.*" She held out a damp washcloth and a tea towel.

Keelie was reaching for the washcloth when Ms. Talbot put her hand up, her frown deeper than before.

"You've set me back two minutes, Keelie. Be considerate." She turned to Mrs. Butters and smiled grimly. "Mrs. Butters, Keelie will come back soon. She's got to see her father first. Follow me. We're almost done."

Almost done, she'd said, as if Keelie was a chore to finish quickly. She ignored the looks and giggles from the people walking by. She must have looked like a little kid, dirty and chastised, running behind her angry mother.

Mrs. Butters followed them up the road, either muttering to herself or speaking to them. Ms. Talbot charged ahead, not paying any attention.

Keelie heard a crowd cheering. The sound came through the trees, and as they arrived at the top of the path she saw the brightly colored flags of the jousting field below. The cheers came from the covered grandstand.

Two knights in armor galloped toward each other on giant horses, each holding a long spear. It looked real. She slowed down, then hurried up the path to where the trees cleared. Here she had a better view of the battle below. One knight and his horse were dressed in black-and-white stripes, and his opponent wore green.

Keelie slowed, sure they were going to miss each other. It seemed too dangerous to do for real. With a giant clash, the knights' spears hit the brightly decorated shields they carried. The knight in black-and-white was knocked back, almost lying down on his horse's back, before snapping back up in his oddly shaped saddle.

They'd done it; they'd really hit each other. Amazed, Keelie noticed the crowd was on its feet, cheering and screaming, just like at a football game.

As he turned his horse, she saw that the green knight's shield had a lion on it. He stretched out an armored hand. A squire on the ground tossed him a lance.

"Keelie Heartwood!" Ms. Talbot's voice floated over the crowd's noise.

Keelie tore her attention from the joust. It was the best thing she'd seen so far.

She hurried toward a clearing with several buildings, not that she was anxious to get this over with, but every time Ms. Talbot called her name, everyone turned around and looked.

The wooden post at the end of the path had four signs on it. The top one read "Rose Arbor, Teas," then "Galadriel's Closet" and "Village Smithy, Swords, Armor, Horses Shod," but it was the last one that caught Keelie's eye. It read simply "Heartwood." She glanced at her map. Sure enough, this was it. The end of everything.

Her heart pounding, Keelie entered the clearing. Ahead of her, Ms. Talbot waited, arms folded, in front of a two-story wood-and-stone building with a thatched roof straight out of a fairy tale. It looked familiar, and she immediately knew why.

Her father had sent her a replica of it for Christmas the year she'd turned five. The play set included a two-story medieval house with little animals and furniture. He'd sent her a copy of his shop.

Ms. Talbot stepped into the shadow of the building's open first floor, and a tall, slender man appeared briefly near the shadow's edge. Keelie couldn't see his face, but she grasped her bag more tightly, clutching it to her chest like a security blanket. It had to be him.

Zeke Heartwood. Her father.

Keelie quickly crossed the clearing and stepped onto the cool flagstone floor of the building. She was surrounded by wooden furniture and the fragrance of sawn lumber. She felt the presence of the furniture around her, but instead of the unwelcome feelings wood brought on, she felt she was surrounded by friends. Browsers still lingered here, and she pushed past them through the narrow walkways between displays, looking for the man she'd spotted earlier.

A nearby table glowed like warm honey. It was beautiful. Her hands trembled and her breathing was unsteady. It was probably more to do with the wood than the proximity of her father. She was so not going to cry.

Put an end to it. Even if she threw up or burst into blisters, she'd stop this awful shaking. She let her quivering fingers trail along the tabletop. The surface was like silk, yet her fingertips tingled from the contact, as if they'd been scraped. A vision of a tree with a dainty canopy of saw-toothed leaves came into her mind. Alder, she thought. She frowned and rubbed her fingertips to rid herself of the feeling. Her odd gift really had followed her here. She thought it might have been her imagination, but it was true. There hadn't been much wood on the plane or in the cab, and she'd always avoided living trees. Impossible here.

Freak. An echo of the taunt had bounced around in her skull since kindergarten. She'd learned to keep her odd curse to herself. It was nothing useful, like telling the future. She could only identify wood. Some people channeled spirits, she channeled trees.

It had only been handy once, when she'd astounded her class by correctly identifying all the hardwoods on campus without once glancing at the field guide. Her biology teacher had commented on her unique perception. Her friends had been impressed and thought she'd been studying, but Mr. Brooks had watched her closely. He'd noticed she'd come up with the name after touching each tree's bark. Too bad she'd ruined the moment by barfing. She'd barely made it to behind a bush before yakking up lunch.

She thrust her hand into her pocket to shelter it, to stop the trembling. It touched the rose quartz, and the buzzing and tingling receded. Had it been the rock? She pulled her hand away.

A nearby box beckoned, the grain of its wood pronounced, like veins on pale skin. She longed to touch it. Her fingers tightened into fists and she thrust her hands back into her pockets, grabbing for the rose quartz. The wood sense faded again, allowing her to appreciate the beauty of the furniture. She gasped with pleasure as she saw a group of benches and chairs. Twisting vines had been used to hold the rustic pieces together, making them look like court furniture for a forest fairy kingdom. Gleaming crystals sparkled from knots on branches and from crannies created by the binding vines. She was never going to drop the rock again.

Something furry rubbed around Keelie's ankle. Startled, she cried out and tried to back up, then tripped. Hands in her pockets, she couldn't regain her balance and landed, hard, on her knees. Not again, she thought, dismayed. Her cell phone clattered onto the stone and split into two muddy pieces. The rose quartz went flying.

After a while, the pain subsided enough that she could breath again, although the buzzing was back. A huge orange cat sat nearby, gazing at her with huge eyes the color of leaves. Its look seemed knowing, as if it recognized Keelie and knew why she was here. And resented her, she thought.

"Believe me, I don't want to be here," she muttered, rubbing her sore knees. Two falls in one morning. She wasn't usually a klutz. The cat blinked and looked away with typical kitty disinterest.

Keelie sat back, stretching her legs out. Her knees throbbed and her pants were scuffed. A little speck of blood had soaked through on one knee. Ouch. She was afraid to look. A wave of nausea overtook her. Not from the sight of blood. She could handle that. It was the wood, pressing in around her. She scrambled for the rose quartz and sighed with relief as her fingers closed around it.

"Are you okay?"

She looked up. Ms. Talbot stood over her.

"I'll live," Keelie said, feeling a little more like her California self. "I'll definitely have some bruises, though." Chunks of dried mud coated the floor where she had fallen. "At least it knocked some of this mud loose."

"You wouldn't be muddy if you'd stayed with me," Ms. Talbot said.

A slim, long-fingered hand held part of her slimy, mud-covered cell phone out to her. She reached for it, but the phone vanished, and the cool fingers clasped her stained and filthy hand. She looked up, startled.

The slender man from the shadows stood where Ms. Talbot had been a moment earlier. She forgot to breathe as she looked into the familiar, yet strange, image of her own face. He had the same weird green eyes, the same bone structure, the same hair. Here was the source of her looks. Not Mom, with her straight black hair and almond-shaped brown eyes. Keelie's throat constricted.

She wanted the warmth she saw in those eyes to be for her. Would she betray Mom if she let him claim her? She'd wanted this moment since she was little. Mom knew it. Keelie swallowed, and then said it.

"Dad."

"Keelie." She felt his fingers tremble slightly against hers. His eyes were wide, looking at her as if he was memorizing her. His hand tightened around hers.

She suddenly remembered him holding her high up by his shoulder, safe with his strong arms around her. How little had she been, that she could sit in the crook of his arm? They'd walked through woods filled with giant trees, and he pointed out the names of the trees in the lush forest canopied in bright fall colors. He'd pointed to an alder tree and said that a dryad lived in it. Why did she suddenly remember that?

Mom's face flashed through her mind. She saw again

the little wrinkle that formed between her eyes when she disapproved of something. Keelie felt weak and silly for giving in to this need for a father. Just because she felt sorry for herself was no reason to call Zeke Heartwood "Dad," a word that to her was as full of love as "Mom." A word that had to be earned.

How could it be possible to want love from someone who had abandoned you when you were a toddler? Laurie would've laughed at her if she'd been here. She would have told her not to be so needy.

Her cheeks grew hot. She didn't want her father to see her cry. She quickly snatched her hand out of his and stood up. She hitched her messenger bag over her shoulder and reached her hand out for her cell phone.

He searched her face with those woodland green eyes—the same color as hers, unusual enough that strangers asked her if she wore colored contact lenses. She'd secretly been proud that this was something she'd inherited from her father. A piece of him that was a part of her forever.

Sometimes Mom would stroke her hair and say, "Keelie, you have beautiful eyes." She'd have a faraway look on her face. Mom's brown eyes could be cold and dark, like little rock chips, and there was usually very little wistfulness about her.

Her father handed Keelie her cell phone and the battery. She snapped it together and shoved it back into her bag, not bothering to wipe it clean. "Where's Ms. Talbot?"

He seemed disappointed. Good. What did he expect, a love-fest?

"She left," he said, still kneeling on the flagstones.

The blood drained from Keelie's face. Her lips felt cold and stiff. She didn't care for Ms. Talbot, but she was her last connection to the life she shared with her mother, and now she'd abandoned her at this medieval freak show.

"She didn't say goodbye," she cried, and hated the piteous sound of her voice.

Her father stood up, towering above her. "She said she had to catch her plane back to California. Don't worry, Keelie, it's going to be okay. I won't leave you."

"Again, you mean?" Keelie fought back tears. His hurt look made her feel good. She'd been hurting for two weeks. Take that, Zeke Heartwood. That's what happens when you uproot someone and force them to leave their home.

A woman cleared her throat. "Excuse me, but how much is this dresser?" She looked at Zeke, waiting for an answer.

The woman had bleached blonde hair with half an inch of roots showing, and she wore a laced leather vest with no blouse underneath and a long leather skirt. Mugs, a sword, and a leather pouch hung from a black belt with silver spikes. She wore wide leather bracelets, Xena-Warrior-Princess style, bristling with silver spikes.

None of the costumed women Keelie had seen so far had been dressed so outrageously.

Her father seemed to study Keelie's reaction, then turned to the lady. "I'll be right back to answer your questions. I need to see to my daughter."

Despite her resolve to be less needy, a lump formed in Keelie's throat when he called her his daughter.

"Let's go up to our apartment," he said. Our apartment.

One of the mud players who'd teased her earlier entered

the shop. He carried a paper grocery sack with a mound of yellow fabric sticking out of it. He looked a little sheepish when he saw Keelie.

"Hey, Zeke," he said, casually eyeing the woman in black leather. "I thought your daughter might like to borrow these. Seeing how folks might mistake her for one of the Muck and Mire Show Players in her present garb, we thought we'd seal her fate." He grinned and handed the bag to her father.

Zeke opened the bag and pulled out a pile of fabric. He shook it, and the material fell open to reveal a tunic that seemed clean but was dirt-stained to a dingy brown, and a huge, full yellow skirt. He turned it around, examining it.

Horrified, Keelie saw that the skirt had big, red hand prints painted on the backside. The last item he removed from the bag was no better—a purple bodice with frayed pink ribbons. On the front and back were big square patches with huge zigzag stitches.

"That can't be for me," she whispered.

"You'll need garb for every day," her father said. "You want to fit in, don't you?"

"Fit in where, the circus?" Heat crept into her cheeks at the thought of walking around in that hideous outfit.

The mud guy laughed, but her father frowned at her, as if he'd suddenly realized that daughters weren't all sugar and spice. Take that, Keelie thought.

"They're clean," Zeke said. "You'll only have to wear them until we get you something else. Thanks, Tarl."

"You aren't going to make the poor kid wear that Technicolor clown outfit, are you?" The bleached blond Renaissance biker babe looked outraged.

The mud man shrugged. "Whatever. Just trying to help."

Yeah, Keelie thought. Help her be ostracized. She'd keep her normal clothes on forever, if she had to. She began to feel itchy from the dried mud sticking to her skin, though. She'd kill for a hot shower.

"Honey, you'll only make her a laughingstock if you make her wear those rags. She needs decent garb." The blonde caught Keelie's gaze and shook her head. Men, she seemed to say.

Keelie smiled at her for the help, even though the woman's concept of decent clothes was probably illegal somewhere. Funny that the walking fashion nightmare stood up for her. She looked from the mud man to her father to the biker babe. She would never fit in with these people. And she didn't want to live in a pretend world, playing dress-up.

The medieval biker babe started to wander away, browsing through the furniture. Zeke looked relieved. Tarl the mud man followed her around with his eyes.

"Hey, I'm camped down at the Shire," he called to her. "Mine's the big Viking tent with the wooden dragon out front. Stop by for a beer later."

The woman looked him up and down. "Sure. I'll come by. After dark, okay?"

Keelie was nauseated. The thought of these two ancient and homely relics doing it was too gross.

Zeke didn't seem to notice anything weird. "Thanks

for the clothes, Tarl," her father said. "I appreciate you coming to the rescue." He exchanged a knowing look with Tarl the muddied nutcase.

What was that about? Maybe it was about how Zeke was now saddled with a daughter? Some "just us guys" thing? Or maybe it had to do with the Rennie biker babe. Ugh.

She looked around the shop at the female shoppers who'd occasionally gaze at her dad with hungry looks in their eyes. Yeah, she'd definitely cramp his lifestyle.

Tarl the mud man smiled at Keelie, but she didn't return it. She turned away and pretended to look at her nails, then noticed the dirt caked under her French manicure. Ew!

"I'll see you later, Zeke. And you, too, Keelie."

Keelie acted as if she didn't hear him. She knew she was being a brat, but she didn't care. Let old Zeke figure out what he'd gotten himself into. Maybe he'd ship her back, like a Christmas puppy that grew too big. She pictured herself arriving at LAX with a note pinned to her shirt: "SORRY. DIDN'T KNOW GIRLS COULD BE SO OBNOXIOUS."

She ran her hands along a wooden chair. It hummed with energy underneath her hand. She snatched her hand back and stared at the chair. Her wood reaction was much worse here. Mom had said it was an allergy from her dad's side of the family. Now wasn't the time to ask, though. She could see she'd really ticked off the old man.

"Let me show you where you'll live," her father said. He looked tired.

No, now was definitely not the time to ask.

"Come on, you can change upstairs." He handed her the grocery sack, the ugly clothes stuffed back in.

Reluctantly, she accepted it. Not that she planned to change. Not into those clothes. Not into his daughter. She was her mother's daughter. She would always be Keelie Hamilton. She was stuck being a Heartwood, but it was just another name to her. She was Katherine Hamilton's daughter.

"What's the Shire?"

"No place you need to go." He nodded at a woman as he passed by. "It's the campground for Faire workers who don't have sleeping space in their shops."

"Why can't I go there?"

"Because I said so."

She laughed. He stopped and looked at her.

"What? You think you can tell me what I can't do? Get over yourself, old man."

"I know this is very different from L.A. But you don't know how different it really is. Until you do, you'd better stick close to home."

"Home is 125 Hemlock Drive, Los Angeles, California. I'd love to stick close to home, Zeke."

His shoulders tensed, but he turned and walked on.

As she followed her father through the maze of furniture, she ticked off a mental list of her life goals: finish high school, attend college, then law school. She would become a lawyer like Mom had always wanted her to. Maybe she'd make partner one day. That had always been Mom's dream, and she'd throw herself a party when it happened.

"Did Ms. Talbot tell you anything about my luggage?" she asked. "The stupid airlines lost everything."

Her most valuable possessions were inside those suitcases.

The tangible objects that connected her to Mom: the purple jumpsuit that Keelie had worn on the first day of kindergarten, her tattered Boo-Boo bunny, and the scrapbooks with Mom's pictures. She didn't think she could look at them right now, but she wanted them back.

He shrugged. "She gave me your folder. We didn't really have time to talk. She said everything I needed was in the file: vaccination record, birth certificate, and school transcript."

Sudden tears trembled on her lower lids. She widened her eyes a couple of times to spread the tears around so that she didn't have to wipe them away. Everything he needed to know about her, in one folder? He didn't know anything about her. He'd missed most of her life. Now her mother's attorney had reduced her existence to three pieces of paper. Keelie turned her head. She wouldn't cry. She would never let her father see her cry.

Thunder boomed, and rain splattered the saturated ground. Crowds cheered from the jousting field, too excited or too dumb to get out of the rain. Keelie wondered if her golden knight had won.

Lightning forked across the black clouds, the brightness blinding her for a second. Fire burned her. Her head felt as if it were splitting. "Help," she cried. "In the meadow—fire."

Dimly, she saw her father, mouth open, staring at her. "What? Fire, where?"

Keelie clutched her head, trying to hold back the pain. "There's a tree on fire. In the meadow. It's calling for help." Her father took off running, leaving her there, alone, and without an aspirin. What was going on? Was she getting voicemails from trees now? Where the heck was this meadow?

She sat on the flagstoned floor, not trusting the nearby wooden chairs, in case they sent messages through her backside. She didn't know where to go, so she'd wait for her father to return. She knew where she ranked on his priority list. Dead bottom.

As soon as she could, she'd call Laurie and get their plan moving. Keelie had to get back to California.

three

"So what should I call you? Zeke? Lord Heartwood?" Keelie sat on her father's overstuffed green sofa, swaddled in a leaf-colored quilt, a mug of hot tea in her hands. Her straggly wet hair tickled her cheeks as she looked around the apartment above the shop.

It had taken him two hours to return, and it would serve him right if she died of pneumonia. At least she'd be with Mom.

"Call me Dad."

"How about not?"

"Knot's the cat. I'm your father."

"Well, you don't act like one. Why'd you take off like that? It was just a dumb tree."

His smile faded. "How did you know that the tree was on fire? Did you see the lightning bolt hit?"

Keelie was relieved he'd supplied the answer. "Yeah. And I saw smoke."

He didn't look like he believed her. "I ran because fire is very serious up here. We live in a forest. If it had spread, our lives would be in danger."

"Oh. That's the first thing anyone's said that makes sense in this wacky place."

From the window beside her, she could see the jousting arena at the bottom of the hill. The jousters were gone, and the field was empty except for a couple of workers picking up garbage.

She wondered if her golden knight had won and pictured him bending down for a kiss from the girl with the perfect Goldilocks hair. She frowned. Bad image. She needed to imagine him kissing her.

What was she thinking? She wouldn't be here long enough to hold his hand, much less kiss him.

"So, what'll it be? Dad?" Her father was still angling for a title.

"How about not?" She'd already called him that, but it was a mistake. She'd been swept away by the moment. "Dad" sounded so intimate, so close. Everything they were not.

"How about Father, then?" He picked up his own mug, embellished with a leaf motif.

"Formal, but acceptable," she said. "Do you prefer Zeke

or Lord something or another when I talk about you to others?"

He grinned at her. "Lord something or another? Now who's being formal?"

She grinned back. Despite her recent dark mental trend, she was usually pretty nice. And she was pleased that they were having their first normal conversation. She didn't want him totally out of her life. Where would she go for holidays?

She wondered what kind of freak show Thanksgiving celebration they'd have here. It would probably include that evil hairball.

After her father's return she'd fallen into a mud puddle as she was preparing to climb the shop stairs. Her capris were soaked, stained with brown slime, all because that stupid shop cat tripped her again. On purpose, she was sure of it.

As she sat in the cold puddle, her underwear glued to her skin, she'd seen the cat run up the steps past her father, who gave him a stern look before he jumped down gracefully to join her.

Her father reached down to scratch the cat's ears. He lifted his chin and purred, eyes closed.

"What's with that cat? I never knew you had one."

He sighed as if already exhausted from dealing with her. "You have to watch out for Knot. He's a sneaky cat."

She looked at her father, incredulous that he owned a cat. He'd had time for a cat, but not for a daughter? "You know Mom was allergic to cats."

"So she said." He didn't sound convinced. So now Mom was a liar, too? "Knot is different from most cats. He was the only cat your mother would pet." He smiled at some long ago memory. "We used to be a happy family, believe it or not."

Goose bumps flecked her skin. A happy family. Keelie searched her father's face and saw pain in his eyes. Maybe at one time they had been a happy family, but he'd screwed it up when he left. Any chance they had to be a family again, just the two of them, was haunted by that fact. Thirteen years of nothing did not entitle him to be called Dad or Father. She'd call him Zeke.

The cat opened his eyes and looked at her, almost as if issuing a challenge. Could cats be that smart? She wanted to boot his heinie out the window.

The cat was a relic from her childhood, from the time when Mom and her dad were together. She stared back at the evil feline. It didn't seem that old. How long did cats live?

"Knot must be really old."

"Very. But he comes from a line of long-lived felines. He might outlive us." Her father smiled.

"Hypothermia kills millions every year, Zeke. I may be the next victim."

"There's a big tub in the bathroom," he said, pointing to the only real room in the apartment. "You can wash out your clothes in the sink. I put the bag with Tarl's costume by your bed. You won't have to wear them for long, just until we get your luggage from the airline and get you fitted for decent garb."

She wrinkled her nose at the memory of the hideous

mud costume. "Thanks, I think. At least they're dry. What's garb?"

"It's what we call the costumes we wear here. Since this is a Renaissance Faire, you'll have to wear Renaissance costumes, at least during the day when the mundanes are about."

"Mundanes? It sounds like a disease."

He laughed. "They can seem like one, too. But it's just what we call the visitors."

"Oh." She put a world of feeling into that little syllable.

He looked at her, silent. "Of course, we also call them our bread and butter, and we're always polite to them. Courtly, in fact."

"I won't forget it." Did he think she was a baby? She'd wear the clown outfit until her sweater set and capris were washed and dry. He could wait to hear that she wasn't about to dress like the inmates in this asylum.

Meanwhile, she'd call the airlines and use her lawyer voice to demand that they find her luggage and return it to her. Mom would be proud of her for taking action, being firm, and for Keelie thinking of herself as a lawyer.

She'd use the lawyer voice to keep the "mundane" clothes, too. No way she'd play one of Oz's little Munchkins.

Her father went downstairs and she jumped up to examine her new home. Temporary home, she reminded herself. The main living area was an airy, open room. Wind chimes hung from the four huge wooden beams that crossed the ceiling. The white walls were hung with tapestries full of unicorns and flowers. Two areas were curtained off, carving out private rooms. One had the curtain pulled back with a tasseled silk rope. A tall, wood bed was inside, its high mattress covered with colorful pillows. A homely paper sack was on the floor next to it, a red hand print clearly visible on the yellow cloth spilling from the top.

She walked around, not touching anything, her eyes jumping from one thing to another, trying to take it all in at once. It was like walking into a fairy tale house.

A sense of belonging and freedom welled up inside of her, although this was the total opposite of her California home. Mom preferred the dark cherry wood furniture that had belonged to her Grandmother Jo. The huge pieces had always seemed so oppressive, and they had not been friendly. She avoided it, preferring her own bedroom's chrome and fiberglass retro look.

The tinkling chimes made a constant music, a soothing song. She smiled. Mom would have called it drafty.

Keelie noticed a cluster of framed photographs on a corner table. She walked over and picked up a frame with hearts carved across the top. Keelie, age six, grinned back at her, proud of her missing teeth.

All the photographs were of her. He had every school photo taken of her since she attended kindergarten, including last year's ninth-grade picture.

She spun around as the door reopened behind her.

"Keelie, I'll be in a meeting by the front gates until late, and then we can talk," said Dad. "If you're hungry, grab something from the fridge. Don't wander off. It gets dark fast."

Keelie spun on her bare feet. "You're going back to

work? I just got here." She wanted to be alone, but it seemed unfair of him to desert her. Of course, he was good at it. He'd had practice.

"I want to spend time with you, too, but there's a Faire vendor's meeting."

"I'm so sorry Mom picked such an inconvenient time to die," she shouted. She froze, shocked. She wasn't an out-of-control freak. What was happening to her?

He looked stunned. "No, Keelie, that's not what I meant at all."

Her face hurt from holding back the latest round of tears. "Just go, okay? I need time alone." She sobbed and swallowed hard to stop the next sob from bubbling up.

"When you get dressed, you can go explore," he said. "There's lots to see, although everyone's closed up. Stay away from the Shire." He sighed. "You can stay up here, too, if you wish. Ms. Talbot said that you'd be here next week, so I'm not ready for you, but since you're here, we have to make do. It's my responsibility to care for you, and that includes financially, with my business. That's what I meant, Keelie. You're not a burden or an inconvenience."

He walked over to her and kissed her on the cheek. She accepted the kiss but didn't look at him. She really did need time alone—her stomach rumbled—and some food. She was hungry and confused.

After he left, she found the little bathroom behind a plank door. A huge claw-footed bathtub with a hand-held shower took up most of the room, along with a gleaming porcelain sink, the bowl painted with twining green leaves. She found fresh towels in a basket and lavender-scented soap in the tub. This was more like it. It reminded her of the bathrooms at Chico Hot Springs, where she'd vacationed with her mother.

Cleaning up took a long time, but at last she was mud-free. She felt like a different person, especially after she dressed in the stupid clothes the mud man had loaned her. Just as she'd suspected, she looked like a fool. She thought of the beautiful girl with the pink and gold hoopskirt and the perfect golden hair, the one who would be kissing Sean the golden knight. Keelie looked down at the frayed pink ribbons on her purple bodice. She peeked over her shoulder. The red handprints on her bottom all but glowed on the yellow skirt. The blouse was dingy, but clean. At least her skin was free of crusty mud. She should have packed an extra outfit.

She attempted to finger comb some of the tangles out of her hair. Her detangling spray was in her luggage, along with her salon shampoo, conditioner, straightening iron, and gel. Curls and ringlets had popped out all over her head from the moisture in the air. She threaded a strand of her brown hair through her fingers. Except for the owl lady, nobody at this festival had short hair, which was fine. She didn't want to fit into this place, anyway.

Keelie touched her cheek where her father had kissed her. That had been weird. She hadn't even tried to move away. The whole day had been twisted. Sometimes she wanted to run away, to return to civilization, and other times she wanted to be the little girl in his arms. It must have been a reaction to the stress of her mother's death and the move.

Maybe what she needed was to keep busy, to keep moving so that she didn't have time to think too much. Thinking led to thoughts of her mom, and how much her life had changed, and then the tears would start again.

She glanced out the multipaned window that faced the jousting field. The rain had stopped, and jousters were practicing in the lengthening shadows of the field below. Now that the Faire was closed, she decided to check out the after-hours action, although really she just wanted to see if Sean was there without Princess Perfect-Hair Elia.

She looked down at her feet. No shoes, but if she stepped on patches of grass, then her feet would stay clean, or at least free of mud. After all, the jousting field was practically next door. She ran back to the bathroom, where she'd left her dirty clothes on the floor. Her capris were a disaster, but she wasn't going to do laundry until later. She rummaged in the pocket for the rose quartz and tucked it in her bra. Luckily, the top was baggy enough that no one would see the weird lump.

A quick search of the tiny kitchen area showed that there wasn't much to eat, but she found a canister full of oatmeal cookies. Perfect. She shoved one in her mouth and carried two more, then slammed the door behind her and picked her way down the wooden stairs, bare toes tingling. Yellow pine from Georgia.

Hopping down the hill from one green grass patch to the next was more difficult than she'd anticipated. When she got to a spot where the next patch was four feet away, Keelie regretted giving up ballet. She jumped and landed squarely in the middle of a puddle. No mud, thankfully.

The jousting field was labeled by the sign next to the grandstand that had earlier been full of tourists. Mundanes, in the local lingo. All around her, armor clanged, horses and riders called to each other, and harnesses jingled. She wondered which way the Shire was. Her map of the site, soggy like all of her belongings, was deep in her purse back at the apartment. The workers' campground probably wasn't on it.

Two armored knights, helmets removed, stomped past, as muddy as Keelie had been earlier. They didn't seem to mind. One waved to her as they passed. She started to lift her hand to return the wave, but they had gone on.

Two clumps of grass grew between her and the rough wooden barrier at the edge of the field. A giant horse was tied to one of the posts. It turned its massive head and looked straight at her, then whickered a greeting.

It was almost as if he wanted to meet her. She'd never been near such a large animal, but she wasn't frightened. Keelie judged the distance to the next clump and jumped, but missed. Water flew everywhere.

The horse tossed his head as if in approval, and Keelie laughed. She stopped, startled, as she realized it was the first time in days that she had laughed.

Ankle-deep in water, she giggled. The horse nudged her with his nose, and she petted him. "Pleased to meet you, too," she said. She offered him an oatmeal cookie. The horse chomped it noisily. Horses liked cookies. Who knew?

"I should have known you'd be one of the mud people."

Keelie turned and saw Miss Goldilocks Perfect-Hair standing arm in arm with Sean. Great. They'd both gotten a long look at the handprints on the back of her skirt.

She decided to tough it out. She extended her right hand. "Hi, again. We didn't introduce ourselves properly. I'm Keelie Heartwood. I'll be living up the hill with my father." It felt strangely good to say that.

Lord Sean bowed, smiling. "I am Lord Sean o' the Wood, and this is Lady Elia."

The girl looked down at Keelie's outstretched hand with disdain. "Ladies curtsey, Katy." She dipped gracefully and fanned out her pink skirts. "Like this."

"Oh. Like this?" Keelie gathered her hideous yellow skirts daintily in each hand and dipped, extending her left foot, then deliberately smacked it down on the mud in front of her. Slimy brown mud splattered in all directions.

"Oh, you klutz!" Lady Elia shrieked, spreading her wide skirts, searching for spots. The girl's hate-filled eyes turned to Keelie, taking in the mismatched, tacky clothes. "You did that on purpose," she hissed. "And you will be sorry."

"I'm already sorry. And the name's Keelie."

Elia stalked off, nose in the air. "Come along, Lord Sean. It's going to rain again any second."

Sean stared at Keelie, fighting to keep a smile from turning into a full-fledged grin. "Lady Elia hates to get wet."

"I've heard that about witches. Don't they melt in water?"

One of the knights gathered nearby guffawed. Sean shrugged and followed after Elia.

Thunder boomed overhead. Keelie snatched the quartz from its hiding place in her bra, holding it tight in case she got another tree voicemail. The sky had darkened again, and wind thrashed branches high overhead. The little crowd scattered, and a rider came to lead away the horse tied to the post.

As big raindrops started to hit the ground, Keelie was left alone. There was no sign of the real world. The gray sky hid any airplanes, the only sounds were rain and the distant shouts of Faire workers scurrying to shut down for the day. No sign of her mother or Ms. Talbot or her old life existed.

What was left was this green place, alien and wet, so unlike California that she needed a guidebook to figure it out, and filled with people who didn't want her here.

Rain sheeted down, plastering her hair to her head. Her costume hung in heavy folds, although her legs were warm and dry under the layers of cloth.

Slowly, she started back up the hill, away from the abandoned jousting field, not caring if she forded suddenly created streams, bare feet splashing heedlessly through mud and water.

Keelie had to accept the fact that she was stuck. Stuck in Medieval Hell...but she wouldn't be here for long.

four

Keelie was beyond wet, but she still hurried toward the shelter of her father's shop. Others were rushing through the rain. As she turned onto the path that led to her father's shop she saw the familiar face of the goth girl who had given Ms. Talbot directions earlier. She seemed to be headed to her father's shop, too. Keelie ran into the darkened furniture shop, relieved to be out of the rain. The girl came splashing in a second later.

"Did you find your dad okay earlier?" She dropped the hood of her cloak.

"Zeke? Sure did. I'm Keelie." She held out her hand and the girl shook it. Her hand was cold and wet.

"I'm Raven. My mom has the herb shop at the bottom of the hill."

"Raven. Cool name."

The girl shrugged. "It's a liability in business classes. Nobody takes you seriously."

"What business classes do you take?"

"I go to NYU in Manhattan. You?"

"Rising junior in high school. I'm from Los Angeles. I plan to go to law school at UCLA."

"Cool. Having urban withdrawal?"

"In the worst way. How do you stand all the medieval weirdness?"

"I grew up on the Faire circuit. I kind of like it. It's home. But I love Manhattan."

Manhattan. Mom had been there several times on business and had promised to take Keelie some day.

"Do you know where the Shire is?"

"I was heading that way now. Big party. Want to come?"

At last things were going her way. A new friend, a college business major no less, and she knew where the party was. "Sure, love to."

Raven headed into the back of the shop.

"Where are you going?" Keelie didn't think her new friend should be wandering around her father's shop. Unless—but no, Zeke wouldn't go for someone that young. She hoped.

"Your dad keeps cloaks back here in the workshop. Have you met Scott yet?"

"Who's that?"

"Zeke's assistant. You'll…like Scott." She handed Keelie a black hooded cloak, then helped her to fasten the big hook at her neck.

"Will he be at the party?" She pulled up the hood, feeling like a monk. A pair of worn hiking boots were propped by the workshop door. Keelie stuck her bare feet in them, glad they were dry.

"You'd better hope not. Scott will tell your dad. He's such a workaholic, though. He's probably asleep somewhere warm." Raven laughed and pulled her own hood up. They headed out into the pelting rain.

"Why would he tell my dad? Er, Zeke?"

"He's such a suck up. And guaranteed, Zeke won't want you partying with the Shire folk. It can get wild down there."

"Wild like how?" She thought of Sean, tangled in sheets with some woman. Not Goldilocks. It hurt to even think about that.

"Drinking, wenching, fighting. The usual."

"I met a cool guy earlier. Lord Sean o' the Wood. Know him?"

Raven stopped and gave her a Darth Vader look. "Yeah, I know him."

"So—?"

"So nothing. He's a jerk. And you won't see Lord High and Mighty Sean or his kind at the Shire. They have their own private campground."

"Where's that?"

"In the woods. You won't want to go there. They hate

company. You think they're rude in public? Go knock on their door."

The path they followed went through a dark woods. She held tight to Raven's cloak and in the other hand she held the quartz. The unfastened boots flapped around her ankles.

"Raven, I can't see anything."

"Don't worry, I've been this way a million times since I was a kid. Just stay on the path. If you go into the woods you won't know where you are until morning."

Keelie shivered.

"See the open space on the left?"

"No, just dark and rain."

"There's a big meadow there. First we cross the bridge. Can you hear the stream?"

"Nope. Just rain."

"Listen, dumb ass."

She heard a gurgle under the sound of the rain. "Okay, I think I hear the stream."

"Okay, once you hear it, the bridge is just ahead. Cross the bridge, five steps. Then the meadow's on the left. Pass the big stone. Fifty steps to the campsight. By then you'll see the camp lights."

They crossed the bridge, Keelie's boots clomping on the planks and an echo coming from beneath.

"Heartwood." The thin, reedy voice sounded like it was coming from under them.

Keelie yanked on Raven's cloak. "Did you hear that?"

"No."

"Someone said my name."

"You spook easily. I'll bet you're fun at a slasher film."

"Mom said I was too young to see them. So we're going to a party at the Shire?" The cloak surged forward, making Keelie hurry.

Light glowed yellow in the dark ahead. The rain had lessened a little, and she could hear distant conversation.

"Almost there. You can let go of my cloak now. I swear, I thought you'd choke me to death on the bridge."

"I'm telling you, I heard someone say 'Heartwood.'"

"Probably someone making out under the bridge."

And saying her name? That didn't seem likely. Unless it was her father under the bridge with some woman.

The campground was a mixture of store-bought tents of all sizes, pop-up campers, big RVs, and fantastic custom tents. They passed a tall, long tent glowing white from within. A stylized wooden dragon topped the front pole.

This must be Tarl's tent, she thought, then hurried past as she heard the female moaning coming from inside. As she rushed past, a man's silhouette appeared on the tent wall, potato-shaped and obviously naked. Keelie had been hoping to score some food at the party, but now her appetite was gone.

"The party's in the last tent on this row. The tents are arranged in a circle, and then there are rows making streets inside of the circle."

They stopped in front of a medium-sized Coleman tent. Laughter and light greeted them as they pulled aside the front flap and entered. A cloud of sweet blue smoke rolled out.

She'd smelled pot before at parties, but never so much

of it in one place. The inside was lit by pillar candles on dishes, and the floor was covered with oriental carpets and big pillows on which the party goers lounged.

"Hey, Raven. Who you got there, girl?"

"This is my young friend Keelie."

Keelie waved at the greetings that rose around her, hating Raven for calling her young. She took her cloak off and put it in the pile of wet garments by the front door.

A smiling pirate with Johnny Depp eyeliner patted the carpet next to him. "Sweet Keelie, bide here a while."

She slipped out of the boots as Raven had done.

"Sit over there by Aviva," Raven said, pointing toward a dark-haired girl in a belly-dancing outfit.

The Johnny Depp lookalike grinned and patted the pillow next to him. Flattered, Keelie lowered herself, only to jump up again when his hand cupped her backside. She glared at the pirate.

"Sorry, sweetling. I thought you had printed instructions on your booty."

"Ha, ha. No." She sat down and arranged her skirts so that no handprints showed. She needed different garb, pronto.

She listened to the conversation, sitting up, very aware of the man next to her. He edged a little closer.

"You're shivering, lass. Snuggle up to Captain Randy and I'll keep you warm."

How old was he? She didn't want to scoot away like some scared child. If she were poolside at a friend's party back home she'd know just what to do.

Raven had settled in across from her, leaning on the

muscular chest of a wild-haired drummer, his drum abandoned at his feet. She seemed comfortable.

Keelie experimented with leaning back a little. The pirate put an arm next to her, allowing her to cuddle against his shoulder. It felt warm and nice.

Her pirate took the bottle that was being passed around. "Mead," he whispered in her ear, his breath tickling her. "Sweet as honey. Try it."

Keelie eyed the unlabeled bottle suspiciously. Not that they'd be passing around antifreeze, but it didn't seem safe. She rubbed the mouth of the bottle with her cloak, then took a sip. It was good. Captain Randy laughed as she took a long swallow.

"Warms your tummy, doesn't it?"

"It sure does."

He took the bottle from her and put his lips to it, not bothering to clean it off. Apparently it didn't bother him to share her germs. He winked at her as he drank, and her heart fluttered.

She hoped he couldn't feel the little trembling that had started up in her shoulders and neck. She couldn't figure out if she was scared or excited or both.

His breath blew across her neck and she shivered. His arm went around her waist, steadying her.

"Hey Raven, dance for us!" The cry was echoed by others, and the drummer reached lazily for his drum and started a heartbeat-like rhythm. Raven stood and moved to the beat, belly dancing, her hips sliding side to side, her back arched as her arms snaked sinuously. The beat changed to a darker, faster pace and she shimmied, the muscles in her waist showing as her top lifted with her movements.

Keelie stared, mesmerized, feeling detached from her body. The smoke that filled the tent didn't bother her now and she was feeling warm.

Raven's dance was very different from the fat lady at the Moroccan restaurant. Raven's moves were assured and sensuous.

The partygoers were leaning forward now, avid eyes on Raven's body. She smiled enigmatically, as if she was laughing at them. Keelie felt the pirate's hand on her waist, pulling her closer. She let herself be drawn against him.

This was the best party she'd ever been to in her entire life.

The pirate's hand caressed Keelie's side, fingers moving along her ribs and dipping inside of her bodice in rhythm to the drums. Her breath came faster. If she looked at him, he might take it as permission to go further. She looked up at Raven, instead. Beautiful Raven, the life of the party.

She pivoted on one bare foot and her eyes met Keelie's just as the pirate's fingers touched the bottom of her breast. Keelie's breath stopped. What would he do next? And what should she do? This was the place to let go, right?

Raven's eyes darkened, and her right hand made a cutting motion. Instantly, the drums ceased.

"Aw, Raven." Complaints rose from around the circle.

"Keelie's got to go to bed, folks. Let's continue this on a drier night. Come on, Keelie."

"I don't have a curfew. I'm having fun right here." Keelie turned to Captain Randy for support.

"Let her stay, Raven. I'll escort our fair maiden back when she's ready to go home. What reason do you have to ruin her night?"

"I have two reasons." Raven put her fists on her hips. "One, she's fifteen."

Randy's smile slipped a little, but then he looked at her appreciatively. "Young minx."

"And she's Zekeliel Heartwood's daughter."

The hand left her waist. She turned, puzzled, and saw him scooting farther away on the pillows. "What?"

He looked in her eyes and leaned forward to kiss her cheek. "Good night, sweetling. I'll see you again."

Keelie floated out of the tent, loving the Faire, especially the Shire, but peeved at Raven. Who did she think she was, her sister?

Outside, Raven handed Keelie her cloak. It had stopped raining, and the moon shone thinly through the clouds.

"Have fun?"

"Oh, Raven, I didn't know you could dance like that. It was awesome."

"Yeah. It's a party favorite. I'll teach you if you want."

"When? And can I get one of those little outfits with bells?"

"Sure. They sell them here at the Shimmy Shack, Aviva's shop." Raven walked briskly up the hill. "So, you and Captain Randy were all cozy."

"Is that his name?"

"Not exactly. That's his Faire name. His real name is Donald Satterfield. Off-season he's a supermarket clerk in

Denver. He lives in his mom's basement and plays computer games all day."

"No." She thought of her handsome pirate. Of his hand on her breast. "Why is it okay to be felt up by a pirate, but not a supermarket clerk?"

"Pirates choose to be criminals. You have to be a lazy bastard to be a loser."

"He has a job." Supermarket clerk wasn't sexy, but it was work.

"He's twenty-eight, Keelie."

"He doesn't look that old. So you quit dancing because you saw him touch me?"

"Good eye."

They'd crossed the bridge and she didn't hear her name this time. All she could think of was the feel of the pirate's hand on her breast. Wait till Laurie heard about this.

As they climbed the hill toward Heartwood, she noticed that the apartment above the shop was still dark. Zeke wasn't home yet. Good thing, because she smelled like mead and weed. Luckily, the walk had cleared her head.

"See you tomorrow, Keelie." Raven peeled off, heading down the path toward the herb shop.

Upstairs, a loud yowl of protest split the silence as she turned on the light. In her father's chair, Knot the cat glared accusingly.

"Good thing you can't talk." She headed toward the bath to erase her sins.

■ ■ ■

Keelie stretched her toes underneath the toasty warm blanket. As she fingered the soft fleece and snuggled down deeper, she thought about the pirate's warm body pressed against hers.

Pirate?

Bolting upright, Keelie was suddenly wide awake, remembering the party the night before. Instead of pot smoke, she smelled baking cookies. Mom didn't bake. She always bought the little elf cookies from the supermarket. A lump formed in her throat. Oh, Mom!

She remembered that Mom would never again buy supermarket cookies. Mom would never hold her again. Mom was dead. Keelie felt a little guilty about the fun she'd had the night before. This place was a fairy tale from hell, apart from the Shire. The Shire was fun.

Mom would've been horrified, especially if she knew how Keelie had let the pirate cop a feel. Lifting her shirt to her midriff, Keelie brushed her fingertips along her ribcage where the pirate had touched her. What if she ran into him at the Faire?

Keelie didn't care what he did in the real world, but she wasn't sure she wanted to repeat last night. Of course, his seductive talk might have been part of his act. Had she fallen for the personae instead of the person? What was real here? She didn't want to embarrass herself by thinking there was more to last night. She'd be cool, like Raven.

Keelie flopped back down and looked up at the bedposts. They were twisted vines, the four posts entwined overhead to form a knot from which flowed billowy white gauze bed curtains that hung to the floor on both sides of the bed. Beautiful. If Mom were alive, if she were just visiting her father, she'd be happy. Especially if he'd asked her to come, and she would hang out with Raven and they would be friends. Keelie could come visit him when she was back in L.A. Living with Elizabeth wouldn't be like being with Mom, but it would be familiar, and she and Elizabeth could talk about Mom, who'd been her best friend, and Keelie and her own best friend, Laurie, would be sisters. She needed to talk to Laurie, to set their plan in motion. Keelie could be back in L.A. before the end of the week.

Rolling over, she hugged the big down pillow tight to her chest and pulled the blanket to her chin. She'd cried a lot yesterday. Wouldn't that just be her luck. The one time she tried to let them flow, they wouldn't.

She closed her eyes and willed herself back to that waking moment, when she thought she was home asleep in her own bed and Mom was downstairs baking oatmeal cookies.

An obnoxious licking noise interrupted her daydream. Keelie opened her eyes and rolled over to discover Knot eating something from a ceramic bowl on a wooden tray by her bed. A glass of orange juice was beside the bowl, along with a green card with something written on it in elegant handwriting. She reached for it, risking a swipe of kitty claws, and read 'For you, Keelie.'"

The cat lifted his head from the bowl, clumps of oatmeal hanging from his whiskers like grotesque boogers. A glint of smug satisfaction glowed in his green eyes.

Keelie's stomach rumbled when she caught another

whiff of the oatmeal, but seeing the grody cat made her lose her appetite. So much for her father's breakfast.

Wow. Someone had made breakfast for her. That was a first. Mom had been big on self-sufficiency and independence.

She reached for her orange juice. Knot hissed and swatted at her with his paw. She hissed back, then snatched the orange juice and drank it down without stopping. She plunked the glass down on the wooden tray, where it clinked against the bowl. The cat glared at her with his weird green eyes.

Apparently, her father loved Knot, but not her. Anger bubbled up in Keelie, flowing like hot lava. Knot turned away from her and went back to eating her oatmeal.

She reached for the pillow on the bed and threw it at the cat. The pillow missed him, but it hit the edge of the tray, which toppled onto the floor. The bowl of oatmeal crashed, and the almost-empty juice glass with it. Glass shards and oatmeal globs in an orange juice puddle marred the smooth hardwood floor.

The stupid cat jumped from the table onto the floor, turned around, and glowered at Keelie. He swished his tail as if saying, "Ha, ha, you missed." Then he sauntered off, picking his way through the oatmeal and broken glass, not a speck of oatmeal on his fur.

Footsteps thundered up the stairs, then the door crashed open. Her father pushed aside the curtain. He looked scared. "Are you okay?"

Knot meowed piteously as her father rushed to the side of the bed. "Keelie, are you okay? What happened?"

She wanted to scream, *"No, I'm not okay. I want to go home."* But she didn't.

She stared at the cat. "He did it."

Knot meowed, hunched down as if he were the injured party.

"Knot, you rat," Zeke said mildly. He looked at the mess on the floor. "Stay there. Don't get out of bed. You could cut your feet."

He returned with a roll of paper towels printed with unicorns and a wooden trash can.

He didn't seem to own anything that wasn't made from a tree. He threw the big pieces from the broken glass and bowl into the trash can.

Father handed Keelie her once-white Skechers, still stained with mud.

She accepted them, and should've said thanks, but didn't. Anger still percolated through her. Instead, she looked away from father's gaze, "Why do you call him Knot?"

He smiled. "Why not?"

She didn't return his smile; instead, she gave him her perfected teen glare. Mom called it her matador glare because if Keelie were ever to be in a bullring with a charging bull, that look would send the bull running, tail tucked between its legs.

His smile faded. "Your grandmother looks at me like that whenever she's displeased with me."

"Past tense, Zeke. My Granny Josephine died two years ago from a stroke."

"I heard. I'm sorry about your Grandmother Josephine, but I was speaking of *my* mother. Her name is Keliatiel.

You were named after her. And when I spoke with her last night, she could barely contain her excitement about seeing you again."

Keelie stared at her father. Another grandmother. One her mother had never bothered to mention. The thought of having another real live grandmother stunned her. Why?

Father snapped his fingers. "Good news, too. The airline sent a courier out late last night with one of your suitcases." He patted her on the shoulder as he stood up. His fingers were long like hers, but his were strong and brown from the sun. "I'd better get a dustpan and get the rest of this glass."

He stepped out of the room. Knot sat down, lifted his back leg up in the air, backside to Keelie, and proceeded to groom his fur with his pink tongue.

"Gross." Keelie put her feet into her shoes and walked over to him. She nudged him with her foot. "Take it somewhere else, stupid cat." She wondered what her long-lost grandmother thought of Knot. Did she love cats? Would she love Keelie like her granny Jo had loved her?

Knot gave her a baleful stare, then hissed. He swatted at her shoe, then with his tail at full mast, he sauntered out the room.

That was a spooky cat. She wouldn't be surprised if he had a side job riding on the back of some witch's broom on Halloween. However, she'd gotten what she wanted. Knot had left the room.

The sound of men shouting floated through the window. She moved aside the white curtains with one hand and looked down onto the jousting field. Men were already in armor and practicing on horseback.

"Here you go, Keelie," her father said. He plunked a suitcase onto the bed. Disappointment made a sharp pain in her gut. Or maybe it was hunger.

The recovered luggage was her small green tapestry overnight bag: the one she'd packed her underwear and bras in. She'd been hoping for one of her big bags. She looked over at her mud-splattered pants and at the Muck and Mire Show dress that hung on the back of a wooden chair. She still didn't have anything decent to wear. From now on, she'd never forget to pack an extra set of clothes in her small bag. Lesson learned.

She walked over to the bed, flopped down on it, and placed her hand on the overnight bag's green handle. She wasn't going to cry. She wasn't going to scream. She wasn't going to react. She wanted to numb her mind and her body.

Zeke came in and sat next to her on the bed. Father's smile was hopeful, but reserved. As if somehow this suitcase was a failed peace offering. "Not the one you wanted, I take it."

She had to admit, Father caught on quickly. "It's my underwear. I thought it would be my clothes." Normal clothes that connected her to life in California. Connected her to Mom.

"I'm sure by the end of the day, your other suitcases with your clothes and the rest of your things will be here," he said. He sounded so sure.

Hope bloomed inside her. "You think so?"

"I've got a feeling. In the meantime, get dressed and go down to the tea shop. Mrs. Butters has muffins and scones baking right now, and by the time you arrive, they'll be fresh out of the oven."

"Sounds good." She remembered Mrs. Butters from the day before. "She's the round gingerbread-man's wife?"

Zeke looked puzzled. "What gingerbread man?"

"From the story, Dad. Remember? The ones you never read to me?"

"I'm not big on fairy tales." He patted her knee and stood.

Keelie watched him walk away, noting how tall he was. She tried to imagine her corporate-executive mom and her hippie rock-star father hooking up, way back when. There were a lot of unusual things in the world, things that defied explanation, and she guessed this was one of them. Opposites attract, she thought. Either that, or mead and weed was popular then, too.

She unzipped her overnight bag, laid it open, and smiled. The contents smelled of lavender and citrus, just like her room back in Los Angeles. She grabbed a pair of Hanes cotton panties and a cotton sports bra. Clean undies. Who'd ever think it would feel like a luxury?

In the bathroom, Keelie grimaced at her hair. She'd gone without conditioner, and with no tools to fix her hair she was doomed to have boinging curls to go with her gross dress. She ran wet hands over her hair and brushed it flat.

She washed her face in cold water and brushed her teeth with toothpaste and her finger. Her toothbrush was still in the holder in her house in L.A., the victim of rushed packing. Stupid Ms. Talbot. She needed a toothbrush, and more. She had to find ye olde drugstore; maybe Raven could help. She was so not asking Zeke.

Of course, that might embarrass him more than her. She imagined asking him for tampons in front of all his groupies.

She looked in the mirror at her scrubbed, reddened skin and remembered Elia's peaches-and-cream complexion and her perfect golden hair.

"Great," she said. "If my hair does go wild today, I'll look like a brown-headed dandelion." As she watched, her hair started to twist into curly spirals.

She gave up and slipped into her bra and panties, but her clothes were still muddy. The Muck and Mire Show costume on the floor was damp but fairly clean. She didn't relish wearing it again, but if she could go without conditioner, she could wear that ridiculous costume one more time. When in Rome, do as the Romans do, Mom used to say. And when at the Renaissance Faire, do as the Renaissancers do. Keelie sighed. Was the rest of her life going to be like this? One compromise after another? Maybe Zeke would be good for a new skirt. Not that she was staying, but the red handprints were too humiliating.

Then she sniffed. What was that horrible smell? It smelled like cat pee. The bedroom door stood partly open. Her heart thumping, she looked over at the bed and stared straight into Knot's weird green eyes. His tail swished back and forth as he squatted, strangely, in her suitcase.

Keelie stomped over to the cat and swatted at him. "Get out of my stuff, you'll get cat hair all over it."

Knot leapt up from the suitcase, landed on the bed,

and bounded out the door. Keelie covered her nose and mouth. The smell was worse. She looked around for the source of the stink, hoping it wasn't what she thought it was. No such luck.

He'd used her suitcase as a litter box.

"Knot, you are so dead!"

five

"I'm going to kill you, cat," she muttered. She stood outside on the mud-free bottom step, looking for Knot. The foul feline was nowhere in sight. Smart kitty, she thought. Evil, but smart. He probably knew that if she got near enough to strangle him, she would.

At least the rain was gone. The sky was clear and blue. She took a deep breath, then wrinkled her nose as she caught a whiff of cooking meat. Probably those gross turkey legs that she'd seen people gnawing on like barbarians. Not for her. She wouldn't buy into the argument that eating with your fingers was medieval. Plastic cups weren't medieval, and there had sure been plenty of people slurping from them the day before.

What she needed was a cup of coffee and some scones. Where was that tea shop?

She pulled at the drawstring of the leather pouch she'd found in her curtained bedroom area. Inside was her rose quartz, better than a gallon of calamine lotion for stopping that wood itch, her money, and the folded map of the Faire site.

She unfolded the map. Her father's shop was on the far left side of the grounds, with the tournament fields on one side of the hill and a lake on the other. It was time to replace the breakfast that the little oat-booger kitty had messed up.

Keelie's hearing locked onto the sound of her father's voice in conversation, followed by a low, appreciative murmur. Another woman, she thought. She should have guessed. Old Pops was the Faire's version of Matthew McConaughey. All the old chicks loved him.

She stepped onto the still-wet ground and walked to the edge of the booth. Her father was speaking to a tall guy dressed in an oversized tunic. So it wasn't a woman. Good.

She needed to talk to her father, alone, to discuss returning her to California. Father dropped a small leather pouch and leaned over to pick it up. A passing woman in tight jeans and a red halter top ogled his backside, clad in leather pants under his short, belted tunic.

Gross. She walked after the woman. "He's not for sale," Keelie said. She pointed to the other side of the shop. "Furniture's over there."

The woman's eyes widened, and her mouth dropped open. Keelie saw her father frown. Whoops. Rude to a customer, ten demerits.

Keelie whirled and left, giving the woman a good view of her handprints. If she wanted to look at backsides, she'd give her an eyeful.

She rounded the corner and stopped by the railing that separated the path from the steeper slope of the hill that Heartwood was perched on. The sight of the activity on the tournament field caught her attention. A man cantered by on a massive warhorse. He wore a tunic and his trousers were tucked into tall, slouchy boots. With his long, brown hair blowing behind him, he looked just like a picture in a storybook.

She scanned the field for Sean.

Whoa, hold it. What was she thinking? They were from two different worlds, and as soon as Dad heard her plan and let her move back to Los Angeles with Elizabeth and Laurie, Sean would be just a pleasant memory.

On the field, a flash of fur the color of fall leaves streaked in front of the big horse. Her heart drummed against her chest. It was that stupid pee cat, about to get squashed under the horse's massive hooves. The rider was looking the other way.

"Knot, get out of there," Keelie shouted. Just because her underwear smelled like a litter box didn't mean she wanted him to end up squished.

Either the cat didn't hear her, or he chose to ignore her. He was chasing a field mouse, and she clutched the wooden railing as the cat followed the panic-stricken mouse back toward the horse in a trajectory that would take him under those dinner-plate-sized hooves.

Stop, she whispered to the horse. *Stop*. The rail under her hand felt warm. *Pine*, a tiny part of her mind thought, the rest of her concentrated like a flying arrow on that small bundle of doomed fur. She suddenly felt the presence of every tree around her, distinct, like people in a crowd. Her hands flew up, away from the fence.

A whoosh of air flowed around her, then through her, a breeze that ruffled her hair, though the leaves of nearby trees were still. Keelie watched, astonished, as the horse halted in mid-stride, legs suddenly straight, body leaning back in a hard stop. The rider's surprise was complete, too, as he tumbled over the horse's head to land on the sandy dirt of the ring. Knot ambled up to sniff at the fallen jouster, then hissed and swatted him, snagging his claws in the man's breeches. The man yelped and grabbed his leg.

Had she done that? Impossible. A weird coincidence.

Knot turned and looked toward the hill. He seemed to be staring at her. From here, Keelie could only imagine the eerie green of his eyes. She stuck her tongue out at him. If she had been down there, he would have swatted at her, too. Ungrateful cat. She didn't know why she was even worried about him, after what he did to her.

"I've been upstairs," her father said behind her. He must have missed the drama on the field. His eyebrows lifted. "I saw what happened to your suitcase." He shook his head. "What can I say? We'll need to add underwear to the growing list of supplies you need."

"Yeah. That cat is so busted," she said.

"I didn't leave you cash for breakfast. You must be hungry." Zeke reached into a leather bag and withdrew a ten-dollar bill. He unfolded it and placed it in her palm.

She looked down at it. "That's it? In California, I can't even buy a latte for this."

Zeke's smile ironed out, then flat-lined. "This isn't California."

Keelie took it. "Can I have more for the washing machine? There's a laundromat around here, right?"

"Yes, by the front gates, behind the Administration Office. Let me get you some cash from the register."

"I'll take the money now, but I'll do my clothes later. Did you know your obnoxious cat almost got himself killed just now?" She told him about what had happened on the field, leaving out the part where the wind had flowed through her and the horse seemed to obey her wish.

Zeke shook his head. "Knot's got a mind of his own, and sometimes we can't tell what he's up to. Come into the shop a second and let me scrounge up some change."

The gangly guy in the humongous tunic kept his back to her as they approached the counter.

"Scott, this is my daughter Keelie."

Scott didn't turn around.

"Scott?"

He turned around, and his face seemed irritated.

"Keelie, this is Scott, my apprentice. I teach him woodworking, and he helps me out. He lives in a room out back."

Keelie didn't smile back either. Not only did Zeke have time for a stupid cat, he had time to teach this dork woodworking. She followed her father as he went behind the counter. The counter itself was amazing. It was taller than her waist, and the front edge was carved with imaginary animals, locked in a race around the countertop. The bottom was carved to look like roots, as if the shop itself was part of the Earth.

Hand stuck out in anticipation of money, Keelie looked around the shop. The posts that held up the top floor had root-carved bottoms, too. Weird. Must be a Heartwood theme. Her roots were elsewhere, weren't they?

Zeke handed her some bills, then broke open a roll of quarters and scooped up half of them to drop in Keelie's palm.

"Hey, we'll need those today to make change." Scott frowned at them.

"The cat peed on my clothes. I need to do laundry." Keelie matched his frown.

Scott laughed. "Is that why you're dressed like that? I thought Tarl had pitched that outfit after Daisy complained last year."

"Scott, why don't you show Keelie where to eat cheap? I'll bet you can show her how to make that ten dollars last a week."

Keelie was mortified. Oh great, she'd be strolling around with über-dweeb and people would think they were a couple. Captain Randy, for one. And if Scott saw Captain Randy and her together, he'd no doubt tell Zeke all about it.

"I can't go, Zeke. I have to finish this piece for Mr. Humphrey. He's picking it up on Friday." Scott didn't seem any happier about it.

Zeke clapped a hand on Scott's back. "Don't worry. I'll take care of everything. The Faire's just opened, so this is a good time for Keelie to see the sights before the crowds get in the way."

Ignoring Keelie's outraged stare, he waved Scott toward her. "On Sundays things don't get busy until after one in the afternoon. You can stay out until then."

They set off down the path, each clinging to the opposite side of the path. Scott glanced at her and snorted.

"What?" She couldn't see anything amusing.

"So, now that you have the garb, are you going to join the Muck and Mire Show?"

The skirt. Keelie hated the hideous Muck and Mire Show costume more than ever. It was a symbol, and it was the wrong one. Her Baywood Academy uniform had been the symbol that informed the world that she was somebody. Only the brightest and best connected got into Baywood. The blue and black of the Baywood uniform showed everyone that she was smart and her mother was important. Here she was a goofy-looking misfit.

"Are you laughing at me?" Keelie stopped in the middle of the path, hands on her hips. Scott's eyes widened, and he tried to stop, but laughter just bubbled out of him, the vermin.

"Don't you want me to?" He wiped his eyes. "You're dressed in that outrageous outfit. Like a clown." He hiccupped.

"Look at you. You've been here far longer than me, and you're wearing something that belongs to a giant. At least you have a choice."

She didn't have a choice in anything. Where to live, what to wear. Who to walk down the stupid path with. His laughter was suddenly too much.

She turned and ran. Racing down the hill, she veered right, speeding past a colorful barge tied at the lakeshore, full of fancy-costumed people. She ran past tradesmen setting up shop and artists opening their studios.

She heard Scott follow her for a while, but then she couldn't hear him anymore. Not that she'd turned to look. He'd never catch her looking to see if he was there. She wanted to be alone, to get away. From Scott. From her father. From this whole freakish wonderland.

The air felt good on her face, and her muscles stretched and sang as she lengthened her stride. She loved to run, and the proof, her cross-country racing ribbons, were in the missing suitcase. People looked up as she passed, but no one tried to stop her. She hadn't run for weeks. It felt great.

After a long time, she circled back to the Heartwood clearing. From the path's edge she watched her father and Scott unload lumber. Back to business. No one was concerned about her. She wondered what Scott had told her father about his early return. She could bet that it wasn't the truth.

Her stomach growled. She could use a muffin and a tall latte. She pulled the map of the Ren Faire site from the pouch slung around her waist and examined it. She was tempted to cut through the woods, but she'd been warned to stay on the path.

She started down Water Sprite Lane, hurrying over the bridge she'd passed last night. No voices today. The meadow was full of trees, just as Raven had described. She shut their voices out of her mind and ran.

The teashop was a ramshackle building, half-timbered and leaning. It seemed to be held together by ivy, which grew, dark green and lush, all up and down the sides. There wasn't a rose bush in sight.

Keelie walked onto the deck, which was huge, and covered by an arbor draped in—what else?—ivy. Maybe the ivy had eaten the roses.

Inside, Mrs. Butters was pulling a tray from an oven. The gingerbread woman smiled kindly at Keelie, who didn't return the smile. She didn't want to get used to anyone being nice or friendly to her. It was better this way. Keelie Heartwood was out of this place the first chance she had.

"Good morning, Keelie. What can I get for you?" The gingerbread woman smiled, her little black-raisin eyes shining in her brown face. Keelie resisted the urge to lean forward and sniff her.

"A couple of muffins, please." Too many carbs, but after this morning it was a well-deserved treat.

"What kind do you want?"

"Do you have any blueberry?"

"Of course. But they're for the mundanes. For us I have some with unicorn fruit and crystal seeds. Of course, this may be a bit more to your liking." The woman reverently held out a golden mound-topped muffin speckled with bright bits of red berry. "Fairy winkberry. It's your father's favorite."

"Fairy winkberry," Keelie repeated, hoping she wasn't losing her hearing.

The woman's eyes twinkled. "Yes, fairy winkberry. I don't make these very often, for the berries are rare in these parts, but one of the jousters happened upon a blooming plant near the meadow the other day and brought me back a basket."

Berries sounded more normal than crystal seeds. For all she knew, the crystal-seed muffin could have quartz bits in it. She remembered the toothless guy from the day before. No doubt about it. He could've been a crystal-seed muffin victim.

"Okay. Fairy winkberry. But since it's so big, I'll have just one. And a tall chai."

"I'm afraid I don't have chai, but I do have a lovely herbal tea that goes great with the muffins." She pulled a tray from a stack and put the muffin on it, with a lacy paper doily underneath it.

No chai. Of course not. Keelie remembered going to the coffee shop at the mall with Laurie and the gang after school. Chai and coffee were their favorite hot drinks. This place was totally primitive.

"How about a coffee then, dark roast?"

"Aren't you a little young for coffee? I think Zeke would object." The feminine voice behind her sounded disapproving.

Keelie quickly turned to see who had spoken to her. It was the herb lady, Raven's mother, dressed in purple and white, her billowing sleeves embroidered with little green herb plants. Her bracelets jingled and chimed with her movements.

Heat crept up Keelie's cheeks as she looked down at her mismatched Muck and Mire Show outfit. And the woman smelled divine, like something from an exotic land. Mom had never worn perfume. She'd thought it was unprofessional.

The memory of her mother brought Keelie back to reality. Who was this woman to question whether or not Keelie could have coffee? To call her dad Zeke and pretend she knew what his rules were? Mom let her have coffee. And it wasn't any of this woman's business if she did. Her motherly act was irritating.

She was probably out to impress her dad, Keelie thought. And if that's the case, she's auditioning for a part that doesn't exist.

"I think that's for me to decide," Keelie said. "I'm old enough to make my own food choices."

"I know that your dad eats as naturally as possible, just like your grandmother," the herb woman said, unperturbed. "Besides, it's going to be too hot for coffee."

She didn't want the nosy herb lady to rat her out, but she wasn't giving in yet. She turned back to Mrs. Butters. "Do you have Coke?"

The herb lady frowned.

"No," Mrs. Butters said. "But the turkey leg stand opens in about an hour, and they sell soft drinks there."

Keelie sighed. What kind of eating place didn't sell Coke? This was taking the medieval theme all too seriously. "Okay, give me the herbal tea."

The muffin lady and the herb lady smiled at each other. Keelie looked away. She didn't want to make friends with anyone who treated her like a child, but the herb lady's gentle smile made Keelie ache for Mom's smile. The smile that said, "No, you can't have it," in a loving but firm way. The one that said, "I love you enough to say no." That smile.

She could feel her throat swelling up like it always did whenever her mother's smiling face appeared in her mind, aware that she'd never see her smile again except in photographs. Mom would never, ever say no to Keelie again. She vividly remembered their last fight. She'd wanted to have her belly button pierced like her friends Laurie and Ashlee. Keelie ran her hands over her stomach. She could do it now if she wanted to. Who was going to stop her, the herb lady? Her dad?

The minute she got back to L.A., she would get her belly button pierced. Mom couldn't stop her, and for sure her father wouldn't stop her. When she came to visit, he wouldn't notice, either. He was too busy with his trees, customers, and that dumb cat to notice that Keelie had done something that she'd always wanted to do. It would be a sign of her independence. And she'd drink gallons of coffee, the strongest she could find.

Keelie absentmindedly accepted the tray with the huge golden-domed muffin and the cup of hot tea. The herb lady handed the muffin lady a green cup just like the one Keelie had seen Father drinking tea out of earlier this morning.

Keelie plopped her tray down on a table in the farthest corner of the deck. She picked up the muffin and touched the bits of fairy winkberry. Probably a cutesy name for cranberries.

The herb lady sat down in the chair opposite Keelie. Keelie glared at her and started to pick apart her muffin. She took a bite, starving but determined not to scarf it down in front of this woman.

"We weren't introduced earlier. I'm Janice. I think you know my daughter."

"Where is Raven today?"

"Tending my shop so that I can do some errands." She sipped her tea. "I knew who you were the minute you stepped into my shop. You look just like your dad. You smiled a little then."

"Your shop smelled nice," Keelie said.

"Thank you. You're welcome back any time. I heard your luggage didn't come in with your flight yesterday. Don't you hate that?"

Keelie dropped the muffin back onto the tray. "Yeah, and what can I do? I'm stuck with these stupid clothes like I'm stuck being here at this stupid fair."

Janice folded her arms. "It stinks, doesn't it? Being ripped away from the school and people you knew and loved and all of a sudden you're here. I lost my mother when I was sixteen. She died of cancer. I guess that's why I turned to herbs. I wanted to heal the world, but I couldn't forget the awful days in the hospital. No regular medical school for me."

Keelie's resolve to be surly thawed a little. "Yeah, well... I just want my clothes." She wanted her mother back, too. She realized that she was mad. She was mad at

Mom for dying, she was mad at Dad for showing up in her life now that Mom was gone, and she was mad at the world for moving forward when the most important person in the world was no longer here to say no to her.

"Zeke was so excited that you were coming. He kept telling everyone. We thought it would be next week, though. This Faire's almost over, and he thought you'd come closer to the end."

Janice didn't give up. Couldn't she tell that Keelie didn't want to have this conversation? If Janice wasn't leaving, maybe she could get some information out of her.

"So the Faire's almost over? What happens then?"

"Some of the workers are locals, and they do this for extra cash, for fun. For others, your father for instance, it's part of a circuit. There are Renaissance Faires all over the country, at different times of the year. Lots of the artisans and performers will head to another Faire after this one."

Surprised, Keelie wondered where they would be headed. And what about school? She'd been given her final grades, but what about next year? Maybe Dad was taking her to California. Wishful thinking. "Where will you go?"

"The big Faire in upstate New York. It's called Wildewood Faire. It lasts three months, and then winter comes, and some go south, others go home until the spring."

Keelie found herself eating her muffin. It was delicious. The fairy winkberries tasted like a mixture of strawberry and vanilla, and they burst in her mouth with sunshiny warmth. She sipped her tea. It tasted good, too, darn it.

"Keelie, go easy on your dad," Janice said. She hesitated, then added, "He was devastated by your mother's death."

Keelie's like-o-meter swung to extreme dislike. How dare she? She stood up. "I better get back to the shop. Zeke will want to know where I am." Yeah right, just like he'd missed her for the last fourteen years.

Janice pointed to her tray.

"Aren't you going to finish?"

"I've lost my appetite."

Now was the time to have a conversation with her father. And she needed to get back in case some of her luggage showed up, and before that evil feline could do something to it.

"See you around," Keelie said politely, and wrapped the rest of her muffin in a napkin, just in case. Janice smiled sadly, as if aware that she'd said something wrong.

Keelie stepped out of the tea shop and out onto the sun-dappled main pathway. The trees here were not old giants. Tall and slim, their leaves looked green and tender against the blue of the sky. She'd never been around so many trees before, but she hadn't had any weird episodes, except for this morning. She pushed the thought aside. It had been a coincidence.

She decided that she liked the trees. She raised her face to the sunlight, enjoying its warmth on her cheeks. She remembered reading about an enchanted forest in a fairy tale book, one that she'd only had for a little while. Mom had hated fairy tales, and now she could understand why. She'd always said that Dad lived in a fairy tale world, and Keelie believed it now. This place was unreal.

Keelie had been raised to be grounded in reality. Her feet were firmly planted, like the roots of a tree. She was Keelie Heartwood, an independent teenager who made her own decisions. Sort of. She touched the skirt over her belly. She was going to get her belly button pierced as soon as she could. Why wait? Mom couldn't stop her now.

And right now she would tell Zeke she was going back to California to live with her friend Laurie. She didn't believe that he wanted her here, that he bragged about her coming. He'd probably be happy to hear it. She could tell that she was cramping his lifestyle. She'd still be in California if Mom's will hadn't named him her guardian instead of Elizabeth. No one would have known any different.

If Zeke said no, she could sue for emancipation. She and Laurie had looked it up. She couldn't wait to talk to Laurie. Her cell phone was mucked up, but with a little cleaning it might work. If not, she'd use Zeke's phone and pay him back for the call.

The mud squished under her shoes. At least it wasn't pouring down rain like yesterday, and she had on clean underwear. Things were almost looking up. She walked by the herb shop, inhaling the woodsy aromas coming out of the shop. Janice the herb lady was still at the tea shop. Keelie hesitated. She wanted to go in and look. She itched to touch some of the dried herbs displayed in flowerpots. She wanted to crush them between her fingers and smell their scents.

"Do you want to go in and look around?" The round, frizzy-haired woman in the booth next door was standing by her door, holding yet another of those mugs that looked like Zeke's.

"No, thanks. I was just getting some fresh air. There's not much of it back in L.A."

"So I've heard." The woman smiled. "I'm Ellen, the potter." She lifted the mug. "These are mine."

"Oh. Everyone has one. I thought having one meant something."

"You mean like a special symbol?" Ellen laughed. "All it means is that I badgered them into buying one."

Keelie laughed. She liked Ellen.

Janice was coming up the path, carefully balancing her steaming mug. Her long skirts swung gently around her.

Keelie crossed her arms to cover her ugly bodice.

"Hello again, Keelie. I see you've met Ellen." Janice smiled. "Let Keelie pick out a mug, Ellen. It'll be a gift from me. An apology. I shouldn't have spoken to you the way I did."

Keelie blinked. Like-o-meter readings rose steadily. An apology? She was being treated like an adult. "Thanks."

"Great! Come on in, kiddo, and pick one out." Ellen vanished into the little awning-shaded shed.

Keelie entered and sniffed. It smelled like raw clay, an art room smell that she'd always loved. Glass shelves lined the windows of the tiny shop, loaded with vases, cups, and funny little statues of dragons.

"I've got one I think you'll like," Ellen said. She pulled a green mug off the shelf. It wasn't the biggest one, but it had a leaf shape pressed into the side. She handed it to Keelie. "Look inside."

Keelie took the mug. It felt as if it belonged in her hand. She tipped it to look inside, and smiled. The bottom of the mug had a beaky-nosed face sticking out of it. The funny little creature was winking at her.

"How fun! I'll see this little guy whenever I finish my coffee, or whatever weird herb drink I'm allowed to have."

"That's the idea," Ellen said, ignoring Keelie's sarcastic drink remark. "Hand wash only. Not that you'll find a dishwasher anywhere around here."

Keelie laughed. "I'll bet." She lifted the mug to eye level and looked at the leaf more closely. "An oak leaf. I love it. This is perfect."

"Glad to hear it." Ellen turned suddenly, distracted. "Oh, my kiln's almost ready. If you'll excuse me, Keelie, I've got work to do."

"Sure." She caught herself before she offered to help. It would be fun to get her hands in the clay and make stuff. She poked a little dragon figure holding a crystal. She might as well have a little fun in the short time she was here. There were all kinds of mysterious shops in this place. And shopping was shopping.

Janice was waiting for her outside of her shop. A woman was inside and a couple in shorts was walking up the hill toward them. Tourist time.

Mundanes, Keelie reminded herself. Janice looked pretty in her purple gown. Maybe if Keelie had to stay here awhile, she could ask Janice for help with a better costume. She gave herself a mental pinch. Hello, Keelie? What was she thinking? Stay here in Weirdsville?

"Did you get a nice one?" Janice smiled at the green mug Keelie carried.

"Yes, thank you." She held it up for the herb lady to see.

"An oak leaf," she said, noting the figure on the side. "Why did you pick that one?"

Keelie shrugged. "I like leaves and trees." This was new. Trees used to be creepy.

"You are definitely your father's daughter," Janice said. She looked serious again. "And I'm sorry I said what I did, Keelie. It was none of my business."

Keelie shrugged. She didn't know how to respond.

"You plan on returning to Los Angeles?" Janice asked.

"As soon as possible. A friend of my mom's is willing to get custody of me if Zeke agrees, which I'm sure he will. As soon as she calls to check on me today, we'll be able to push through the arrangements. Everyone's been nice to me—" She thought of Knot and Elia the stuck-up princess wannabe. "Most everyone. But this place is not for me."

Janice frowned. "Are you sure you've given the Faire or your father a chance, Keelie? If you stay, you may discover things about yourself that you never knew were possible."

A chill went down Keelie's spine. She couldn't tell Janice that she was forgetting the sound of her mother's voice. That if she lived with Elizabeth and Laurie in L.A., her Mom would be with her that much longer.

"Yeah, well, I liked my life in L.A.," she said. "And if Zeke wants to get to know me, then he can come live there with me."

An odd expression crossed the woman's face. "He wanted to come see you, but he has to live among the trees."

This lady must be smoking some of her herbs, Keelie thought. "Yeah, whatever. I'll see you around."

Despite her desire to explore the store, she'd stay away. Janice was pushing it with Keelie, and Mom was right. She'd never wanted her to explore plants, trees, and healing because she was afraid it would interfere with her education. Keelie smiled, remembering that Mom had never approved of her volunteering at the hospital with her Grandmother Jo, but Gran and Keelie did it anyway. She could play with herbs after college and law school.

She hurried away from the shop, as if even wanting to go in contaminated the dreams Mom had for Keelie. Farther down the hill, the sword shop was open, and Keelie looked at the different types of real swords that hung outside, tied to the display bar they hung on. Sean had worn a sword. Wasn't it dangerous for everyone to be armed?

Another store farther down the path caught her eye and she hurried over to it. The Dragon's Horde had a sign hanging from chains that said "Rocks and Crystals."

Maybe she'd find more pink quartz.

The shop seemed older than some of the other buildings. Carved posts held up the little roof over the front door, two dragons writhing up toward the slate roof tiles. She'd seen slate tiles in gardens before, but never on a roof. The inside was dark and cool, like a cave. Baskets and carved stone bowls held jewels and rocks of all sorts.

A deep voice asked, "May I help you?"

Keelie searched for the owner of the voice, but she couldn't find him. Then a little man stepped out from behind the counter. He had a curlicued mustache, and he was dressed like a swashbuckler from an old Hollywood movie, a tiny musketeer.

He removed his extravagantly feathered hat and bowed with a flourish. The feather kept bobbing long after he'd stopped. "Do I have the pleasure this day to meet a new member of the Muck and Mire Show Players?"

"Not on your life," she answered peevishly. This Muck and Mire Show thing was getting old. "I'm Keelie Heartwood."

"Ah," the small man said, twirling the ends of his mustache. "I should have figured that out. Must need some more coffee." He headed toward the back of his store. "It's the devil's own brew. Want some?"

Keelie was surprised. He was offering her coffee, not telling her that her father would disapprove. This was a first for Camp Loserville. "Yes, please. I take it with a little cream, if you have it."

"But of course. Sugar? No? Ah, well, you are probably sweet enough as you are."

She blushed, as if he were a handsome knight. What he lacked in height he made up for, triple-strength, in charm.

He took her new green mug and filled it from a delicate silver carafe with a cobalt blue glass insert. He poured thick cream into it from a matching creamer, then handed her mug back to her and waved her toward a pair of leather-topped stools.

She sat, then sipped. The coffee was strong and fragrant.

He gestured with a spoon. "Me, I like it very sweet,

but no cream. My name is David Morgan, by the way. My friends call me Davey. Sir Davey, around here."

"How do you do, Sir Davey?" she said solemnly. He treated her like a grown up, with respect, and she believed in returning the favor.

"I am well, Lady Keelie." He sat on the stool opposite hers. A sip, an appreciative roll of his eyes, and then Sir Davey studied her.

"Ah, my dear. You don't mind if I call you my dear, do you? I'm older than I look. Ancient, practically."

"I don't mind," Keelie answered, smiling. Her smile muscles creaked, out of shape.

"Excellent. I saw what happened at the jousting field this morning. An unfortunate cat, that Knot. Quite a scene with Sir Oscar's war horse. He was very lucky."

"That crazy cat almost got himself smooshed," Keelie declared, rolling her rose quartz talisman between the fingers of her left hand.

"Yes, indeed. But don't expect him to be grateful to you for saving him."

Keelie slammed her mug down. "What? Me?"

Sir Davey smoothed his mustache. "I saw what I saw, my dear. So tell me, how long have you been practicing Earth magic?"

six

Confusion bubbled up inside Keelie. She closed her hand over her rose quartz. What had he seen? She hadn't done anything special. "Magic? As in David Copperfield? I'm afraid you've made a mistake. And I guess I have, too."

Sir Davey looked surprised. "In what way?"

"I thought you were normal. I can see you're just another one of these granola guys."

"Granola guys?"

"Yeah, fruits, flakes, and nuts. Thanks for the coffee, but I have to go."

Sir Davey put a hand up, but she'd seen the smile. So he

thought she was funny, too? Well, ha on him. She was so out of here.

He didn't try to stop her as she walked toward the front of the shop.

Keelie started to step outside when Sir Davey called, "Watch out."

He'd grabbed her arm before she could step into the road. Keelie tried to wrench herself free, but his grip tightened.

She formed a fist and pulled her arm back. If the short dude didn't let go, she was going to pound him on his large hooked nose.

The reverberating boom of horses' hooves thundered, echoing from around the bend in the path. She stepped back out of the main path into the doorway of the shop. The dwarf's grip relaxed, and she jerked her arm free.

Armored knights rode by on their majestic steeds, the sound of their mounts' hooves punctuated by the percussive bang of steel against steel as their armor rattled. Some plate armor shone like silver, others were dulled, or scuffed, like pots that had been scrubbed too often. One rider wore black and gold, and he carried a green banner with a silver lion emblazoned on it. Keelie sucked in her breath, impressed by the sheer power of the horses and knights.

For a few seconds, she was willing to suspend reality and pretend she was in Camelot waiting for her Knight of the Roundtable to return from his quest.

She watched as the last rider rode by. As he passed the doorway, the horse splattered mud on them. She brushed away the cool dollops of dirt from her arms and sighed.

She was doomed to be mucked up for the rest of her time here.

Sir Davey removed his hat and stared at it sadly. It was dotted with flecks of mud and little clods of dirt. Fortunately, the feather came through unscathed. "Bloody pretentious hooligans, endangering everyone with their galloping around."

One of the jousters wheeled around and returned, slowing his horse to a walk. Then horse and rider stopped right in front of her. The knight removed his helm, and Keelie's chest tightened. Sean. She hadn't recognized his armor without the green and black cape.

Sean tilted his head to the right, smiling down at her. His hair slipped away from his ear and she noticed that it was pointed, like the elves in the *The Lord of the Rings* movie. Was he wearing a prosthetic as part of the show?

She fingered the upthrust end of her right ear. She'd always kept it covered, but here it seemed to be a desireable birth defect.

"I like your curls, Keelie." His green eyes were as dark as evergreens.

Keelie stood like a blockhead, unable to utter a single word. Had he seen it?

Sir Davey stepped outside holding a rapier pointed toward Sean. "Be off, varlet. She's not for the likes of you."

Heat crept up Keelie's neck. She wanted the ground to open up and swallow her.

"Sir Davey, please." She glanced up at Sean. His eyes narrowed as he stared at the little musketeer.

"And has the lady appointed you her protector?" asked Sean.

"No, but Zekeliel Heartwood, her father, wouldn't want her around the likes of you."

She wished she could smack Sir Davey on the head to silence him. Keelie stepped closer to Sean's horse.

"I don't really know him," she said. "We just met. He doesn't speak for me."

Sean's dazzling grin made the dimples on the left side of his cheek pop out. She yearned for him to reach out with his hand and pull her up on his horse, then gallop away with her. It would be so romantic. Instead, Sean placed his helm on his head, then lifted the visor.

"There may be more of the likes of me and my kind in Keelie than even Zeke Heartwood wants to admit, Sir Jadwyn," said Sean.

Keelie looked from the dwarf to Sean. "Excuse me, but in case you two have forgotten, I'm standing right here. And I thought your name was Davey."

The little man shrugged. "I said they called me Davey. Jadwyn's another name."

She gazed up at Sean. "What did you mean? More of the likes of you and your kind? In me? Not a chance, Sean. I like horses, but that doesn't mean I'm going to take up jousting."

A man on an impressive white horse stopped beside Sean. "Lord Sean, the Queen requests your presence in the ring."

Sean smiled at Keelie, then he winked. "I wish you a

wonderful day, Keelie Heartwood." He circled his horse around and followed the other jousters.

Even though Sean hadn't answered her question, and obviously wasn't friendly with the glowering Sir Jadwyn, Keelie's heart cartwheeled because Sean said she was of his kind, even in her mud-pit clothes and curly, short hair. He had even winked at her.

"Lady Keelie, stay away from him. He may look young, but he's older in more ways than you can imagine. It's best you get back to your father." Sir Davey just didn't look like a Jadwyn.

She heard him but pretended she hadn't. This place was full of folk who thought she needed mothering. The only person who fit that job description was gone.

Her eyes remained fixed on Sean's retreating figure. Could he really like her? He looked seventeen. Sir Davey said he was older. Could he be twenty? That was just three years older. Not as old as Captain Randy. She imagined her friends' reaction back at Baywood Academy as they gathered around her locker to hear about her boyfriend, the twenty-year-old actor and stuntman.

She returned to the counter, picked up her mug, and took another appreciative sip. "Thanks again for the great coffee."

He arched a steel gray eyebrow, still brushing flecks of mud from his hat. "See that you go straight back to your father's booth and don't be conversing or congregating with any strange folk."

"Then I can't speak to anyone, can I? Everyone is

strange around here." With a jolly little wave, Keelie left the shop, mug in hand.

"We'll talk about that other matter another time," Sir Davey called.

That other matter? Earth magic. She remembered that Janice had told her that if she stayed she would discover things about herself that she hadn't thought possible.

Not if she could help it. She thought the words "law school" over and over until all thoughts of magic were scrubbed from her mind. Good thing she'd stayed away from those crystal-seed muffins.

Even though she was heading back to her father's booth, she could still explore a little more. She wondered if there was a place at the Faire where she could get her belly button pierced. She wondered if Raven had a piercing.

She spied the jewelry booth where she'd bought the quartz and strode over to it. She hadn't gotten a good look before, with Ms. Talbot hurrying her along like a mad corgi with a stubborn sheep.

No body jewelry, but on a velvet display board, a small silver necklace glistened. A fairy pendant dangled from the chain. She touched the fairy, marveling at the itty bitty wings.

A woman in an elaborate Renaissance dress with a high, tight bodice and huge, dragging sleeves shaped exactly like her huge, dragging nose walked over to Keelie and said through Shar-Pei wrinkles, "Please don't handle the merchandise unless you intend to pay for it, little girl."

Keelie looked closer. Under the big dress was a huge bosom. It was Tania, playing the Evil Queen instead of the

Melon Smuggler. Keelie let the fairy necklace slip from her hand back to the display board.

Little girl? Humiliated, Keelie wanted to run, but decided she'd walk away with her head held high.

When she turned around, she almost walked right smack into Elia, Princess Better-Than-You, who raised her pert nose as her gaze lingered over Keelie. Elia carried a harp today, and hugged it closer as if contact with Keelie would contaminate it.

Elia's perfect rose-tinted lips lifted into a sneer. "What happened to your hair? Did you cut it?"

Tania laughed.

Keelie didn't bother to answer that it only looked shorter because it was curly. It would have been a waste of time. The girl lacked any human feelings. Keelie stepped around her.

Elia followed. "Hey, I was talking to you, California girl. Who cut your hair? I want to know so that I can warn all my friends not to go there." Elia laughed.

Just keep moving, Keelie thought. Don't even mess with her. There isn't a brain underneath all that golden hair.

Anger boiled within her. She clenched her fist tightly around her mug. She wanted to punch Miss Perfect in the nose.

Keelie was surprised to hear Elia's footsteps continuing behind her. She wouldn't give her the satisfaction of turning around. Elia ran her hand over her harpstrings, and sweet music filled the air. She began singing in a lilting voice:

"A girl there once was with locks so shorn
She looked like a sheep, not human-born,
Who could blame her for being forlorn?"

A crowd of spectators, including the stilt walker that Keelie had seen on her arrival yesterday, had gathered to listen to the performance. Elia strummed her harp again and smiled at the people as if she were an innocent angel. Then she continued her singing:

"Her garments were soiled, all covered in dirt,
A sight she was, and filled many with mirth."

"That doesn't even scan, Lady Lame," Keelie muttered. Closing her eyes, she tried to recall the wisp of power she'd felt earlier. She imagined the harp strings breaking. She felt the trees all around her, as if gathering to protect her. This was far different from the claustrophobic feelings she'd had in the past. They felt friendly, as if they'd said, "Got your back."

A breeze touched her face, soothing, like the windchimes in her father's apartment, and she opened her eyes, surprised.

The wispy wind blew right through her, leaving a piney green smell that clung to her like incense. The tall pine trees that grew behind the jewelry booth began to sway. A hanging gold Renaissance dress oscillated in the wind like a dancer doing a jig. Several loud pings sounded nearby, and Elia screamed.

Keelie looked with a mingled combination of horror and delight. Elia's harp strings blew in the breeze like silky strands of spider silk.

A pointed ear tip showed as Elia bent her head over her harp. Just like Sean's. A Faire fad, or were they all related?

Elia looked up at Keelie, her green eyes glowing with hatred. Something darker slid behind their vivid color, then floated up to ring her irises in black.

Whoa. Keelie backed away from the scary-eyed girl.

"You did this. I don't know how, but somehow, you did this," she cried out as she rocked her harp in her arms.

More and more people crowded around the sobbing girl. Tania had joined the crowd and scowled at Keelie. "What did you do to her?"

"I didn't do anything. I was standing right here. I didn't touch her harp." She hadn't touched the harp, but she'd wished it. Was this Sir Davey's Earth magic? The cat and now the harp. This was way beyond what she'd been able to do in California.

Elia looked up at the gathered crowd with tear-filled eyes. "I shall be unable to play today for not only are the strings of my harp broken, alas, so is my heart."

What a drama queen!

Keelie started to back away, but a hand squeezed her shoulder. The elegantly costumed jeweler held her still.

"Don't move," Tania said. She looked around at the gathered mundanes and hauled Keelie back behind the jewelry booth and shook her shoulder. "You've caused enough trouble, girl. You mud people need to stay in your own area. If I see you here again, I'll call security."

"I didn't do anything," Keelie said, breaking free of the woman's claws. She glared at the jeweler, who looked back at her angrily and made another grab at her.

"Go. Get away from my shop," Tania hissed. She turned to look at Elia, still sobbing on the path. The woman spat on the ground and rubbed the spit into the dirt with the tip of her shoe. She muttered something under her breath.

Over the woman's shoulder, Keelie watched Elia turn slowly, as if smelling something in the air. She thought the girl was looking for her, but she locked eyes with the jeweler.

Tania gasped.

Elia took one step toward her. "Do you think your puny curses can harm me?"

The woman stepped back, pale. She really looked afraid. Keelie was disgusted. This must have been a show for the mundanes. She wished she'd been let in on it. That was the lesson to remember. Everything here was fake.

Sean appeared on foot, followed by some of the knights she'd seen earlier. Elia ran to Sean, harp strings fluttering behind her damaged instrument. He put his arms around her, but his eyes were on Keelie. Elia pointed toward Keelie, then started to cry again.

Keelie backed away. Elia lifted her face from Sean's shoulder and smiled wickedly at Keelie. As she suspected, the tears were fake.

She was confused. Was anything real here? She quietly wove her way through the growing throng of people and once clear of the crowd, started to run, not caring where she went. At this rate she'd make the long-distance track team back home.

When her side began to ache, she stopped. She had to gulp in several deep breaths to calm herself. She was by the entrance towers. A family paid their admission and passed through the gates. The dad walked with two little boys and behind them the mom pushed a little girl in a stroller. They looked so normal.

Keelie wanted to yell, *"Turn around, don't enter. This place isn't for normal people."*

She watched as the two little boys, dressed in raincoats and carrying wooden swords, shouted "Huzzah." Wind whipped their hair back, and they yelled into it. Their father turned back to hurry them along.

"Rain's coming, boys. Let's get out of the mud." Above them the sky had darkened again, and the wind brought the smell of ozone. "Weirdest summer ever, right, guys?"

Keelie turned away from their protests that mud was fun. It hurt to watch the happy family. Had she been like the little toddler in the stroller? Were Mom and Zeke ever happy together? Her dad who couldn't live away from the woods? Dad. He wasn't a dad to her. He was her father in name only, and he was fifteen years too late to be "Dad."

She gazed at the entrance and froze. Keelie couldn't believe what she saw. Could it be? It couldn't be. It was. An anachronistic gadget in this feudal festival—a pay phone, hanging on a wooden fence between the exit and the restrooms.

She reached into her pocket and found the change the lady from the tea shop had given her. She pulled it out: a nickel, two quarters, four pennies, and six one-dollar bills.

Hadn't she seen the toll-free collect-call commercials on television? She'd call Elizabeth. She would make immediate arrangements for Keelie to come home once she told her of the horrible conditions that she had to endure here.

Two men dressed in leather vests, white muslin shirts, and cloth breeches scurried past her and out the exit.

"If she flies past the grounds, we'll never be able to catch her," said one man. "She'll die out there."

"Aye, we'll need to alert the management. I've never known a bird more tenacious than that one," said the other man.

She wondered what that was about, but it didn't concern her. She was on her way home. Keelie lifted the phone from the cradle. She stopped as she heard music nearby, the sound of a harp. Had Elia followed her? She looked around, but there was no golden-haired witch in sight. The harping stopped, and then she heard the dial tone and punched in one of the 1-800 numbers she recalled. An operator answered, "To whom would you like to make a collect call?"

"Laurie Abernathy in Los Angeles, California. This is Keelie Heartwood." Keelie gave the operator Laurie's number. Thunder rumbled above her as the phone rang. Keelie's heart pounded against her ribcage, and on the other end of the receiver, a familiar voice said, "Hello?"

The operator said, "Will you accept a collect call from Keelie Heartwood?"

"Yes!"

Laurie's voice was like warm sunshine after a cold, rainy day. It was home and school and listening to new CDs by the pool. Keelie wanted to transform herself into little bits of microscopic Keelie pieces and travel through the telephone cord over the fiber optic network to be with her friend.

A dark shadow swooped over her. Keelie looked up into the sky to see what it was—

—and screamed as razor-sharp talons reached for her eyes.

seven

"Keelie? Keelie, is that you?"

Keelie heard her friend's voice, tinny and far above. She'd dropped and rolled onto the ground, arms over her head. A harsh screech sounded directly overhead. She flinched as something brushed her back.

Eyes closed, she pictured the claws extended like powerful scythes, ready to shred her face. She pulled her legs up tighter and tucked her face into her arms. A hawk. A huge one.

Keelie's muscles felt frozen by the frighteningly shrill cry and flapping wings. The pay phone cord dangled somewhere above her head, and Laurie's voice was replaced by a woman's monotone voice, "If you would like to make a call, please hang up and try again."

Keelie closed her eyes tighter and covered her head. All those years of earthquake drills in school finally came in handy. She listened for more of the bird's movements; instead, she heard only the irritating beeping of the phone. She twisted her head and peeked between her fingers. Blackening, swirling storm clouds, but no movement. She cautiously moved her arm. No hawk hovering above her, waiting to tear her into shreds.

She rose to her knees and scanned the surrounding trees. Still no hawk. Relief flooded through her. It was gone.

Keelie stood. Something skimmed the back of her head with a light stroke. Panic returned. She remained perfectly still, then inhaled sharply when the hawk landed lightly on the nearby fence. Its claws dug into the wood as it attempted to balance itself, wide wings tented.

Mouth dry, she gazed into the bird's golden eye as it scrutinized her. It turned its head, and her fear lessened, replaced by sympathy. The other eye was milky white. Blind.

Keelie had never been this close to something so majestic and beautiful in her entire life. Its blindness didn't mar the power, and being this close to it touched something inside her—tripped a switch deep within her soul.

A warm breeze ruffled the bird's feathers. The irritating beeping from the pay phone receiver pulled Keelie's attention away from the hawk, and back to the fact she'd lost her connection to Laurie: her connection to home.

Keelie reached for the receiver, picked it up, and

stretched closer to the pay phone to push the buttons to call Laurie. She smiled at the hawk. It watched her, unmoving, until she pressed the metal buttons. The bird cried out again as if asking her, "What are you doing? Why do you want to leave?"

She left the pay phone and walked over to touch the wooden fence. It was cedar, and in her mind she saw rows of planted trees. Tree farm.

The hawk cried out. Keelie turned to see the two men who had rushed by only minutes before. They walked through the tower gates, then stopped when they heard the hawk cry out again. Keelie looked from the bird to the men. "Is this your bird?"

One of the men called out, "Don't move, kid."

The other one held out an arm encased in a thick, stiff leather glove. "Come, Ariel, come to me," he called out.

The first man motioned cautiously to Keelie. "Don't move. She's dangerous."

Yeah, now you warn me.

The hawk turned its head from the men to look once more at Keelie. This must have been the bird that had flown away during the raptor show when she'd arrived yesterday.

Above her, the trees whispered to each other. She felt their touch in the breeze against her cheek. Feather light.

Feathers. She sensed that the hawk wasn't going with these men, but maybe she would come to her.

Ariel the hawk turned her golden eye to Keelie and as their eyes locked, the two connected. Understanding flowed between two hurt souls, bound in pain. At that moment, Keelie knew she had a friend at the High Mountain Renaissance Festival.

She edged closer to Ariel. "Will you come to me?"

The hawk bobbed her head as if saying yes. Ariel inched her talons down the fence closer to Keelie.

"Move slowly," the gloved man called. He drew the glove off and tossed it to her underhand. It fell at her feet. Ariel shifted her weight back, as if ready to jump on it, then settled down.

"Put the gauntlet on, then put out your arm. Be careful, her talons are as sharp as knives."

Keelie tugged the glove onto her hand, moving carefully so that she wouldn't scare the hawk. She was glad for the protection from Ariel's sharp claws.

Ariel bobbed her head up and down, examining her, then launched herself toward Keelie and landed on her extended forearm. She was large, but not as heavy as Keelie had thought. She kept her head back, afraid of the wicked beak so close to her face. Ariel lowered her head and leaned forward. Keelie mirrored the move, and Ariel touched her forehead to Keelie's.

"Holy cow!"

"Will you look at that?"

Ignoring the wondering cries of the men, Keelie and Ariel touched, feather to skin, until at last Keelie raised her head.

"We both should've flown free when we had the chance," Keelie whispered against the smooth head.

At the raptor mews, Keelie learned Ariel's sad story from the two men. Some teenage boys had shot at her with a BB gun, and the pellet had permanently blinded her left eye.

No longer able to see to hunt, she had been brought to the raptor rehabilitators. Since Ariel could fly, she kept attempting to escape. Each time she'd returned when she was hungry, but her impaired vision put her in danger of being injured.

This was the first time she'd flown to a person, and the men seemed in awe of Keelie as they flanked her on the walk to the mews.

"Thank the stars and the planets, Ariel has returned to us," said a tall, slender woman with odd, brush-cut hair. Keelie recognized her; it was Cameron, the lady who had held the snowy owl the day before, and the only other woman at the Faire with short hair like hers.

"You must be very special. She lets no one touch her, other than Tom and me." The woman motioned with her head toward the man who had given his leather glove to Keelie.

Warmth rushed through her at the praise. Wind from the rising storm flipped a curl onto her forehead, but she didn't dare brush it away.

Cameron turned toward the men. "Have you been introduced to Keelie Heartwood?"

The men stared at her intently.

"Is she, now?" one said.

The other nodded as if he'd learned something special. "Makes sense."

The woman frowned at the wind-whipped trees overhead. "Storm's getting closer. Let's put the rest of the birds up."

The men hurried away. Keelie's shoulder ached from holding up the bird. She rolled her neck, trying to get the blood moving again. "How did you know my name?"

"We met yesterday, remember?" Cameron shifted her birdlike gaze to Keelie. "Have animals always liked you? Did you know you also have a gift for healing?"

"I've never been around any animals, other than my friend's cat." She didn't answer the question about healing. What a joke. Mom had always considered medicine an unsuitable career for her.

Cameron opened the door to a large steel cage and beckoned to Keelie.

Although she didn't want to do it, Keelie reached into the cage with Ariel still on her arm, and placed the hawk next to a large branch inside. Surprisingly, the bird hopped over to the perch and settled right down, as if flying away was no big deal and now it was time for a nap.

"Amazing," said Cameron. Her smile widened as she watched Keelie put the hawk away. There was no disdain or condescension in the woman's eyes.

"If you aren't the squeamish type, Keelie, you can come by tomorrow and feed Ariel her lunch."

"What does Ariel eat for lunch?" She imagined a bag of hawk chow.

"Rats."

Keelie's face must have shown her disgust.

"Are you up to it?"

She watched Ariel on the perch. The hawk's milky eye

faced her. She was not totally blind, Keelie thought. The white eye was like a lens that allowed her insight into the hawk's soul, and Ariel shared the pain of losing her freedom.

Feeding rats to birds was gross, but she couldn't imagine not coming here. Cameron took the glove from her.

"When?"

"One in the afternoon," said Cameron. Her eyes darted back to the birds and then to Keelie. She was like a bird herself. "I'll be here."

Keelie walked away, but turned to catch one last glimpse of Ariel. The hawk had closed her eyes.

"See you tomorrow, Ariel."

On her way back to her father's booth, Keelie noticed that a lot of people were leaving, anxious eyes on the lowering clouds.

She was starving again and stopped to buy a corn on the cob dripping in butter. When she paid for it, she overheard a mundane say that they were under a tornado watch.

"Excuse me, sir. What time is it?"

"Four o'clock. What are you dressed as, kid?" The man was grinning at her skirt.

She glanced down. "I'm a fairy princess. What else?"

She left the guy staring openmouthed after her and hurried back up the path. Tornado watch. There weren't any of those in California. What was she supposed to do? Her only experience with tornados was at the movies. *Twister* and *The Wizard of Oz.*

She watched a wrinkled man in a long beard hurry past her, his purple robes flapping in the wind. Come to think of it, this place was very Oz.

She had stayed a long time at the Raptor Motel, longer than she'd meant to. Dad would be worried, but then he'd said she should explore the Renaissance Faire, and she had explored it. He probably hadn't missed her at all today. She bet he'd been busy with his furniture and his groupies.

It was funny how quickly time passed once she was with Ariel. She'd totally forgotten Laurie, too, though she needed to call her again. Tomorrow, she thought. After she'd fed Ariel.

She came to a sudden stop. She'd been so busy attending to the messy buttered corn that she hadn't paid a lot of attention to her surroundings.

There it was: the Muck and Mire Show's stage. She looked down at her bodice, and then glanced back at the handprints painted on the back of her skirt. She had to smile in spite of her hatred of the costume. The man named Tarl, who had brought her the dress, stood nearby talking to a small man.

She remembered the silhouettes and moans coming from Tarl's tent down at the Shire the night before. She didn't think she'd be able to talk to him with a straight face. The guy he was chatting with looked a lot like Sir Davey Morgan. She looked closer. It was Sir Davey Morgan. She hoped he didn't embarrass her by talking Earth-magic nonsense.

Part of Keelie wanted to run away and not speak with the men, but the compassionate part of her that had been awakened by Ariel wanted to stay. Tarl had been genuinely nice to her, coming to her rescue. It was an atrocious rag, but it was a kind gesture. More than she could say about some people. The image of Elia came to mind. Janice the herb lady had been nice to her, too, but Keelie figured she was just trying to to get in good with her father. And then there was Raven. Raven was cool, the big sister she'd never had.

On impulse, she decided to go up to Tarl, thank him for the clothes, and let him know that her luggage should be arriving soon. She'd try not to giggle at the image of his naked, potato-shaped silhouette.

He noticed her and waved.

She waved back and walked up to Sir Davey and Tarl. The image of Tarl's naked silhouette against the tent came back. Ew.

Clearing her throat, Keelie tried to think of the right words, but they sort of tumbled out. "Thanks for the clothes."

Tarl smiled. "You're welcome, Keelie. They look good on you. I'd like you to meet Sir Davey Morgan." He motioned with his hand toward the miniature musketeer, "And this is Keelie Heartwood."

Sir Davey bowed, and this time his ostrich feather swept through the mud. "I've had the pleasure of meeting Lady Keelie earlier, Sir Tarl."

Lady Keelie. She liked that. "Your hat," she exclaimed. The plume on his hat was now thin and brown, ruined by streaks of mud.

Sir Davey removed his hat and examined it, eyebrows furrowed. He pushed it back onto his head. "Good, clean dirt never hurt anyone, did it, Tarl?"

"Dirt is my life, Sir Davey." The big man glanced at a

group of Muck and Mire Players. "I'm going to get back to the others. We're working on a new skit. Care to join us?"

"I think I've had more mud to deal with in the past twenty-four hours than I will ever want to deal with again in my life," Keelie said.

Sir Davey waved his hand over the mud stain on the hat. Mud chips flew from the plume. Keelie couldn't believe it. The once brown and scraggly tip of his ostrich feather was now pristine white, as if it had been dipped in newly fallen snow.

"How did you do that?" she asked. "Is it a magic trick?"

"Tell me, Keelie Heartwood, as a child did you ever make mud pies?"

"Mud pies? Me? No."

"You missed out on a very important part of your childhood, young lady."

"How can missing out on making mud pies be bad?"

Sir Davey settled himself on the edge of the stage. He patted the plank beside him. She sat down.

Sir Davey picked up a handful of mud and squished it between his fingers. "This is part of the Earth."

"Right." She could do without the Captain Obvious science lesson.

Sir Davey arched a steel gray eyebrow at her. "Don't you think that's important?"

She shrugged.

"Think about the artists who work with clay, and kids—little children are artists, and they create from their heart. Have you seen children playing in the mud, in the sandbox? They don't say, ew this is gross!"

Keelie had to smile at Sir Davey's imitation of a valley girl accent. "Okay, I played at the beach a lot when I was a kid. But never with mud."

"Ahh, she admits to playing." Sir Davey grinned at her. "And in sand. Even the elementals are amazed at this confession."

"Elementals?"

"I'll explain later. First I want you to feel the mud. Hold out your hand."

Repulsion made her shiver. "I've had enough mud, thanks."

"Don't be a wimp."

"A wimp?" She extended her right hand, palm out. Sir Davey plopped the ball of mud onto her palm.

"You can create from the heart without your mind interfering with the process." He put his hand under hers and closed her fingers over the mud. It squelched between her fingers.

"Gross." But it wasn't.

It gave off an earthy smell, totally unlike the scented Play-Doh Keelie had played with when she was little.

Sir Davey shaped another ball of mud with his small fingers. Keelie formed her mud back into a ball and let it fall back onto the stage. She poked her index finger into it.

"I used to make homemade cups for Mom in art class when we did clay in elementary school. The art teacher would fire them in the kiln. Mom used one for her pens on her office desk."

Keelie poked another hole into the lump of mud.

Sir Davey kept shaping his mud into something. Keelie couldn't tell what it was, but it brought back a memory.

"When I was in second grade, I made a big bug pin for Mom. It was an ugly bug, too. I painted it black with pink polka dots, but Mom wore it to church on Easter Sunday. It clashed with her yellow floral designer dress, but she said that my pin was a work of art, and that she would be the envy of all the moms on Easter."

Sir Davey opened his hand to reveal a mud-brown replica of the bug pin she'd made Mom. Grief squeezed her heart. Keelie didn't question the magic any longer. The sadness oozed out of the space in her heart where she'd kept it, locked up as tightly as her anger. Sir Davey's mud bug had loosened the door.

She closed her eyes, trying to stop the tears before he could see them. When she opened them again, the bug had disappeared and in its place was a homely lump of mud.

"The Earth below us connects us all. We all stand on it, and we depend on it for nourishment," Sir Davey said. "Sometimes it can be dirty and messy, but it can also be nurturing and healing. And Earth is just a small part of your world, Keelie. Don't forget that in the days and months to come."

She heard her father calling. At first she thought it was part of Sir Davey's lesson, but then she realized she really could hear his voice. He stood a few feet away.

"Keelie, there you are. Where have you been all day? I've been looking for you everywhere."

She shoved all the sad feelings away, along with some

of the oozy ones. It was like locking away a secret treasure box. Keelie didn't want Dad to find her sad feelings, and somehow, she thought he'd be able to sense them. She added an invisible barrier of bricks around them.

"Zeke. Good to see you." Sir Davey bowed his head toward her father, who nodded in reply.

"Davey. I see you've met Keelie."

"It has been my honor." Sir Davey hopped off the stage and bowed to Keelie, and even though his snowy ostrich feather touched the ground, it remained white. "I enjoyed our talk. Come see me tomorrow and I'll show you how I did it."

A little shiver went through her, and she realized, surprised, that it was anticipation. She smiled at Sir Davey. He put his finger to his lips. Our secret.

"Come on, Keelie. Let's go home," Zeke said.

"Your home," Keelie corrected.

He sighed. "Come on."

They were a long way from the wood shop, and their silence made it seem even longer. When they neared the shop, Keelie raced ahead, climbing the stairs quickly and throwing open the door. Her eyes swept the room, looking for her luggage, but to her dismay, there was still no sign of her suitcases.

Her father seemed to be analyzing her face. "Looking for the cat?"

"No, my stuff. I thought it was supposed to arrive today."

He sighed even louder than before. "The airline called

and said it would be a few more days; it seems your clothes and other belongings have been flown to Istanbul."

"Istanbul? That isn't by any chance a suburb of Fort Collins?"

"Turkey. As in the country of."

Keelie dropped onto the bed. "I can't believe it. Those idiots can't deliver a simple bag." Much less ten of them.

"They've been tracked from Los Angeles to Hawaii, and then Hong Kong. Now they're en route to Istanbul."

"I thought I could live a couple of days without my clothes, but now it might be weeks, right? I can't walk around in this ridiculous outfit anymore. It's too humiliating."

"I agree. It doesn't really suit you," her father said. "But you need more than garb. I thought I'd take you shopping tomorrow."

She stared at him, then a spurt of laughter escaped her. "You? Take me shopping?"

He shook his head. "Unbelievable, I know. We'll experience the malls of Fort Collins. And you can go to Galadriel's Closet for a couple of Rennie outfits."

Mall. Just the word made her happy.

"It won't be so bad, I promise." Keelie pulled her feet up onto the bed. "Honestly, how long have you been at this festival in Fort Collins?"

"Three months a year for the past seven years," her father said.

"That long?" She counted back. Since she was nine. "Have you ever been to the mall?"

"I've never been to any mall."

"Never? Excuse me, what century is this?"

He laughed. "Fear not, daughter. I don't think it will be hard to find."

"Can you even drive?"

"Keelie, I can function in the mundane world."

"Some would call it the real world."

"Speaking of the real world, the books from your new school should arrive this week. I think it's important that we get started on your studies as soon as possible."

If her father had wanted to get her mind off her clothes, telling her that her books would be arriving here from her new school did it. It was almost summer.

Keelie picked up a green pillow with a beautiful gold-embroidered tree and hugged it close to her chest.

"Let me get this straight—you're expecting me to do schoolwork over summer break? And here, not at school with other kids my age?"

"In three weeks' time, we'll be traveling to New York for the Renaissance festival there. We'll be there for eight weeks, and you'll keep up your work by correspondence. When we return home to Oregon, you won't be behind the rest of your class."

"You think I'm going to New York and to Oregon with you." She didn't bother to make it a question. The answer was obvious.

"Yes, Keelie, I do. You're my daughter. We're family. We belong together."

Hot anger blazed its way through her. She threw the pillow onto the sofa. It bounced off and landed on the floor. She jumped up and kicked it.

"Mom and I were family. You ditched us, remember? I

belong in California. That's my home. Not Oregon. And not with you."

He looked hurt. Good.

"Keelie, I am so sorry you're hurting. I know you miss your mother very much. But you belong here with me."

"Did you even think about what I've lost? Not just Mom, but my friends, even my room?" She was mad at herself now. Was she going to cry? "You made all the decisions. One minute I'm at home, the next I'm here in this, this—" She waved her hands around, the words gone.

"It's another world, isn't it?" He looked around the room. "My life has changed, too. I'm not used to having a child around. Or a woman."

"Oh yeah, I'll bet your groupies are all in grief counseling now."

His eyes widened. "Groupies?"

"Don't tell me you don't notice all the women throwing themselves at you all the time. And what's with all this Keliel stuff? And the Spock ears everyone's wearing? This place is beyond bizarre." Keelie kicked the cushion again. "I want to go home. To California. I want my old life back."

"Even if your mother still lived, you would have come to me eventually," he said.

"That is so conceited. Like I was suddenly going to want a father, after years of nothing?"

"You needed to come here to learn how to control your gift." He looked serious.

She looked at him. He knew? She'd gone through hell

her entire life thinking she was some kind of genetic mutant, and he knew about it?

"Did Mom know?" she whispered, her lips numb.

He looked down, avoiding her gaze. "Yes. It's one of the reasons she left."

"She left? She said you left." Her world was suddenly sideways. Had Mom lied to her?

"We were in Oregon, and she took you and went back to California." His voice grew softer with each word.

"So why didn't you sue for custody? Of course, I'm fifteen now and it wouldn't work. After twelve, you get to choose where you live. I wouldn't pick here, that's for sure."

Her father was suddenly still, as if he was holding his breath. "Is that what your mother told you? She said I left you and that I didn't want you?"

"Well, not in so many words. But we were in California, and you were off being a gypsy. And you never asked for custody or even visitations." All of her friends with divorced parents had scheduled visitations.

"Visitations? Custody?" He looked totally bewildered, and a little angry, too. "Unbelievable. Keelie, your mother and I were never divorced."

eight

Earth magic, magical gifts, never divorced. The words spun through her head, making her dizzy. Keelie flopped onto the tall bed and hugged a pillow.

Tears burned her eyes, and she closed them tightly. She wouldn't cry. Why not, though? Who would see? She buried her face in the pillow and let the tears come.

She wanted to throw or break something, to tear something up until all of her anger melted away.

Colorado, New York, Oregon. But not California.

Never.

Never.

Never.

Something purred near her head. She opened her eyes. There, like a furry pile of autumn leaves, was Knot, curled into the corner behind her pillow.

"What are you doing in here?"

He purred louder.

"Go away."

The inner rumbling increased.

"That horse would have stomped you into itty-bitty kitty pieces if I hadn't shouted at it."

The purring stopped.

"Ungrateful beast."

It started again.

"I hate cats."

He sounded like a car engine.

"I hate you, especially."

The cat opened his weird green eyes and blinked at her.

With each insult, the gnawing anger inside of her dissipated a little.

"You're ugly."

Knot stretched and yawned.

"You shed fur everywhere."

The cat sat up.

"I should kick your butt for peeing in my suitcase."

Knot licked the fur on his tail with his pink tongue.

"Ew! Gross!"

The cat hopped off the bed and meandered over to the door. He sat down, his head turned expectantly toward Keelie.

She scooted off the bed, walked over to him, and stared

down at the insolent feline, her hands on her hips. "I'm not your door girl."

He blinked up at her.

"All right." She cracked the door and the cat squeezed out. She reasoned that if she didn't let him out, he might spray the room. It would be unliveable. As it was, she might never get the noxious smell of his urine out of her underwear and suitcase.

She heard her father speaking to a woman at the base of the stairs. Keelie could see his back and heard her low response. Keelie closed the door but left it open a wee smidge so she could hear and see.

"I don't know how to get through to her," Zeke was saying.

The woman answered, "Give her time, Zeke. Keelie has just arrived to a whole new world. It's the total opposite of what she's known, and on top of that she's grieving for her mother."

It sounded like nosy Janice. Keelie didn't need anyone going to bat for her. If she was blowing her father's mind with her rebellious attitude, then her plan was working. He would want to get rid of her all the sooner. And that meant she could live with Laurie in Los Angeles.

Keelie was doing him a favor.

She watched as her father's shoulders slumped. "I should never have agreed to be hands-off with Keelie's upbringing all those years ago. But that was what Katy wanted. She was so afraid of what Keelie would become. As if keeping her away from me would change the facts."

Keelie sucked in her breath. It wasn't Mom's idea for

Zeke not to see her. How dare he blame his absence all these years on Mom!

"What are you going to do? It's obvious what she is," the woman said. "The whole Ren Faire's buzzing about her. She needs to know, Zeke, and be taught some control. She's already wreaked havoc. That cat, for example. And poor Elia—not that she didn't deserve it. But if the mundanes notice, it would mean real trouble, for all of us."

Keelie almost jumped out of her hiding place. Had they gone crazy?

Her dad sat on the stairs, long legs sprawled out. He leaned his head on his hand. "She doesn't want to learn about her gift. Katy let Keelie think we were divorced, that I abandoned them."

So it was true. Keelie's head felt heavy.

Knot hopped into her father's lap, and he absentmindedly scratched him behind the ear. The cat closed his eyes and swished his tail.

"Stinker," Keelie mouthed silently.

Knot opened his eyes. They glowed like freaky green swamp gas. What was even freakier was that the cat stared right at Keelie as if he heard her. He began purring so loudly that she could hear his thrum upstairs.

Keelie quietly shut the door. The whole Ren Faire was talking about her? Well, la-de-da. She was leaving anyway.

No way she was going to wait around for Zeke to have another life-changing chat with her. She waited until Zeke left the stairs and returned to work, then put her shoes on and took off down the hill. She needed to see Ariel. She had a lot in common with the imprisoned hawk. Maybe she could just talk to her.

The sky was a lot darker than usual for this time of the evening, even though the tornado watch had been called off. She'd probably be missing dinner, if Zeke was planning to cook. More likely he'd send her back to Mrs. Butters. What a weird little woman.

Keelie passed merchants putting up their wares and locking their shops. A few glanced at her, then quickly turned back to their tasks. Keelie frowned. Was it her breath? Here she was dressed like one of them, living here, and she was being treated like a leper. Not that she wanted to be the local princess. But, still—would it hurt them to say hi?

She slowed as she reached the Birds of Prey show stage. A little sign next to a giant pine read "The Mews." Behind it was the place where the bird cages were kept. It was dark and silent.

What if she went in and woke the birds up? The great owls and vultures and hawks? The squawking would bring down a crowd. She stopped and looked around. Sir Davcy's shop was not too far away, but she didn't feel like another lesson on dirt and mud. Thunder rumbled above, but it seemed far away.

Maybe waking the birds was a bad idea. She needed warmth and to be around people. She thought of the Shire. Keelie turned toward the path. Maybe she would take more than a couple of swallows of the bottle when it was passed around. She needed something to warm her on the inside as well as the outside.

Last night, the tent had been warm and dry. She wondered what tent Sean slept in. And if he slept alone. Maybe Raven knew. She'd go to the Shire and ask her. She whipped around and started back down the hill, staying close to the merchants opposite Heartwood, in case Zeke saw her.

She walked past Galadriel's Closet and scooted quickly down to the bridge. She remembered Raven's instructions. "Over the bridge, past the meadow," she muttered. Stay on the path.

As the shadow of the bridge came into view, she saw lights to the left. Bingo. She remembered the lovers doing it underneath the bridge last night. With so many tents and buildings around, you'd think people would pick some place warmer and dryer. A troll didn't under live under the bridge. Or did it?

She thought about the slugs and frogs and spiders that no doubt did live there. Creepier than a troll, in her book.

She touched the handrail. Her hand buzzed, tingling. And she knew. Redwood from California.

"Far from home, aren't you?" Keelie murmured. Quickly, she withdrew her hand. And inhaled. She had to stop this. She just needed to be around the other kids that hung out at the party. Hopefully, she could find Sean. She imagined placing her hands against his chest as he wrapped his arms around her. She envisioned the warmth of his body soaking into hers.

"Keliel." Her name wafted around her like half-remembered perfume. A ghost of her name, carried on the faint breeze, and drawn out, as if the speaker were singing, but forgot the tune.

She looked around nervously. Keliel. The voice had plainly called her by her given name. Not Keelie, the nickname her mother had called her. Who besides her dad and Ms. Talbot even knew it?

The rain-laden breeze ruffled her hair. "Keliel," the voice moaned, and it sounded as if it was coming from beneath the boards under her feet. "Keliel, swim with me."

What the heck? She looked down. Not cool. She thought of walking up this path yesterday with Raven, talking about horror movies. Creepy films where girls walking around in the dark alone always ended up as chick nuggets.

The girls in those movies were too stupid to live. She didn't consider herself stupid, so why the heck was she out here in the dark? She wasn't going to stick around to find out whoever or whatever knew her name. Her real name.

Suddenly, she realized that it was quiet. As in, not even any insects. No light. She looked behind her, up the path toward Heartwood. No light showed. Only the moon illuminated the path. Fast clouds moved in the purple sky around it.

She looked around, then stopped. There was a light. It was on the other side of the clearing. She wasn't afraid, she told herself, breaking into a run. Gravel in the path crunched underfoot as she sped toward the light. It must be the Shire.

She was off the path now, trying to ignore the buzzing on her skin as she passed tree after tree. So many. Pine, pine, oak, hawthorn. Something about the hawthorn was different. She didn't stick around to find out.

She ran faster, eager to get to the light. She veered north, the moon at her right shoulder. The meadow she ran through was fragrant with tall grass. At the end of the meadow was a forest. The light came from there. Suddenly, a cloud of bugs sprang out of the weeds. Fireflies. Hundreds and hundreds of them.

Storm clouds covered the moon, and it was suddenly dark. Pitch black. No stars. No way of orienting herself. The fireflies glowed brighter, seeming to gain light from the darkness. They hovered, a living wall.

She stopped, afraid. Bugs didn't get brighter. These fireflies didn't twinkle, turning on and off like regular ones. They just glowed. Like lightbulbs. She backed away. She didn't want to go through them. Her stomach ached, as if it had been clenched for a long time. She shivered. She had to find a way home. She wanted her mom.

Maybe she could ask the voice at the bridge for directions. Okay, maybe not. This was weird. She wasn't afraid of the dark. And she sure as heck wasn't afraid of bugs or lights.

She forced herself to take a step forward. Fireflies were just little bugs. Bugs were creepy, but fireflies were like lady bugs. Raven would forge ahead and not be afraid—she'd march right into the creepy dark, and whatever was in the woods would be afraid.

Keelie took a step toward the forest, then another. The lights were closer, and then they were gone, and she was at the edge of a village. An honest to goodness village, not the crappy mudfest of the Faire.

Why didn't her dad's place look this good? She stepped

onto the pine-needle cushion of the forest floor and felt immediate relief, as if an unknown pain had been relieved.

A stone tower pushed toward the tree tops, embellished with carved, jeweled dragonflies and stone leaves. Really, Dad had the forest thing going on, but these people took it to designer level.

It was no Bel-Air mansion, but if she was roughing it, this was roughing it with style. A beautiful smell clung to the place. Like going into a Bath & Body Works. What was that smell? It was like Christmas here. A subtle hint of cinnamon imbued the mostly pine forest.

A movement at the base of the tower caught her eye. Elia was inside, wiping down her harp. Holy cow. Keelie crept closer. She lived upstairs from a wood shop, and Elia lived in a stone tower, like a princess? So not fair.

Before she could get closer, a man appeared. He looked like something from *The Lord of the Rings*. Tall, with long blonde hair and a long, cold face, he wore crimson robes that swept the forest floor as he stepped in front of her, barring her way.

"Whoa. Am I glad to see you. Can you tell me how to get back to the Faire?"

"Who are you? How did you get here?"

Elia came to the door. "Father, is something wrong?" She saw Keelie and froze. "Keelie? How did you get past the Dread?"

This guy was Elia's dad! Immediately, Keelie saw the family resemblance. Sneering must be in their genetic code. Elia angled her head in that snarky I'm-better-than-you tilt that irritated Keelie. She'd have to do an impression of Elia for Raven.

But, the Dread? What was that, their guard dog? "I didn't see any Dread. I got off the path and got lost. Really, if you show me the way back I'll be out of your hair in a minute. By the way, love the outfit. Where did you get it?" Gold embroidered leaves trailed around the wide sleeves: a back-to-nature theme with bling, bling. It went with the designer feel of the camp.

Glowering at Keelie, Elia's dad swung a silver chain back and forth like a pendulum. "You're Heartwood's brat. His little human half-breed."

Keelie's eyes were drawn to the strange pendant, a vine of thorns twined around an acorn. She shivered as the man's glance caught hers. The thorn-imprisoned acorn spun around hypnotically. Clasping his hand over the pendant, he shoved it up his wide sleeve.

As it vanished, she regained her courage. "I am Keliel Heartwood," she confirmed, giving him her full name. "And who are you?"

His eyebrows surged together in a glacial frown.

A voice spoke a name in her mind, green and fragrant with sap, counteracting the strong odor of cinnamon.

"Elianard. That's your name."

He stepped back.

"How did she know, Father?" Elia's voice was almost frightened.

Suddenly, an overpowering darkness enveloped Keelie. The trees swayed, but she couldn't feel the wind; instead, it was hot. Very hot and sticky. Sweat dripped down her back as she stumbled away from the blurring images of Elianard and Elia. His crimson robes becoming a morphic swirl of crimson and darkness. A nasty giggle surrounded Keelie as she woodenly ran away from the camp. She had to get out of here. Now. She couldn't stay any longer. If she did she wouldn't be able to breathe.

Something scratched at her legs as she ran. She only knew one thing: Get out of the forest. Green ropy fingers with sharp pointy nails snagged her skirt. She saw briars and thorns, but she thought she saw eyes and limbs tangled in the mess.

Keelie ran up to a beech tree and wrapped herself around it. She pressed her face into the smooth bark. Its life-giving sap pumped through its trunk like the red blood that flowed through Keelie's body. A branch touched her hair with sticklike fingers in a comforting gesture, sort of like Mom use to do when Keelie was upset. Raw grief burst forth. Unbidden tears flowed down her face, but it washed away the fear, revealing a hollow hole inside her heart.

She said in a soft whisper, "Mom, where are you? Which way to the Faire?" As if in answer, Keelie heard water flowing nearby. It had to be the stream. She lifted her head up toward the branch, and for a second she swore she thought she'd seen some primitive puppets made of sticks, grass, and leaves way high in the uppermost branches of the tree. She shook her head. Ever since she'd arrived here at the Faire, she'd seen things that she'd sworn were there, and when she looked they weren't. It was like the lines between reality and pretend had blurred. Did she really want to see stick men?

No.

Keelie stepped away from the tree and brushed away her tears. If Raven were here, she would have marched over the bridge and all the way back to New York. But what if Keelie heard the eerie voice again? Taking a cue from Raven's example, Keelie summoned her bravado, what was left of it, and marched with determination. What was another weird voice in her head? She was going to get back to the Faire, and she was going to get back to California ASAP.

She started to touch the redwood handrail but pulled her hand back. Enough. Her wood-channeling days were over. From the corner of her eye, she saw a small shape run in and between the trees. It was too fast to be a raccoon, and it didn't move like anything from *Animal Planet.* She shuddered. No. She wasn't going to let her boundaries between reality and imagination blend like two primary colors.

She just had to get over the bridge and get her ass back to the Faire. "Over the stream, through the woods, back to Daddy's bungalow, I go." Her whispered song faded as she heard the watery voice from under the bridge.

"Keliel. Danger."

She stopped.

Twigs snapped in the woods. In between gathering dark clouds, the moon silvered the forest as the red blur streaked through the trees. From the distance, thunder rumbled. Adrenalin pumped through Keelie as she ran across the bridge.

On the opposite side she tripped over a rock, tumbled down the bank, and landed face-first in the shallow water.

As she pushed up on her hands, something heavy and solid landed on her back. Whatever was on her pushed Keelie's head back underwater.

Water filled her nose, her mouth. She couldn't breathe. She kicked her legs as she tried to roll over to get the thing off of her. She opened her eyes, but she couldn't see anything. The eerie voice that she'd heard under the bridge was clearer, sharper. "Touch the bridge."

Keelie searched frantically for the bridge. Inches from her head was the bridge post, but she couldn't reach it. She forced her way over to it, using her elbows in the sandy bottom as the heavy thing on her back pushed her head farther down into the water. The tips of her fingers scraped the wood. Energy flowed through her. The solid weight on her back was suddenly gone. Keelie flung her head up, gasping for breath.

Rivulets of water streamed down her face and over her body as, teeth chattering, Keelie rose to her knees.

Shock and cold coursed through her. Someone had tried to kill her. Or something, she thought as she stared at a pruny-faced little man with a red cap and pointed teeth, gesticulating wildly at her with his hands as he danced a jig on the other side of the stream. He looked like a Christmas elf gone bad.

"Death to the daughter. And grief to the father," he sang in a tinny, singsong voice. *The Twilight Zone* moment was interrupted by a bundle of orange fur that landed in front of the repulsive Rumpelstiltskin.

Knot hissed as he swished his tail back and forth like a

deadly whip. Teeth bared and ears flat against his head, a deep growl rumbled from his throat.

"Get him, Knot," Keelie yelled, then stopped. What if the hideous thing hurt Knot?

The little man growled back, snapping his teeth together. The cat crouched lower, his bottom moving back and forth, ready to attack. Keelie held her breath, unsure how this would end. She crouched, too, and felt for a stick. If Knot needed her, she'd play Whac-A-Mole with the little creep.

The red-capped man reached down to the ground and pulled up a black, decayed mushroom. A horrid stench filled the air as it disintegrated. The little man danced a jig, and more rancid mushrooms popped up from the ground. Old autumn leaves from the forest floor swirled around the hideous creature in a leafy tornado, hiding him.

Knot attacked, but when he landed there were only old dried leaves and mushroom goo. He waggled his left front leg and then his right front one to dislodge the fungus yuck from his paw pads. The smell was outrageous.

He meowed and turned his head toward Keelie. His swampy green eyes glowed like two full green moons. He headed away from the stream and through the woods, with his tail swishing back and forth. His orange fur gleamed with phosphorus luminosity.

"You know this place better than me, old cat." She followed him. He was hateful and obnoxious, but he'd come to her rescue. She glanced once more toward the bridge, but saw only darkness.

Neither the little red-capped fiend or the owner of

the voice under the bridge was visible. She shivered and raced to catch up, shoes squishing loudly in the otherwise quiet forest. Only thunder pierced the strange quiet of the woods and the moon had disappeared behind a coverlet of clouds.

Lighting forked in the sky, and in its momentary brightness, she saw the path. She sighed with relief.

From a distance, she heard her father calling.

Knot yowled in return and then disappeared into the woods in the direction of her father's voice. Just like that cat to come to her rescue, then get her into trouble. Despite nearly being drowned by a manic midget in a really bad elf suit, Keelie knew her butt was about to be barbecued, parent-style. She wrapped her arms around herself in attempt to shield her body from the cold, from the woods, and from whatever creepy stuff was happening around the Faire.

As Zeke walked quickly toward her, Knot accompanied him, meowing like he was telling Zeke what had happened. Her father nodded as if he understood him and walked faster. The snot cat was ratting her out.

He stopped, inhaled, and then he reached for her and hugged her close to him. "By all that is blessed in the Great Silvus, you're safe."

Keelie stepped back from his fatherly embrace.

Lowering his hands, Zeke clenched them into fists. "Half the Faire's been looking for you. You've been in great danger."

Keelie's teeth started to chatter, but she wasn't about to

confirm or deny. He'd left her almost fourteen years ago. Mom and Dad were never divorced.

"Were you at the Shire? That place is off-limits, Keelie. I thought you understood that. You were in great danger."

"I know. I was there."

"And you're grounded. And you are not to walk by yourself—ever. Sir Davey or myself will accompany you."

Fabulous. A new level of lame.

"I'm not in nursery school, Zeke. I can take care of myself."

A glow from nearby made her glance away from her father's angry face. Was it that tiny dude, come back to finish the job? This could turn out like that horror movie about the evil leprechaun she'd seen late one night on the SciFi channel. Mom hated the SciFi channel.

The glow got closer. It was a lamp, held up by Sean. How embarrassing. She scarcely heard her father's angry words as she thought of the extreme humiliation of being reamed out on the path while the Faire's number-one hottie could hear. Where was he ten minutes ago when she needed to be rescued?

"The regular rules don't apply here. I should have warned you, but you've only been here one day and already you've disobeyed me. I can't trust you. I was going to allow you to use the telephone to call your friends in California, but that's out now until I see that you can obey my rules."

Grounded? What could be worse? She saw Sean, who'd overheard everything, turn to someone, and the person stepped into the light. Elia. Elia, grinning broadly. If that manic midget needed a victim, Keelie had a recommendation for him. After she kicked his butt for trying to drown her.

Time to turn the tables on dear old dad. A little sympathy play might get her sentence reduced.

She summoned a sniffle, a convincing one since she'd probably caught pneumonia. "I got lost in the woods and found Elia's father. Elianard frightened me."

"Where did you meet Elianard?"

"At his place. Gotta say, they live much better than you do. How does he rate the stone tower? Kind of fairy tale, but cool."

Zeke stared at her as if he'd just noticed that she was soaked. He picked a thorn out of her sleeve. "What happened, exactly?"

"I fell into the stream and got attacked by a grumpy yard gnome with pointy teeth. Knot rescued me." She tried to make light of it, but her muscles tightened and she started to shiver. The gnome had really tried to kill her.

She stared at the cat. So awful to be indebted to the beast that had ruined her clothes. "We need to call the police so they can arrest that demented gnome, lock him up, and throw away the key."

"This gnome, did he have a red cap?"

"Yeah, do you know him?"

"No." Zeke sounded offended that she would even ask the question. "But this confirms what we suspected. It's not a gnome. I'll have to notify the others."

"Hey, how about some justice for me? I want to file a police report. I want to see his butt hauled off to jail. I want Rumpelstiltskin in a lineup."

Zeke sighed wearily. "This is a Faire problem. We'll handle it."

"What? You haven't been down to the Shire, have you?" She leaned closer to get a whiff of his breath. He smelled like cinnamon.

Raven came running down the path, holding a blanket over her arm.

Janice was close behind her. "Keelie, are you okay? I heard you got wet."

"Been talking to Knot? He's such a chatterbox."

Raven snorted. "Okay, long evening, tired kid. You need to get dry, O delusional one." She unfurled the blanket. It was a wool cape with a hood. She settled it on Keelie's shoulders and put the hood up.

Keelie thought she probably looked just like she felt—like Death.

"I can't believe you let her stand out here, freezing to death, Zeke." Janice fussed over her, twisting the cloak closed. "She needs dry clothes."

"These are my only clothes." Keelie sniffed for effect.

Both women turned to Zeke, openmouthed.

"I don't have any underwear, either. Knot peed on them. In my suitcase." Keelie sniffed again.

"That's it. We're taking you shopping tomorrow." Janice looked determined.

Zeke threw his arms in the air. "I was going to. She's only been here one day."

"Let's go to the mall." Raven grinned at Keelie.

"I told her I would take her shopping. We'll go to the mall tomorrow," Zeke said. He sounded defeated.

"You?" Raven looked at her mother, who returned her disbelieving stare. "You've never been to a mall."

Raven laughed. "This I will have to see. Zeke Heartwood in the mall. This is High Mountain Renaissance History in the making. I can't wait to see her reaction when she sees what you drive. I'm coming with the two of you. Keelie will need the moral support."

"Fine, do you want to drive?" Zeke raised an eyebrow.

"No, that's fine," Raven said hastily. "I'll ride."

Keelie hadn't thought of what kind of car her father might drive. "What is it, a Gremlin?" She snorted.

Raven shook her head. "You'll never believe it."

"You'll see," her father said. Thunder rumbled ominously overhead.

It wasn't until much later, when she was in bed, that she realized she hadn't asked her father what Elianard had meant by "little human half-breed."

nine

Keelie ran down the path to the parking lot ahead of her father. She'd spent the morning doing her laundry with Dad's herbal soap. Now her panties smelled like cat pee and lavender.

She'd tried to use the washers and dryers, but had stopped dead ten feet away and out of sight of the occupants.

The little glass-fronted room with the two commercial washers and dryers was full of half-naked pirates. They were drinking mead, throwing dice, and waving their arms, probably telling stories to each other, and not one of them had on more than underwear.

Keelie presumed that their clothes were being washed, but she wasn't about to go near the place, no matter how good they looked. And some of them were lots of fun to look at. She could sell tickets. *The Full Randy*—a new pirate show.

It had been a pain to do the laundry by hand. Next time, pirates or no pirates, she was using the machines, or else she'd be the one that was naked. But that might be moot. In two hours she'd be at the mall.

■ ■ ■

Keelie stared in disbelief at the ancient pickup truck with its rusted hood. She'd rushed through Ariel's feeding for this?

"Like I'm going to be seen riding around in this ski chalet on wheels," Keelie said. "Everybody who sees me get out of this contraption will expect me to yodel."

The thought of shopping at a real mall had made her almost giddy, but the jubilation deflated when she saw Zeke's unbearable ride.

The pickup truck wasn't so bad. It was even kind of cool, in a retro-cowboy way. But the A-frame camper attached to the back of it, decorated like a shop project birthday cake with gingerbread trim, horrified her.

Zeke sighed. "It's the only wheels I have, Keelie, so if you want to go to the mall and buy some new clothes, then you're riding in this 'ski chalet on wheels.'"

"I don't see how you draw the chicks with this," she said. "This buggy broadcasts 'Granola Acres Retirement Home' loud and clear."

"This is just transportation, Keelie. And I'm older than I look, but I'm not retirement age."

"How old are you?" It hadn't occurred to her before to ask his age.

"Old enough to be your daddy." He opened the camper. "Would you like the grand tour, mademoiselle?"

She was going to refuse, but the smell of cedar wafted from the dark interior like a forest perfume. Irresistible.

Her hand reached out, fingertips touching the wood of the camper frame. It was blue spruce and cedar, from a remote northern forest in Alberta, Canada. Lovely.

She was growing used to the internal wood identification system she seemed to have been born with. In L.A. it had been faint, but here, surrounded by old forest, it was like a sound system turned up full blast.

The inside of the camper looked like a dollhouse. A small stove and refrigerator lined the back, next to a minute countertop and sink. Garlands of garlic and dried red peppers hung from a cup hook overhead.

"This is so cute!" As long as it stayed parked right here.

She ran her hand over the homemade quilt with awesome tree appliqués that was tucked over the mattress on the shelf bolted to the wall.

A smaller shelf below the big one held a round pet bed lined with fleece and decorated with reindeer. Even if she hadn't guessed that it was Knot's bed, Keelie recognized his orange cat hair. An evil smile tugged at her lips. So, the wittle bitty kitty had a reindeer bed. She'd remember to torment him with that knowledge next time she saw him.

She looked out a window and saw the majestic Rockies, rising like giant stone teeth, and the Faire, tucked in at the bottom of the rising rock mammoths like a village from a fairy tale by Grimm.

Keelie glanced around the small interior. It had a cozy, self-sufficient atmosphere to it. She loved it, but something had to be done about the hideous alpine hillbilly exterior.

"Getting the fifty-cent tour?" Raven stuck her head in the door. "So, Keelie, what do you think?"

"This is too cute. Like a little dollhouse."

Zeke smiled at Keelie.

"I just don't want to be seen driving in it." She watched her father's smile vanish.

"Yeah, just think how it'll be learning how to drive it. You're fifteen, right?"

Learn to drive? In this? Keelie grabbed the doorway. Elm.

Zeke looked kind of faint, too. "Learn to drive? Already?"

"Miss fourteen years and it kind catches up to you, doesn't it?" Keelie stood straighter. Learning to drive in this buggy was so not going to happen, but if it made Zeke uncomfortable, she'd let him think she wanted it.

"Mom had a Volvo. Fabulous safety rating." She flicked the doorway with her finger.

Raven grinned up at her. "My mom taught me how to

drive in her old VW van. It was like driving a box. Worse, it reeked of stale patchouli."

Raven shouldered her purse. She looked great in hip-hugging jeans and layered sweaters. As she reached up, Keelie saw a glint of gold at the waistband of Raven's jeans. A belly ring.

Envy stung Keelie. She wanted one so badly. For sure she'd have it before the summer was done.

"Earth to Keelie. Ready to go to the mall?" Raven was grinning.

Mall! Keelie'd been distracted from her mission for new clothes. She wanted—no, needed—to go shopping. It wasn't just about underwear. She craved the processed air, the new-clothes smell of retail heaven, not to mention the scents of fresh high-end coffee brewing, perfume samples, and the mingled smells of the food court—cinnamon buns, French fries, and Chinese food—that would infuse new life into her blood cells. She jumped down from the camper, landing with a splash.

"I'm ready."

If she had to ride in the Swiss Miss Mobile to get there, then by golly, she'd do it. Mom would've been proud that Keelie hadn't let any obstacle stop her from going shopping.

Zeke hopped into the driver's side of the ancient truck, inserted his key, and the engine coughed like a chain-smoking emphysema patient Keelie'd met when she'd gone on pink lady volunteer rounds with Grandma Josephine.

Raven jumped in next to Keelie after she got back in,

squishing her against Zeke, then slammed the passenger-side door shut.

Finally, the engine sputtered to life. Zeke pulled out of the graveled back parking lot where the Renaissance Faire actors and vendors parked their personal vehicles.

The place was crowded with Faire workers in everyday clothes, enjoying their day off. She didn't see Captain Randy. She almost giggled at the thought of just how much of him she'd seen earlier. It gave a whole new meaning to the phrase "pirate booty."

"On weekdays the craftspeople work on their wares, making more stock for the weekends," Zeke explained.

Raven laughed. "Not everyone's a craftsperson. A lot of us go to the laundromat, the grocery store, and do all those errands we don't have time for during the weekends."

Another pickup truck approached them, this one perfectly normal, with no dents, and best of all, no chalet on the back. It was full of long-haired guys. The driver leaned out and blew kisses at them. Captain Randy! Had he seen her?

Zeke shook his head.

Raven rolled her eyes. "That idiot. He was probably at the Admin office picking up his paycheck."

"Paycheck?" It hadn't occurred to Keelie that these guys got paid. She thought they all sold their stuff, like her dad did.

Raven gave her a look. "This ain't Middle Earth. The ones who aren't craftspeople are actors and performers."

"Does Elia get paid, too?"

"You bet."

"Not for her personality, that's for sure." As they approached the highway, Keelie ducked down.

"Need a nap?" Zeke's perfect profile was turned toward the road.

"Nope. Just because I had some kind of *Little House on the Prairie* spasm in the camper does not mean I want to be seen hauling it through the hills like Jed Clampett's kin."

"Jed who?"

Keelie sighed. The man was a media moron. "I'll bet you never watch Nick at Nite, do you? Hello? *The Beverly Hillbillies*?"

"Never met them."

Raven laughed and started to sing the theme song.

"And you're probably old enough to have seen them when the show was new," Keelie added.

He grinned. "I probably am."

"At least the rain's held off this morning." Raven looked at the lowering dark clouds.

"Business is way off because of it." Zeke drove with both hands on the wheel. Mom had driven with one hand on the wheel and a cell phone in the other.

"Elianard doesn't seem to be hurting financially." Keelie remembered his lush robe and fancy house.

"He doesn't show his face much at the Faire. He must have another business," Raven said.

"He's a teacher." Zeke turned on the truck lights as rain hammered them.

Keelie couldn't imagine what the beaky-nosed, arrogant man could teach. He hadn't taught his daughter any manners, that was for sure.

Two hours later, after driving in pouring-down rain around what seemed like every street in the world, they arrived at the mall. Funny—it only should have taken thirty minutes from the Renaissance Faire grounds to the mall, according to Cameron.

Like a typical man, Dad refused to ask for directions. Whenever Raven asked if he could pull over in a service station to ask, he said, "I know what I'm doing." If Mom had been driving, she'd have used her sales sonar to zone in on the exact location. Or her GPS system.

Keelie sighed with delight as she scanned the grand temples of retail. She'd brought her money with her, but she wasn't going to spend it unless she had to. Dad owed her. She'd spend his money first. Plus, she might need it when she left for L.A.

"You girls hop out here, and I'll park the truck."

Keelie hopped out and ran for the doors, not anxious to be seen leaving the Swiss Miss Chalet on wheels.

She and Raven went through the revolving doors and stopped inside by a bubbling fountain. Music wafted through the air above the hushed murmurs of hundreds of shoppers.

Keelie took a deep breath, ready for a hit of that shopping-mall smell. This California girl was so ready.

Instead, the air seemed stale, a recycled stink that seemed familiar, but gross. Artificial. It wasn't the life-reviving result she'd anticipated. The first inhalation of mall air had always filled Keelie with a feeling of delirious anticipation. She stared around at the carefully manicured indoor gardens, the water fountain, the bright colors of store signs, and carefully arranged displays. It all seemed fake.

Don't panic, she reassured herself. She'd been through a lot of stress, and she needed to get inside a store. A real store with real clothes, and then she'd feel like the real Keelie.

"I'm ready for a tall latte and a dose of retail therapy," Raven declared.

Zeke joined them, looking disoriented and totally out of place.

"Where do we start?" he asked. "I take it this is your natural environment?"

Keelie swept her arm in a dramatic gesture, then twirled around on one foot like a ballerina. "This is my world."

Zeke sighed. "Then give me the grand tour."

Keelie scanned the directory and found her favorite store. "La Jolie Rouge is on the third floor. Let's start there."

"I love their clothes." Raven ran her finger down the illuminated glass sign. "Here's the coffee shop. Want to come there with me first, or shall I join you later?"

"Let's get this over with as quickly as possible." Zeke didn't look well.

She wanted to do it all, but if her father was going to declare a time limit, she needed to strategize.

"Get me a double-shot grande latte. And if they have almond biscotti, a couple of those." Keelie looked at her father. "How about you? Herb tea?"

"Green tea," he corrected. "With honey."

"Fair trade honey." Raven laughed. "Okay, folks, see you in a bit." She disappeared into the crowd.

Zeke stepped awkwardly onto the escalator, and Keelie took his arm. She didn't want him to fall down and cut their shopping trip short. He drew himself up, standing straight, and patted her on the hand, but his gaze was fixed overhead, on the skylights, where rain pattered onto the glass panels. Zeke's hair had parted around his ear, and Keelie saw a pointed ear tip.

She touched her round right ear, then felt the left one, the one with the funky pointed tip that she always kept covered with her hair or a headband. Mom had said it was a kind of birthmark. Now she knew who to blame.

Maybe all the pointy ears she'd seen earlier weren't fakes, but she was at the mall. She'd ask him about it later.

In La Jolie Rouge, she raced to the teen section, where she quickly started picking out clothes to try on. She narrowed her choices down to ten shirts and five pairs of hip-hugger pants. Zeke sat on a wooden window seat and leaned his head against the glass wall, arms crossed and eyes closed. Shopping obviously wasn't his fave activity.

A young salesgirl with a pierced eyebrow helped Keelie carry her clothes to the dressing room.

"Where did you get your piercing done?" Keelie whispered, glancing toward her snoozing parent.

The girl, whose nametag read "Gabrielle," said, "The only cool place to go is Uncle Harry Mac's."

"Uncle Harry Mac's?" said Keelie. It sounded like a fast food restaurant.

"Yeah, he's got places all over Colorado. And he does

it all: tattoos, eyebrows, ears, and belly button rings." Gabrielle lifted her shirt and showed Keelie her pierced belly button ring. A tiny fairy charm dangled from the ring. Fairies. She just couldn't get away from the darn things.

"I want my belly button pierced, too," Keelie said.

"So, who's the hottie you're with?" asked Gabrielle. And she pointed toward Zeke, who still had his eyes closed and his arms crossed, except now his head was sort of slumped over to the left, and he was making snorting sounds. Hottie? No way.

"He's my father."

"Whoa, girl." Gabrielle stared at Zeke again, then at her.

Keelie snatched the remaining pants and shirts from Gabrielle. The girl may have had good taste in clothes, but as far as men—gross. Her father.

Keelie tried on a tank top that said Vampire Girl in glittering sequins across her chest. The short top exposed a lot of skin. The jeans hung just right on her hips, though Keelie didn't like the cool air on her butt dimples. What were her girlfriends wearing in California? Keelie Heartwood was definitely a fashionista, not a Rennie.

She ran her hands across her belly button. "We're going to be making a little trip to Uncle Harry Mac's," she said to her little innie. "But no fairy charms. A plain hoop, or maybe my birthstone."

No matter what Zeke said, Mom had promised. Well, she'd promised that they'd discuss it when she got back from her business trip. The world owed her a pierced belly button.

"Are you decent?" Raven stuck her head over the dressing room door.

"What if I wasn't?" Keelie tried to look indignant, but then she saw the hand appear under the stall door, holding a big paper-sleeved coffee cup. "Bless you. You may enter."

Raven came in, sipping her coffee. "Cool outfit. Love it."

Keelie twirled to show her the back. "Think my father will let me buy it?"

"Not a chance. But he's out there canoodling with the shop girl, so you can use that as leverage."

"What?" Keelie stuck her head out of the stall door. Gabrielle was sitting very close to Zeke. He had a perplexed expression on his face. Eek. Keelie had to put a stop to this. She jumped out and struck a ta-da pose.

"Hey Dad, what do you think?"

Gabrielle smiled. "Cool outfit. You got it happenin', girlfriend."

Her father frowned. "Vampire Girl? It's not happening, Keelie."

"What do you mean it's not happening? What do you know about fashion?"

He stood and folded his arms across his chest, like the Jolly Green Giant. "I don't know anything about fashion, but I know vampires. I'm not buying that for you."

Gabrielle's eyes widened. "Cool."

"Oh, come on. I brought my own money, and I'll buy it myself if I have to." Keelie looked toward Raven for a little support. Raven sipped her coffee and watched them as if they were a vaguely interesting TV show.

"I'm buying it."

"Fine. Buy it. Waste your money. I'm sure Knot will agree with me. It's too adult for you, and vampires are evil. You won't wear it."

"What do you mean Knot will agree? Knot is a cat."

"Remember that incident with your underwear?"

Gabrielle looked confused. "Your cat picks your underwear?"

Raven was bent over, wiping coffee from her nose.

"Yuk it up, Raven. You are not helping here." She turned to Zeke and Gabrielle. "I am so not discussing my underwear with you." She didn't specify who "you" was.

In the dressing room, Keelie angrily tugged the Vampire Girl tank over her head. One thing Mom had taught her was not to waste money, even if it was to spite someone. She surveyed the clothes—if this top wasn't happening, then the others weren't happening. Except for maybe a green cotton shirt with drawstrings at the chest and long bell sleeves. Galadriel wear. What was the name of that stupid store? Galadriel's Closet. Probably all the people walking around with their prosthetic ears shopped there. Not her. She covered her pointed ear with her hair.

She stepped out of the dressing room. Zeke was looking through some blouses on a round rack. Raven trailed after them, a hanger over her shoulder. The sales girl had three on her arm. "Yeah, that's way cool. Sort of *Lord of the Rings*-like, you know," Raven said.

Keelie cleared her throat.

"Hey, girlfriend, that outfit is so you," Gabrielle said. She glanced up at Zeke, all flirty. "If your dad says so, that is."

Dad nodded. "That's more like it. You look beautiful, Keelie."

Gabrielle held out some more shirts. "Check these out. Your old man picked them out."

Keelie took them. Great, if you went to a severe private school for fairy princesses. She was not going back with Elia's wardrobe.

A white gauze one with colorful embroidery around the neck was the only decent one. She held it out. "This one doesn't suck too much."

Raven held out her hanger. Black jeans and two tops, one a skinny long-sleeved sweater, the other a beaded gauze poet shirt. All black.

Zeke stared at them. "Decent but depressing."

"Everyone in New York dresses like this." Raven held out the hangers, admiring her choices. "If you don't like these, I'm buying them for myself."

"They're very you," Keelie agreed. "I don't know what to get."

"Something colorful that fits. Something for girls." Zeke looked at Gabrielle for advice.

"Buttons 'n Lace is over there." Gabrielle pointed to one side of the mall. "And Noir Leather is over there." She pointed to the other side of the mall. "Girls wear all of those clothes."

Gabrielle was trying to be helpful, but Zeke glared at her.

"You all decide. I'm checking out Noir Leather." Raven grabbed her coffee cup and stood. "Tarl's girlfriend shops there. You know the one, Keelie. She was scoping out your Dad's butt the other day."

Keelie also remembered the silhouettes on Tarl's tent. "Oh, gross."

Keelie watched Raven go. Keelie was so going to get even with Raven for abandoning her to her father's fashion sense.

After trying on more jeans and shirts, Keelie wore the green top with bell sleeves and jeans that hung on her hips but didn't expose her butt dimples. Dad had bought her five shirts and five pairs of pants. She'd used her own money to buy the Vampire Girl top. She was not leaving it behind. And if Knot did anything to it, she'd have a pair of kitty-fur earmuffs, too.

Holding the two heavy La Jolie Rouge bags definitely balanced Keelie. She felt more like her old self.

Her dad, however, looked paler than she'd ever seen him—even more ashen than when Gabrielle had rung up the clothes and announced the total. It didn't seem to make him feel better when Keelie reassured him that spending five hundred dollars at La Jolie Rouge hadn't been that bad. They had really come out cheap. He just didn't get shopping.

After a stop at a shoe store, where he bought her the latest Nikes, she tossed her muddy Skechers into the box, demoted to work shoes. Zeke had paled again when the cashier said the total was one hundred and seven dollars. Keelie had to pat his arm to reassure him that it was okay.

She pulled the credit card from his hand as he was returning it to his wallet. "Bank of Dread Forest? Is that for real?"

The sales clerk smiled. "Sure is, or at least my computer thinks so. Zekeliel Heartwood. Love that name." Her voice was sweet enough to draw ants.

Keelie pictured fire ants in the woman's super-short skirt and smiled. She gave him back his card. "Dread is Elianard's dog, too. He said he couldn't believe I'd gotten past him."

Zeke choked on a sip of green tea.

They caught up with Raven at Noir Leather. Just entering the shop was an education. An adult education. Zeke hastily dragged her back out and made her wait in the mall while he found Raven.

Keelie stared at the underwear on the mannequins in the window. They looked like Knot had gotten to them. Shredded, with chains.

Raven was loaded with packages, too. "Power shopping."

The last stop was a major department store for pee-free underwear, bras, and socks. Raven was a big help here, and two hundred dollars later, even Keelie had to admit she was wiped. The Bank of Dread Forest credit card had had a workout.

All the women in the Mall of Colorado kept gazing at Zeke as if he was some sort of Adonis, but he didn't return their eye contact. He focused his attention on Keelie. And she liked that.

"Hey Zeke, how about something to eat before we return

to the Faire? There's a food court here." Raven had turned to look down a corridor, nose twitching.

Keelie's stomach rumbled at the scent of real, non-medieval food. Chinese. Suddenly, she craved egg rolls.

"Is it anything like the King's court?" Zeke asked.

"Surely, you jest," said Keelie.

Zeke stopped and smiled at her. "You made a joke."

"Yeah, she's feeling better." Raven poked her shoulder.

The realization that she'd made a joke startled her. It had to have been all the shopping. She was back in the normal world. She had to be careful—she was slipping. He might get the idea that they were getting along.

On the way to the food court, Keelie saw a stand of pay phones. A lifeline to Laurie. Maybe she'd have a moment to slip away and call.

At the fast food Chinese restaurant, Keelie ordered sweet and sour chicken and egg rolls. Zeke ordered some vegetarian concoction with tofu.

As they stood in line for their food, Keelie said casually, "Hey, I need to use the ladies' room."

"Go ahead. I'll find a table."

"I'll come with you." Raven walked with her toward the ladies' room.

"Raven, I really wanted to call my friend in California." She held her breath, thinking that the older girl might tell Zeke.

"Cool. I've got to wash my hands. I touched everything at Noir Leather." Raven left her by the pay phones and walked on.

Keelie punched in the 1-800 number on the metal buttons. No hawks here, thank goodness.

"To whom would you like to make a collect call?"

"Laurie Abernathy. I mean, Elizabeth Abernathy, in Los Angeles, California."

The connection was made, and as before the operator asked, "Would you accept a collect call from Keelie Heartwood?" to the party on the other end.

"Yes. Most definitely." Laurie's voice sounded wonderful, especially here in the shopping mall, surrounded by her purchases. Her spirit felt renewed. She felt closer to Mom.

"Go ahead." The operator's voice disconnected.

"Yo, Keelie, what happened yesterday?"

"Long story."

"How's it going? Is it as primitive as we thought?"

"More so. And you wouldn't believe how weird. I need to get out of here."

"Working on a plan. I've been trying to reach you for, like, forever on the cell phone."

"I dropped it into the mud. It's not working."

"Major bummer."

"Yeah, and worse, my clothes aren't with me. They're in Istanbul."

"Like in Turkey?"

"As in the capital of. At least my father's had to buy me all new clothes. I'm at the mall now. Back to the plan."

"Major problems? Mom may not be so hot on you moving in. She's, like, got a major new boyfriend?" Her voice rose at the end of her most of her sentences, making everything a question.

"Well, I never did exactly firm it up with her."

"Keelie. I thought it was handled."

"I didn't have a lot of time to cement things before the attorney showed up with the plane tickets."

Keelie knew she had to get back before Zeke thought she'd fallen into the toilet. Raven hadn't come out of the ladies' room yet.

"We would have had it all settled if you hadn't run." Laurie sounded peeved.

"I'll come up with a new plan. Maybe I could stay with you until I do," said Keelie.

"Way, girl. Are you sure, though? Like, my mom is having major PMS this week. Even I would consider hanging out in a tent to get away from Grizzly Mama," said Laurie. "She even made me do my own laundry."

"At least you have a washer and dryer." Zeke had found a table. Keelie could see him scanning the area for them. "I'll try to call you in a couple of days. Zeke's watching me like a hawk." Hawk. A pang went through her chest. She was supposed to continue Ariel's feedings.

"Gotcha. Take care, Keelie. I'll call my cousin in Boulder to see if she can help us out."

"Great. Bye, Laurie." Keelie hung up. She missed her friend. They had been together since preschool, and not being together was like not being with a sister.

She closed her eyes. Hold back those tears. Keeping her feelings locked in her box was getting harder. A hand with a tissue appeared in front of her face.

"Thanks, Raven." Keelie took it and dabbed her eyes.

Raven looked sympathetic. "It's tough, I know. Let's eat."

Sympathetic up to a point. They headed back to the table.

Zeke sat with a big mound of vegetarian noodles studded with tofu nuggets. Keelie wasn't hungry anymore. She picked at her food while Zeke ate his.

Raven looked from one to the other, then put down her chopsticks. "I think I have to go back to the leather shop. I think I left something there."

"Do you want us to come along?" Zeke frowned.

"No, eat. I'll be back. You guys talk."

When she was gone, Zeke turned to Keelie. "Are you okay?"

She didn't answer. Her chopstick picked up peas and carrots and piled them into a veggie landfill on a corner of her plate.

"I guess coming to a mall is too much like home and reminds you of your mom."

Keelie looked up at him, amazed that he knew what she was thinking. "Why did you let Mom leave?"

He seemed to be trying to keep his face blank, to hold some deep emotion back. Keelie could give him a lesson or two on that.

"Mom said she didn't want to live in a fairy tale world where she could never belong. Is that the truth?"

Dad lowered his plastic fork. "Your mother needed to be in her world, and I had to be in my world. She was young, as I was, when we met and fell in love."

Keelie placed her hands underneath her knees. "Why did you guys get married?"

"I couldn't imagine living without her. She felt the same

way about me. Or at least she did at first." He slumped, as if he was very tired.

"And because you had me."

"No, I married your mother because I loved her." He smiled, but it wasn't happy. "You came along after we had been married for a couple of years. You were a blessing to us both, Keelie."

When had his eyes gotten bloodshot? Was he going to cry in the food court? Keelie looked around nervously. No one was paying attention. She wanted answers, and this was neutral territory for everyone.

"Then why didn't you guys stay together?" Her voice sounded strained. She was trying to keep it down.

"Even when two people love each other as much as your mom and I did, sometimes it's too hard to blend their two worlds into one, especially after they have children. If there can't be a compromise, then one of them must choose. We tried. Your mother wanted you in her world, but I couldn't join you there. I loved you both, and I thought it would be better for you." He looked sick as he said it.

"I wanted you both, too. Why couldn't you come to California? It's nice there. People love high-end furniture, too. Your stuff is great; you would've made a killing."

"It's pointless to discuss it now. You're here with me."

"Hey, everyone ready to go? I saw the Weather Channel on the news monitor by the restrooms. Tornado warnings all around the range." Raven looked worried. "I don't want to leave Mom alone."

A sharp pain shot through Keelie's chest. If Mom was alive, Keelie would do exactly the same thing that Raven was doing: get back to her mom because she was worried about her. It hurt that she wouldn't have that opportunity again.

Zeke stood up and swayed.

"Whoa, Zeke. Are you all right? You look awful." Raven grabbed his elbow.

"He's looked bad since we got here," Keelie said.

Raven looked at Zeke, who hadn't answered. She bit her lip. "Okay. I drive up the mountain."

"I can do it. Maybe it was the food." He looked down at the Styrofoam tray and plastic fork.

Keelie thought she heard him mutter, "Wood." He managed to walk all the way back to the truck, then collapsed on the bed in the back.

"Looks like I'm driving after all." Raven took the keys from his hand. Keelie lifted the seat of a built-in bench and took out a folded blanket. She unfurled the thick folds and tucked them around her father. He murmured "wood" again, but didn't open his eyes.

She took his hand and moved it until it touched the wall. Her own fingers brushed it. Cedar.

"Cedar," he murmured.

Keelie backed away from the bunk. What was this? Dad had called it a gift. Her mother had called it a wood allergy. It was more. Mom had lied. Keelie called it a curse. Keelie thought of her dancing attacker and the moving stick men and the voice from under the bridge. This little human half-breed needed to hear the truth from her father.

The door behind her was flung open by a gust of wind.

Raven appeared in it. "Come on, Keelie. You have to

ride up front. Too dangerous back here. I need you to navigate and keep an eye on the sky."

"If it's too dangerous, we can't leave Dad back here."

"Zeke will be okay, and we can't pick him up and put him up front. Come on, Keelie. The sooner we get moving, the sooner we get back to the Faire."

She shoved Knot's reindeer bed under Dad's head for a pillow. She looked at her father one last time, then jumped down from the camper and locked the door. She climbed into the truck cab and fastened her seat belt. Above them, the ominous skies were filled with gray and white clouds that spun in lazy circles. The light from the west was a sickly yellow, like a dim bulb burning in a dark room. The wind had died, and in the eerie silence Raven started the truck and backed out of the mall parking lot.

"Keep an eye on those clouds," Raven said. She sounded calm, but her knuckles were white on the steering wheel.

"What am I looking for?" Keelie looked up. Clouds and more clouds. Beautiful, dark, and constantly moving.

"When one of them starts to come down, yell."

"Come down? They're pretty low already."

"Down like a tornado, dumb butt."

Keelie had seen *Storm Stories*. She didn't ask any more questions, just kept her cheek pressed to the glass, her eyes on the treacherous sky.

The trip was faster since they knew where they were going. She didn't spot any tornados. They parked in visitor parking, and Keelie stayed with Zeke while Raven ran for help to get him to Heartwood.

Tarl came alone, but he picked Zeke up as if he was a

baby and carried him most of the way. Before they reached Janice's shop, Zeke was awake again.

"I feel better."

"You look better. Better than dead." Tarl laughed.

Keelie struggled behind them with her heavy shopping bags. She'd stopped to put her old shoes back on. The disgusting mushrooms were everywhere. This place needed to be treated with a bleach bottle.

"I can walk, Tarl."

"I say you can't." Tarl held him closer, and Raven ran ahead to open the apartment door for them. Tarl and Zeke disappeared into his curtained alcove.

Keelie dropped her new treasures in her wardrobe and closed it firmly. Knot blinked at her. "Out. Touch not. I wish I could say it in ten languages."

The cat stretched, butt in the air, and sauntered out.

Tarl joined them for the chicken and rice that Janice and Raven brought up. Janice served Zeke dinner in bed while Keelie put the tea kettle on.

Outside it was dark, and the clouds had been blown ragged. Stars twinkled here and there, only to be quickly obscured again.

Like the clouds, a multitude of questions swirled around her mind about what happened when her parents separated, what she was, and how much her mother had known about it.

Dad had repeated that Mom couldn't live in his world. True, Keelie found it difficult to live in his world, too. She just couldn't figure how Mom and Dad came together in the first place.

Dad. She'd been thinking of him as Dad again. That disturbed her. It was like she was beginning to take his side in things while her Mom wasn't here to defend herself. It was all so confusing.

She remembered the sign she'd seen back on the road, glowing on a hill opposite the highway. Keelie had gazed in the rearview mirror and read the backwards writing: "Uncle Harry Mac's Tattoo and Body Piercing. Open Twenty-Four Hours!"

Just what she'd been looking for. If Zeke was freaked out by the Vampire Girl shirt and the extra-low-riding jeans, he'd totally pass out at a belly ring. Of course, he was passed out now, although Janice said he was just asleep. Whatever bug he had, it had hit him suddenly.

What was she doing here? This wasn't home. Raven and Janice were nice, but Raven was going back to school at the end of the summer, and then the whole Faire would be gone, disbanded for the year. And she'd be stuck with Zeke, and who knew what the next Faire was like. Or worse, the Dread Forest.

Was that her new life? Heck no. She didn't want a new life. She wanted a home, and for her, that meant L.A., and her friends, and the places she'd grown up knowing. No weirdness. No Earth magic, or apparitions, or furniture that talked to her. Los Angeles was normal. But was she?

ten

For the first time in ages, Keelie liked the look of the girl gazing back at her from the mirror. Her new top and blue jeans made her feel like her old self, the happy old self who still had Mom. She pulled her top up to look at her unpierced belly button, imagining the ring she'd put there. Left side, or right?

She placed her fingertips on the mirror and pretended Mom was there, behind her. That Mom was here with Dad, that they were together as a family; but no matter how hard Keelie tried to picture her, Mom didn't appear in the mirror.

She suddenly wondered if her mental image of her mother was right. Was she forgetting something? The way she wore her hair, the little smile that meant she wasn't really mad, those were there, safe in Keelie's brain. But what had slipped away? She felt sick.

Would it ever stop? This throbbing and burning pain in her chest whenever she thought of Mom? Would she outgrow the longing and wishing that life would go back to the way it was before the plane crash? Would it ever go away? Hoping that Mom would walk in the door and that her death was all a bad dream?

The fear that gnawed at Keelie, the one thing that she couldn't cope with, was that she would lose Mom all the way, even lose Mom in her heart—if she allowed herself to love anyone as much. She feared that love might be like a computer file, the old overwritten by the new. She would never let that happen. Then a chill skipped down her spine when she remembered Elianard's words: Heartwood's human half-breed.

The telephone rang. She pushed aside the bedroom curtains and rushed out, but Dad had answered it. No. Even though she'd grown closer to him yesterday at the mall, she still couldn't call him Dad. Mom left his world and he'd let her. He was Zeke.

"Hello?" Zeke glanced at Keelie, receiver to his ear. He looked like his old self again. "Yes, it is," he told the caller. "Oh, really? That's interesting. The entire matching set has been scanned and recorded." He gave her a thumbs-up sign.

Butterflies fluttered in her stomach. Her luggage must be on its way back to her from Istanbul.

"Thank you. Just fly them out from there, and hopefully, we'll get them in a few days."

He hung up the phone.

She couldn't conceal the elation in her voice. "Well, what did they say? When will my luggage be here?"

Zeke laughed. "The good news is that all ten pieces of your luggage have been tagged—in Amsterdam. And they'll fly out from there in the next day or two."

"Amsterdam. As in Holland. As in the Netherlands." The image that came to mind was of her suitcases, alone and looking forlorn on a cobbled street, surrounded by tulips, windmills, and smiling people on bicycles.

"I think your luggage has traveled farther than anyone I know," he said, admiringly.

"Unreal," she agreed.

"I like your outfit," her father said. He sat on his sofa and drank some herbal tea from his mug. He still looked pale. "You look wonderful in your new clothes."

She couldn't stop the smile. Okay, she'd give him just this one. "Thanks. I like them, too. Where's Knot?" She searched for the room for any telltale sign of her fuzzy orange nemesis.

"He's running some errands."

"Errands?"

There was a knock on the door. "Come in," Zeke shouted.

"Hey, Zeke," Scott said, poking his head in the door. His shoulders were so wide that they filled the door. He wore a mud-stained 2002 Sterling Renaissance Festival T-shirt. His gaze wandered over to Keelie. "You clean up well."

"Thanks, I think," she said. She didn't really want him looking at her like that. She didn't offer any comment on what she thought about his appearance. Not out loud.

Scott turned to Keelie with a smile. "Hey Keelie, maybe this weekend during the Faire you might like to go have some tea or something."

Shocked, Keelie's tongue froze. Was Scott asking her for a date?

"You'll be too busy working the booth this weekend, Scott," Zeke said in a firm tone.

Thank goodness Zeke interceded.

"Okay, I get it. Don't ask the boss's daughter out for a cup of tea. I'm putting that on my 'no-no' list," said Scott, rolling his eyes.

Scott looked at Keelie and winked at her. "You look great in your new clothes. You'd better watch out for pirates, errant knights, and other such Faire folk."

Her cheeks burned when he said pirates. Did Scott know?

"By the way, I'm having a big problem with the wood that came in yesterday from Oregon," Scott said. "I was wondering if you could give it the old Zeke touch and tell me what to do."

"Is it the oak?"

Scott nodded.

Envy fired up in Keelie. She hated seeing the easy rapport that flowed between Zeke and Scott. If she'd been around Zeke for the past thirteen years, she could help him with the oak.

Zeke frowned. "Leave it alone, it's a sad case. I'll give it my personal attention."

"Knot's upset, too. We're getting that buzzing, you know. He's running in circles and biting at his tail. I think he needs to be flea-dipped."

"I'll get to it this afternoon as soon as I can," Zeke said. He swirled his tea around in his mug, then took a sip. He still had dark circles underneath his eyes, but he had a mischievous smile on his face. "I'll make spaghetti tonight, and put extra garlic in the sauce. Garlic helps get rid of fleas."

Fleas. That cat was so not going to sleep with her. She scratched her arm.

Keelie glanced at the (what else!) tree-shaped clock hanging above the stove. "Time for me to go to the mews and feed Ariel."

"I'm going with you." Scott waggled his eyebrows up and down, and gave her his dorky grin. He needed to floss; he had a chunk of something brown stuck in between his two front teeth.

"No, you're not. Cameron didn't invite you."

"Scott is escorting you to the mews. I asked him to." Zeke was putting on his no-nonsense parental voice.

She glowered at her father. "I'm in high school. I don't need him," she jabbed a finger at Scott, "to go with me to the mews." She was hoping to run into Sean in her new clothes. Having Zeke's shop boy running herd on her like a Border collie would cramp her style.

"Scott is going with you. End of discussion," Zeke said. "Be back in three hours. Four o'clock. Any later, I'll personally make it my mission to escort you everywhere you go until you're eighteen."

Keelie shrieked. Marching ahead of Scott, she found the deserted Faire jolting. Some of the Renaissance residents wore normal everyday clothes like she'd seen in the Shire yesterday. Some Rennies were in costume. She guessed their brains were permanently time-warped to the medieval ages.

She missed the bustle of the crowds, where even in her mud clothes she could go unnoticed. But, for some reason, in the midst of the quiet and in her mundane clothes, she felt glaringly different.

Scott caught up with her, his legs keeping pace with her brisk walk.

"Heard about your adventures in the Shire with Captain Dandy Randy," he said.

She knew it. Although her cheeks were flushed with embarrassment, Keelie couldn't help but glance over at Scott, and if she had a ball of mud she would've smeared it over the smirk on his face. She wasn't going to bother replying.

Scott continued. "He was telling everyone you were giving away free samples."

Keelie stopped.

Scott stopped, too. He grinned, spreading his mouth extra wide so she got a really good view of his back molars.

"He said what?"

"You were giving away free samples, and they were mighty sweet."

She spun on her heel, heading in the direction of the

Shire. "Where is he?" She pounded a fist in her open palm, envisioning Captain Randy's face with a broken nose. The bastard would probably look good.

"He's supposedly working on some new software game. Perilous Pirate or something stupid like that."

"I'm going to show him a perilous pirate. Me."

"I wouldn't worry. Raven set him straight. Besides, he knows that if he said anything to anyone else, she'd tell Zeke. And everyone knows just because your dad lives and works with us normal people, he's not quite like us. Captain Randy got scared."

"What do you mean, my dad is not normal? Who is normal in this place?"

"Ah, come on, Keelie. You know what I'm talking about."

"All right, all-knowing wise ass. You tell me what's different about my dad, since I just got here and you've spent all this time with him."

Scott studied Keelie, but he blinked nervously several times as she kept her gaze level with his. Suddenly, it hit her: he was pumping her for information.

She could feel the corners of her mouth lift up in a smile. "Let's keep it our secret." Whatever he was trying to get out of her wasn't going to happen, because she was clueless about a lot of things about Zeke. And what she did know she wasn't going to share with Scott. She had other problems, and one was a pirate named Captain Dandy Randy. She didn't want Zeke to find out about her Shire activities from the other night until after she went home to California. Worse, if he found out he might get all fatherly, as he was doing back at the apartment a few minutes ago. He'd insist she come back to live with him until she was eighteen. Not having Mom and Dad divorced had thrown a major mountain range in her plans to go live with Elizabeth and Laurie.

Down Ironmonger's Way, the nasty lady from the jewelry booth walked toward them. Her nose looked kind of normal with her giant bosom to balance it. She wore a pink blouse and blue jeans and kept glancing down at a clipboard. It was weird seeing these Renaissance people in regular clothes. The woman looked up and frowned at Keelie, but then she smiled when she saw Scott. Keelie walked on. She wouldn't give this woman the time of day. Anyway, Ariel would be waiting for Keelie to feed her lunch. Though excited to see Ariel, Keelie didn't relish the idea of touching a dead rat or watching it get eaten.

"Good afternoon, Scott. How was business at Heartwood this weekend?" the jewelry lady asked.

"Hey, Tania. Not bad. You know Zeke. He attracts the ladies, so he's not hurting. How's it going with your shop?"

"With these cursed rains keeping the customers away? Everyone is feeling the pinch. This year's been bad for a lot of us, except for Elianard's crew. They never seem to be hurting economically. Business is up for them." Tania strode closer. "Al at the pub says he has the sight, inherited from his Irish grandmother Janie. He says something nasty has brought its dark ways to the Faire." She cocked her head, waiting for Scott's reaction, but her eyes were on Keelie.

Scott nodded, "Yeah, Cameron's been worried. Said

she's seen a strange little man with a weird laugh hanging out near the mews at dawn and sometimes around twilight."

The woman said, "See. Cameron's one of those I would say has the sight. I heard over at the pub last night that they think the little man in the red cap might be the one that started the fire. One of the belly dancers thought she saw him head over into the woods past the meadow."

Keelie stopped and spun around on her heel. Red cap. Woods past the meadow. More than one person had seen the little manic midget. She hadn't been the only victim. He was an arsonist.

Scott whistled. "Really. I wonder what Admin is going to do."

"I don't know. I bet someone from that land development company put him up to it. Why don't you stop and have a cup of coffee with me? We can talk some more." Tania batted her eyes at him.

Keelie was going to heave.

"Oh, I can't. I'm on an important errand. I have to get Zeke's daughter to the mews," Scott replied.

"She's Zeke Heartwood's daughter?" Keelie thought Tania was going to choke on the words.

Keelie joined Scott, feeling much better. Watching the woman's face as she learned that Keelie was Zeke Heartwood's daughter was worth the delay. She was starting to appreciate her father's importance at the Faire.

"I saw her yesterday, but I thought she was a new performer in the Muck and Mire Show."

"It was so nice of Tarl to come to my rescue and loan me

some clothes, because all of my everyday wear is in Europe." Keelie batted her eyelashes, too. If Scott started on his, the breeze from all three pairs of eyes would be noticeable.

"Europe." She looked Keelie up and down, as if she was tabulating the cost of Keelie's outfit. "My goodness. I didn't realize you were Zeke's daughter." The woman smiled, but it wasn't a genuine smile. It was like the one that Mom's tennis rival wore whenever she and Mom met at the grocery store. Mom would go, "Beverly, darling, how are you?" Beverly would reply, "Fabulous, Katy, darling. I can't wait till our rematch down at the club." Though their verbal exchange would sound amiable, Keelie felt the venom dripping with each word they exchanged. Air kisses at twenty paces.

"Keelie, I know you liked that fairy necklace. I still have it," said Tania. She pointed through the woods in the direction of her booth. "I can get it for you, if you still want it."

Shaking her head, Keelie said, "No, thanks. I really must be going. I have to get to the mews. Cameron is waiting for me."

Walking away, Keelie sensed hostility flow from Tania, just as it had from Mom's tennis rival. Keelie felt very satisfied. More than likely, the fairy necklace would've turned her neck green. Maybe that's why Tania wasn't making any money—shoddy merchandise.

At the raptor mews, Keelie ran to Ariel's cage. The hawk was sitting on her perch and opened her eyes, turning her head to watch Keelie's approach. The hawk's golden eye gleamed, and her posture looked noble. Keelie knew the other eye, milky white, was the reason Ariel could no longer soar, and she felt sad for the poor bird.

"Here you are. You've been delivered safe and sound. I'll be back around three forty-five to walk you back. Have fun with the dead rats." Scott nodded at one of the mews workers and sauntered off.

Cameron approached, carrying a brown paper bag marked "Ariel" in black marker. "Good morrow, Keelie. Ariel's been waiting for you." She gave Keelie two sturdy leather gloves.

"I can't wait." Not.

"Where's your father? I needed to speak to him." Worry lines creased her face.

"He's resting. He's not feeling well after our trip to the mall yesterday." Keelie put the gloves on. "I think it might have been MSG in his tofu."

"Your father went to the mall?" Cameron's mouth hung open.

"Yeah. According to Raven, it was a historical event. I needed clothes. All I had to wear were the mud clothes. The airline's lost my luggage, and Knot peed on my underwear." The comment about Knot whizzing on her underwear always solicited sympathy.

"Knot peed on your underwear?"

Keelie nodded.

Cameron scrunched her face up and shook her head. "Knowing Knot, he might have been telling someone or something you belonged to him. Marking you as his territory, so to speak. Some cats do that."

Keelie stared at the bird woman in total shocked silence.

Somebody had been hanging out with her fine- feathered friends for way too long. "I am so not his territory. I think it was a hate message: Leave now."

Smiling, Cameron said, "Well, Knot has always been a bit unusual, even for a cat. I hope Zeke feels better. Do you think he'll be up for a visit tomorrow?"

"I think so."

Cameron opened the bag. "Okay, Keelie, reach in there and retrieve Ariel's dinner."

The thick leather of the gloves made her fingers feel clumsy. Reaching into the bag, Keelie grasped something thin but heavy. She slowly lifted a large, dead white rat out of the bag. Its tail hung limp and disgusting, but thankfully, its eyes were closed. Keelie looked away, afraid she'd hurl her lunch.

"Gross, but necessary, Keelie. Give it to Ariel," Cameron said.

Keelie made her way to the cage. Ariel's good eye watched her—or rather, the rat.

A bundle of autumn-colored fur ran toward Keelie. What was that sadistic cat doing here? Had he heard them talking about him? Forget him.

Keelie focused on Ariel. She locked eyes with the hawk as she approached, cursing Knot silently for weaving in and out of her legs. When she reached to open Ariel's door, she felt claws at her ankle and stepped back, tripping over the cat. She reached for the wooden cage with one hand to break her fall. As she did, she dropped the rat, which landed with a thud as the cage door popped open.

The cat yowled like a banshee when the chilled rat

landed on him. Ariel stretched her wings once, then flew out and spiraled into the trees.

Knot shot into the woods, as if aware of the chaos he'd caused.

Cameron cried out for him to stop, but the cat kept running, leaving a trail of waving grasses in his wake.

In the air, Ariel paused as if noticing new prey, then shot down in pursuit.

All the birds began screeching and flapping their wings against the bars of their enclosures. It seemed to Keelie that they were cheering Ariel on as the hawk flew in pursuit of the rapidly retreating Knot. Keelie wanted to run, too.

Her second day on the job, and she'd lost the hawk.

eleven

Keelie kicked pebbles as she walked down the path toward Heartwood. She'd chased Ariel all over the Faire. Luckily, Cameron had bribed the hawk back with another rat. At least it had been Keelie's idea, so she'd redeemed herself, sort of.

She stopped in front of the Magic Maze. A group of the badass college kids who manned the booths on weekends were playing soccer on the path and the clearing on both sides of it. She detoured around them and circled the Magic Maze. A little path led through the woods.

Great, a shortcut. It probably led to the jousting fields.

The path was narrow, and she brushed against fragrant branches and her fingers grazed occasionally against the rough bark of the trees that bordered the path. Pine, she thought.

A branch snagged her hair, and she ducked to free herself. Her head yanked back. She reached up to untangle her hair. It was wrapped between two sticks. It was starting to hurt. She pulled at a stick and felt a velvety texture. Then a bony, stick-light hand grabbed her finger, wrapping around it.

Was it a bird? She felt around, fighting the panic that made her shoulders clench and her skin prickle. Was it fur, feathers? It felt like sticks and leaves and moss. And it moved against her questing fingers.

She screamed and ran, tearing her hair loose. It hurt like hell, but she wanted to get away from whatever it was. She stopped next to a tree, out of breath, heart pounding. What had it been?

She looked around. She was surrounded by trees, and everything was quiet. Where was she? She should have been at the jousting ring by now. She was lost.

Something moved in her hair. She froze. It glided down the back of her head, then she felt it on her shoulder. Afraid to look, she cut her eyes to the right. Sticks. She turned her head a little. It was just sticks, held together with moss.

But it wasn't. She could see little hands now, brown and hard and shiny, and eyes that glowed from the moss of the face. The little creature lifted a hand to her cheek.

It wasn't real, she told herself. It was a doll from one of

the vendors. A puppet, left in the trees as a joke. The puppet pointed toward the woods to the right.

She followed the tiny twiglike finger. There was movement in the bushes, probably some animal.

"Danger." The voice was like a whisper of dried leaves. "Run, Keliel."

Okay. The stick knew her true name. The bushes rustled a few yards away. She saw a flash of red.

She ran, following the path, running as hard as she could. Then she heard voices. Human voices. She veered toward the sound and saw light ahead. And then she was out of the woods.

She was at the edge of a clearing. She stopped, heart still racing, and looked toward her shoulder, but the little creature was gone. She knew she hadn't imagined it or the glimpse of red hat.

Enough was enough. The evil little person was stalking her. She thought of Sir Davey, who was around the same height. She hadn't seen her attacker clearly, but she knew it was not Davey.

Ahead of her was a large one-story building with massive timbers and a big wraparound deck filled with laughing people. She walked toward it and saw that it was on the shores of a lake with an island in the middle of it. A wide plank bridge farther down the shore led to the island, which was large enough to hold several buildings.

Now that she was away from the forest, she could think clearly again. She was mad at herself for running, and from what? A bundle of sticks and a manic midget in yard-gnome couture? If this was Earth magic, keep it, she thought. And the little dude was only waist high. Let him come near her again, and she'd show him some Earth magic, Keelie-style. She'd pound him into the ground.

The crowd on the deck seemed rowdy, and she was hesitant about asking them for directions. Then she recognized two of them as the pirates who'd driven by after picking up their checks earlier. Now she was definitely not asking for directions.

The drummer from the Shire tent waved at her. "Hey Keelie! Hungry?"

The man with his back to the rail turned around. It was Scott. Fabulous.

Two of the pirates jumped down from the deck and swaggered toward her. Her heart sank. Captain Dandy Randy was one of them. She had to admit they looked hot in their long boots and pouffy shirts.

"What a luscious bit of wench we have here," the other pirate said. He weaved a little as he walked.

Captain Randy leered at her, but he grabbed the other pirate's arm, making him spin toward him. "She's underage. Throw her back and catch her again when she's ripe."

She glared at him. Thanks a lot, Captain Geek.

The other pirate grinned. "She looks old enough to me." He held up a beer tankard. "To all lovely lasses." He drank deeply, then coughed as Scott's quiet voice rang through the clearing.

"She's Heartwood's daughter."

The beer tankard flew out of the pirate's suddenly nerveless fingers. It arced as if in slow motion, its contents flying out and splashing Keelie's new jeans. Great. She'd smell like a brewery.

The pirates froze, then backed away.

Heartwood's daughter. It sounded like a curse. She was doomed to be dateless. Hooves pounded behind her, like the cavalry in an old Western. She turned to see white horses gallop into the clearing, ridden by colorful riders.

Sean. Sean was one of the riders. And then Elia's horse caught up with him. The last person she wanted to see, especially when she smelled like beer.

She saw that Scott had come to stand beside her. The air smelled of beer, cinnamon, and ozone. Dark clouds had gathered above them, echoing her mood.

She could feel the tension between the group on the deck and the riders. She glanced behind her. Some of the college kids who played pirate were gripping the rail, as if waiting for the fight to begin.

Sean smiled easily at the drinkers. "Great day for a ride. We've come to put the horses up—storm's brewing."

Elia's eyes locked on Keelie, her lips pressed in a thin line. "On your way to the Mire? Oops, sorry. I meant the Shire."

Lightning flashed overhead, followed by the rumble of thunder. The skies opened. Keelie was soaked in seconds. She looked down, dismayed. Her new clothes.

Elia's silvery laugh tinkled overhead. Keelie's fists closed, ready for battle, then she stopped. Elia was dry. No umbrella in sight, but the girl's golden curls were perfect, and her long, green gown was unspotted. None of the other riders seemed to be as lucky. They, and their horses, were wet, even Sean.

They wheeled their horses around and headed for the bridge. Even from behind, Elia was dry. What the heck was going on around here?

Keelie wanted to stick her tongue out but was afraid she'd start a melee. When things got real between her and Elia, she wouldn't drag a bunch of innocent guys into it. It would be just her and the she-witch of the Medieval Hell, *mano a mano*. And somebody's long, golden locks would get torn out by the roots.

Scott grabbed her elbow. Before she could protest, he was dragging her up toward a wide, tree-overhung path. The path she'd thought she was on earlier. They passed a long, low stage with a banner above that announced fencing demonstrations, and a shuttered booth called Aviva's Shimmy Shack. A belly dancing shop! She'd remember this place for sure. Maybe she could come here with Raven when the weather improved.

A shout from behind her stopped them. "Hey, Keelie, come back to the Shire tonight. We're having a drum circle by the meadow. Inside if it's still raining." The drummer waved at her and several of the pirates waved and grinned from the deck.

She grinned back and waved with her free hand. Scott yanked her arm. "Quit fooling around. You are in so much trouble. Your dad said not to wander around by yourself."

She pulled her arm out of his grasp. "Yeah? Well, you were the one put in charge of escorting me. And where were you? Drinking with Jack Sparrow's buddies."

Did he look paler? She hoped he felt sick. Hard to tell with water dripping down his face.

"Where were you? You have sticks in your hair." He was looking at her head.

She reached up, panicked, but the sticks in her hair were just tiny twigs and bits of moss. Nothing moved.

Scott gave her a weird look. "Come on."

Feeling they were even now, she walked fast to keep up with his long legs, pulling debris out of her wet hair.

They passed closed stores and exhibit areas, and then she saw the directional sign she'd seen the first day with Ms. Talbot. She'd gone in the opposite direction. Maybe she'd buy a compass and learn how to use it.

"The drummer, what's his name?"

"We call him Skins."

"How PETA-friendly. Skins said the drum circle, whatever that is, was going to be at the meadow, but I was in the meadow last night, and that's a seriously creepy place."

"Yeah, your dad told me you wandered into Elianard's camp. Stay away from him. He's worse than his daughter." Scott leered at her. "But the Shire is tons of fun."

She ignored the remark. "What about the guy with the red hat? What do you know about him? Does he work here? He's got issues. Like, serial killer issues. Dad wouldn't let me call the police, either."

Scott sighed. "There's a lot you don't understand about the Faire. But you will. The police never get called."

"Never? As in, find a murdered body and just bury it in the woods?"

"Planning to kill someone?"

"Just you." She had to walk fast to keep up with his long stride. "What about the red-hat guy?"

"Talk to your father about him. And the meadow's not so bad. What's creepy about it? The Faire administration keeps the area by the Shire mowed and the kids hang out there. They build bonfires and stuff, far away from the trees."

"That actually sounds like fun. But you don't feel anything strange about the meadow?"

"No. Not near the Shire. This hasn't been a normal season. Besides the weather, there have been thefts and fights, and Skin says there's some bad vibes around the Shire."

"Bad vibes, huh? Now who sounds like they're from California?"

"So no more sneaking off, right?"

"I did not sneak off! I was with Cameron in the mews."

"The mews are on the other side of the Faire grounds."

"I got lost."

He looked at her skeptically. "Remind me not to go walking in the woods with you."

She almost said, why, are you scared? But instead she lifted her chin. "What makes you think I want to walk in the woods with you?"

Why did she say that? She didn't want to encourage him. Sean, yes. Scott, no way. But he didn't seem to notice. Clueless wimp.

She splashed her way back to Heartwood. The wind had changed direction, and it was warmer. That was a blessing, at least. She didn't have to be cold and wet. And she had dry clothes waiting for her. She picked up speed, almost passing Scott.

The lights were on in the workshop, and Scott went through the furniture, now protected by long tarps. Keelie squished up the stairs.

The apartment was dark, but it smelled deliciously of cooking onions. Keelie was amazed to see rays of light shooting up from the floor. For a second she thought it was another woo-woo Faire moment, but then she realized that it was the workshop lights leaking through spaces in the floor boards.

She knelt on the wide plank floor (cedar) and put her eye to a crack. For a second, the images didn't make sense, then she realized she was seeing a huge log, bark still on, strapped to sawhorses. Zeke and Scott stood at either side of the log, examining it.

A deep purring sounded near her, and Knot's furry head bumped her cheek. She stayed still, afraid he'd scratch her eyes out.

"Good kitty." The purring stopped. "Miserable feline." The deep rumble resumed. "You are so weird."

She pushed away from the floor and headed toward the bathroom to towel off. Knot followed, watching with eyes half-closed as she undressed and pulled the tags off more of her new clothes.

"Where were you when I ran into the red-hat midget in the woods?"

His eyes opened wide and he stared, almost as if he understood her words.

"And that little twig puppet? The Henson studios need to know about that technology. It seemed real."

Knot wasn't purring anymore. He was watching her carefully. She stopped brushing her hair. "What? You've never seen a chick with moss in her hair? It's all the rage in the Colorado woods."

A twig bounced from her brush and fell at his feet. He batted it closer and sniffed at it, then started to purr again.

Keelie laughed as she noticed the huge bald spot in the back of his head. "That must have been from Ariel. Serves you right."

Warm and dry once more, she walked to the kitchen, hoping for a cup of tea. A big package was on the table. She glanced at the label. Dread Forest, Oregon? She remembered her dad's credit card. Must be family.

She took the tea kettle down from its shelf and turned on the cold water. Knot sat on her foot. With her other foot, she nudged Knot. He didn't move an inch. The diabolical cat sank his claws deep into her skin. "Ow!"

She pushed him hard with her foot. He let go, sliding on the hardwood floor on his belly. Knot huddled his body into a ball. His tail twitched. He raised his backside up, ready to pounce.

"Come on, psycho kitty, I'll take you on." Keelie wiggled her foot in his direction. He lowered his caboose, sat up, and studied her, suddenly calm as she filled the kettle. She tried to ignore him, but he continued to stare at her, and his eyes began to dilate, turning into large, black orbs.

He meandered toward the bedroom curtain, then sat down.

"Not on your life," she warned. She put the kettle on the stove, turned the burner on, and wiped her hands on a tea towel. Her father had started dinner. There was a pot of spaghetti sauce on the stove, and water was simmering in a stock pot.

"I mean it, cat. Stay away from my new clothes, and stay away from me. You're beyond demented."

The cat purred as if she had given him a compliment. Something blue and tiny stuck out of a snarl of fur by his shoulder. She reached down quickly and plucked it off. A tiny blue feather. What kind of bird had this come from?

Knot yowled and tried to swat her, then thought better of it and walked away calmly, as if it didn't matter.

She lit two white beeswax candles that stood in wooden candleholders on the small kitchen table. The flames flickered, casting a warm glow around the room, counteracting the gloom from the cloudy skies outside.

Zeke came in. "Doesn't it smell great in here? I'm making spaghetti sauce."

"It does smell good."

"Can you help fix it? I've got to head back downstairs."

"Sure." Her stomach growled.

Zeke opened a cupboard and pulled out a colander and placed it on the counter. "We need to talk."

There was a knock at the door.

He didn't remove his gaze from Keelie's. "Come in."

It was Scott. "Sorry to disturb your cozy family scene,

but I'm having a devil of a time. Can you come back down, Zeke?"

Keelie glared at Scott. She bet he really wasn't sorry for interrupting.

Zeke sighed. "I was so tired today that I slept and never got downstairs to look at the tree. It's in desperate shape." He walked over to the candles on the table and blew them out. No more golden glow.

Scott flipped the light switch by the door, and the kitchen light burst into irritating brightness.

"Keelie, would you serve the spaghetti and bring the plates downstairs? We'll make it a working dinner."

"Great. Spaghetti for supper." Scott smirked. "Zeke and I've had lots of working dinners in the shop. Oh, and Keelie, sprinkle mine with pepper. Gives it that extra zest—kind of how the pirates like it."

"Oh, like the pirates I found you with at the pub when you forgot to pick me up?"

Scott glared at her, glancing quickly at Zeke to judge his reaction. "Soon as we finish, I'm headed to the Shire. Big party there tonight. Drum circle and everything. Everyone's going to miss you." He winked.

He was so dead.

"Keelie. Scott. Enough." Zeke shouted. "Let's get to work. Keelie, there's a pitcher of cold mint tea in the refrigerator, too."

"Fine." She felt like their maid.

They exited, but Scott opened the door again. "Hey Keelie. I'll take ice with my tea. *Ciao*."

She wanted to scream. When did she become a waitress?

First, she was serving rat to a hawk, and now she was serving spaghetti to a big dweeb-rat named Scott.

She opened the kitchen cabinets and slammed pottery plates with leaf impressions onto the counter. "I'll give him extra zest."

Keelie drained the spaghetti noodles over the sink, then dumped them into a bowl. Something snagged her new blue jeans. She looked down. Two glowing green eyes glared right back at her. "If you don't let go of my pants, I'll kick your butt."

A heap of chopped garlic was abandoned on a wooden chopping board. "I bet this is for you, but you don't have fleas, do you? Scott does."

Keelie wiggled her foot again. Knot studied her as she calmly stirred the spaghetti sauce, then ran into the kitchen and hopped into a chair as if he was ready to be served.

"I'm not going to give you spaghetti. I'm not your waitress, either."

She walked over to the sink and distributed three equal portions of spaghetti onto three plates. She was about to spoon the sauce over it when she noticed the garlic again. "You know, Scott did say he wanted extra zest in his spaghetti."

She strategically hid the garlic in the huge mound of spaghetti. Inspired, she searched the kitchen spice cupboard. "Jackpot."

She sprinkled chili powder on some extra sauce and mixed it into Scott's serving. "Come one, come all—a new show at the Faire. The fire-breathing idiot!"

Knot purred as he watched her. She placed the three small plates of spaghetti on a tray, reminding herself that Scott's was the dark blue one. She added silverware and napkins by the plates, then hoisted up the tray and headed downstairs. They'd have to get their own tea because she couldn't carry the spaghetti and drinks, too.

When Keelie pushed the door open to the outside stairs, Knot ran past her.

"Brain-damaged feline."

The cat ran down the stairs. She stopped on the last step. She could hear the buzzing of hundreds of little bees. But there weren't any bugs flying around to make that noise.

Zeke and Scott were in the shop, talking. Knot was nowhere in sight. Annoying as he was, she envied Scott. He knew Zeke better than she did. Her father had taken an interest in him and taught him how to work with wood. She'd gotten an occasional toy.

She stepped inside, but neither of them noticed her. Zeke's hands were on a massive, scarred trunk of a tree strapped to sawhorses, like a patient on a surgical table. He touched it reverently, caressing the bark.

Wrong. Something was very wrong here. Keelie felt the air vibrating, like waves coming at her from the tree.

"So?" Scott's hands were at his side, well away from the big tree.

"She's still grieving and doesn't want to be shaped into something else. She was taken before her time. She grieves for the sun. She wants to sink her roots back into Mother Earth."

"What are you talking about?" asked Keelie, pulling a charred piece of wood from the table (oak). She had a brief impression of lightning and fire. A figure moved in the flash.

The men glanced at her, but the big tree trunk was their main concern.

"The wood. Come touch her, Keelie," Zeke said.

"Do you think she should do that?" Scott said. He seemed annoyed.

She smiled sweetly at him and handed him his plate. "For you."

"Where's the tea?"

"Upstairs. Get it yourself."

She reached out to the tree but drew back her hand as she saw a delicate feminine face, twisted in pain, look out from inside the bark. She closed her eyes, then looked again, but it was just a tree. There was no carving.

She backed away.

"*Mommy, the tree people say they know me. They know Daddy.*" Keelie was suddenly back in the park with her mother, small, and reaching up to hold her mommy's hand.

"*There are no tree people, Keelie,*" Mom had said, but even at age five, Keelie knew she was lying. Mom said she had a wood allergy that made her see and hear things. But if she stayed away from wood she'd be okay. Keelie had never mentioned her wood sense to her mother again.

Zeke said, "Is something wrong?"

"It's just my allergy," she said. She backed away from the log. She couldn't touch it. She imagined the tree's despair, and it enveloped her. If she touched it the grief would consume her, and she had enough of her own. It's all in my head, she thought.

But the tree's imagined grief brought back her own. It wasn't supposed to be like this. Mom was supposed to be here, alive and strong, face to the sun and feet on the Earth. Keelie trembled. She wanted to cry.

"Mom." The word came out in a moan.

Dad hugged her. "It's okay, Keelie. I'm here for you. And I'm never letting you go again." She wrapped her arms around him.

Scott shouted, "Oh man, that's hot."

Knot jumped onto the log. Keelie stepped back, but Zeke kept an arm around her shoulder, drawing her closer.

The buzzing noise Keelie heard became louder and more distinct, like little pieces of conversation, the murmurs of different tiny voices blending together.

Knot's weird eyes were round marbles of black rimmed in green. His tail swished like a writhing cobra. His ears were slicked back to his head, making his bald spot all the more prominent. He growled, staring at the air above him.

Keelie looked around to see if another cat was challenging him, but there was nothing around except that weird noise, which was getting louder and louder. Maybe the cat was having a psychotic fit.

Leaping from the log, Knot landed on the ground, then shot across the clearing and climbed five feet up a nearby oak tree. He jumped from the tree and landed on the ground, turning on his back to paw at the air, swatting an invisible enemy. Just as quickly, he whirled onto his feet and ran around the oak's trunk three times, then stopped and smacked his paw at the ground. Then he ran down the pathway past the jousting arena and toward the lake. The buzzing and murmurs of conversation disappeared as if in pursuit of the cat.

"Is he sick?" asked Keelie. It sure looked like kitty insanity to her. Maybe she should've served the cat the spaghetti with the extra garlic. She gazed over at Scott, who had wolfed down his supper, and his face was shiny with sweat, and bright red.

"Are you going to get the tea?" Scott asked. "My mouth's on fire."

"Scott, what's the matter with you? Go get the tea." Zeke scowled at him. He squeezed her arm lightly. "I wanted to ease you into your new life, give you time before you started learning about me and about my family and my world. Guess it's not working."

"What are you talking about? What's this tree got to do with it?"

"It was felled by lightning the day you arrived. Remember, you saw the smoke? You saved some lives that day, Keelie. But this tree is beyond saving, and her magic is trapped within her. As a tree shepherd, I have to guide her spirit onward and transform her magic into healing energy."

"Right. Sort of like an arborist and a priest?"

"Sort of. Not everyone can do what I do, and you have my power within you. More than that, Sir Davey and I suspect that you are much more powerful than me."

"Really?" Superpowers would come in handy, although

tree powers were kind of limited. What could she do, frighten squirrels? She was not believing this. Mom had warned her that Dad was all New Age and weird. He should have come to California. He would have fit right in.

Keelie realized that her mouth was hanging open and closed it. Tears stung her eyes, angry ones.

"There are good fairies, too, and some came to bid farewell to the oak that sheltered them. Knot interfered. Knowing that cat, he'd probably desecrated their mushroom circle by using it as a litter box." Zeke shook his head. He was enjoying this.

"Stop it, Zeke. I thought we had a great time at the mall," she said. "I actually thought you were treating me like family, instead of like a tourist. But now you're going off on this wacky fairy tale riff again." She backed away from him, glad that he looked hurt. He deserved it. No wonder Mom left his world. He couldn't tell reality from fantasy. "I'm not some mundane, you know."

He looked serious. "Keelie, you certainly are not a mundane. Far from it."

"I'm going to help Cameron with Ariel. Enjoy your spaghetti." She crossed the open area and started down the path toward the aerie.

Behind her, Zeke called, "Keelie? Wait a minute, I'll come with you. It's dangerous for you to be alone."

She waved without turning, then broke into a jog, which soon turned into an all-out sprint. By the time she returned to school, she'd be in such great shape that the rest of the cross-country team would be eating her dust. Darkened booths flashed by, their owners in their trailers or upstairs apartments. She slowed as she passed the woods on the other side of the jousting field.

A costumed child was walking through the trees. Keelie stopped as she realized what she was seeing—what she *thought* she was seeing. It was Knot, wearing boots, walking on his hind legs, and brandishing a sword in his front paw. And he wasn't alone. A leafy creature, all tangled wood and vines, fought back, wielding a large staff.

Keelie ran faster than ever, anxious to escape from her overactive imagination.

■ ■ ■

There is too much stress and too much grief in my life, Keelie thought as she stroked Ariel's dark red tail feathers, glad that the hawk, for all its elegance and regal bearing, was just a bird and nothing else.

She could hear her father talking to Cameron in hushed tones. He'd run after her the whole way. She'd never tell him how glad she was to have him there, mad as she was that he treated her like a baby. Fairies? Right.

Ariel watched her with her one golden eye. Cameron had not been around when Keelie had arrived at the raptor mews. James, one of the other performers, had given Keelie permission to take Ariel out of her cage and had shared his spaghetti dinner with her. Normal spaghetti, thank goodness. Zeke had arrived seconds after she had, but he'd disappeared once he saw her with James.

Reeling from the über-strange scene at the woodshop, Keelie wondered if she needed psychiatry. No, if any therapy was going to be handed out, her father and Scott needed to be at the head of the line.

Of course it might have been drugs. Maybe there was something in the herb tea everyone around here drank. Maybe some of Mrs. Butters' crystal seeds. They sounded dangerous.

It all seemed like a big hallucination. Faces in trees, magic mud balls, and invisible bugs with buzzing voices. Knot in his little Puss In Boots Musketeer outfit. She'd never be able to tell her friends that one without cracking up. Then again, "cracking up" was not a phrase she should use too much these days.

How could she explain that cat? Every day Keelie spent at the Faire, her sense of what was real and what wasn't blurred. How did she explain seeing a woman's face in the oak log, if it wasn't a weird allergy-induced vision? How did Keelie logically explain the knowledge about trees that kept bubbling up out of who knew where? The sooner she got out of La-La Land, the better for her. No wonder Mom had taken Keelie from Dad's world all those years ago.

Ariel inched down the arm guard toward Keelie's face and nestled her head against her cheek. Keelie froze. Hawks were not kittens. Was this a gesture of friendship and trust, or was Ariel about to rip her face off?

The hawk's head was hot and hard, yet its covering of feathers was incredibly soft. She made no move to attack, and Keelie could feel that part of her that Ariel had switched on grow larger and larger, making her feel good despite the freaky morning.

Cameron's voice interrupted the moment.

"Keelie, thank goodness you're here," she said, her tone panicked. "I need your help." Cameron was so frantic that she didn't notice the hawk nestled against Keelie's cheek.

"Sure. What is it?" Keelie stood slowly, so as not to scare Ariel. Cameron's forehead was creased with worry, and she was dressed in regular clothes, too—a gray sweatshirt, blue jeans, and Nike tennis shoes. She looked totally normal. Keelie needed normal.

"Moon's been sick all day, and I know that what I'm about to ask you is going to be strange, but I need for you to do it. No questions asked."

Keelie felt her heart sink. For a second, she thought Cameron would ask her to kill the bird, to end its suffering. But no. Cameron would do that herself, when the time came. She loved Moon, the snowy owl. It had to be something else, and Keelie knew that she'd do anything to help Moon. "Sure."

"Follow me."

"Wait a minute." Zeke stepped in front of Cameron. "She can't do this, Cameron. She's not ready."

"It has to be her." Cameron looked around, then lowered her voice. "I know you've heard, too. Moon is in the meadow, at the tallest aspen, Hrok. The Red Cap can't touch her there."

The meadow, land of bad feelings. "What do I have to do? Why me?" Keelie tried to catch Cameron's eye, but she was staring at Zeke, as if willing him to approve.

Zeke seemed stunned, but finally, he nodded and stepped aside. "I'll keep the area safe."

"Wait a minute. I need an answer. Remember me? Keelie? The person you're talking about?"

Ariel seemed to sense their mood. The hawk flew from Keelie's arm back to her perch without anyone telling her to do so. Cameron shut the cage door, then turned to Keelie. "I'll tell you on the way to the meadow. We don't have any time."

The three of them hurried through the odd yellow stillness. Keelie was still wearing the heavy leather gauntlet.

They passed the children's area. The maypole and pony ring looked strange and empty. Within sight of Mrs. Butters's teahouse, they turned left, through a gate marked "Employees Only," and went up Water Sprite Lane toward the meadow.

As they went through the gate she heard drumming. The Shire was close by, and the party was starting without her.

They passed a stand of trees, and the meadow was on their right. It looked wide and friendly in the gloomy daylight, with a thicket of aspens on the far side and other hardwoods here and there. A huge rock was in the center.

Keelie could see the glint of stone through the far trees. Elianard's camp. Despite its friendly appearance, Keelie knew the place was dangerous. She could feel the sense of panic building as she approached and a strange vibration from the Earth in the center of the meadow.

From the tree where her cage hung, Moon hooted and fluttered her wings, banging them against the wire walls.

Cameron clucked soothingly as they approached. Zeke eyed the woods warily, and Keelie fought to just keep one foot in front of the other when what she wanted to do was run to the Shire and hide in a tent.

The aspen trees seemed old, and she could sense them, stern spirits, like guardians in a sacred place. The largest one's upper branches were scorched, a scaly black that looked like a vivid wound against the green of its leafy neighbors.

Even from the edge of the meadow, Keelie could tell the owl was sick. Normally, Moon sat tall on her perch, eyes alert. Exhausted from her exertions, she sat listless, her white feathers dull and drooping, her enormous eyes closed. She didn't move, even with the noise of their approach.

Whatever was wrong with her was probably beyond the help of any home remedy. "Don't you think we might need to call a vet?"

"I am a vet. Modern medicine isn't going to help her," Cameron said firmly. "Early this morning music woke me, and the birds were going crazy, making a racket. When I went out to see who was playing the music that disturbed the birds, I saw immediately that something was wrong with Moon."

"So some nut played music, then hurt Moon? Do you think she was poisoned?" Keelie knew something deeper was going on, but she didn't want to go near those creepy trees.

Cameron looked puzzled, then alarmed. "Zeke, I thought you talked to her. Keelie, do you mean you don't understand your role here?"

"Those fairy tales about Red Caps and farewells to

trees?" Even though Keelie didn't admit it, she couldn't deny that she had an uncommon kinship with trees and wood, and that she had seen some pretty strange things.

"Keelie, I need the healing energy of the aspen tree channeled to Moon. Your father can't heal animals, but I sense that you can. It might not work, but she doesn't have much time." Cameron touched the owl's feathers.

Zeke looked at her. "I'll be here to help you."

"What's with you people and trees?" Keelie stared at them.

The part of her that belonged to her mother said, "Run, Keelie! Don't do it—you're turning into one of them." But the part that Ariel had awakened beckoned her to stretch out and touch the aspen. She did not want to touch that tree, remembering the suffocating sadness brought on by the oak in the workshop.

There were tears in Cameron's eyes. "Please, Keelie. Moon means the world to me. I know you can help her. Can you imagine not helping Ariel?"

"It's not that, Cameron. I don't have any kind of power. You're talking about magic, not medicine." And the trees. Keelie shivered. Something was underneath. Something bad. What did that mean?

"You've got that magic, Keelie," Cameron said.

Keelie thought of Ariel, of the hawk's bony head against hers. Ariel trusted her. She thought of her mother, who always said medicine was overrated and that she didn't believe in anything but the law.

Keelie would've defied Mom to save Ariel. To save

Moon, she would have to defy Mom's memory, her beliefs. Or disbeliefs.

She wouldn't let Moon die, even if it meant opening herself up to that tree creepiness, that bad feeling from underground.

"Okay, what do I need to do? I'm only trying it, Cameron. No promises. But I'm willing to try for you and Moon."

Zeke put his hand on her shoulder. "Good girl. I'll keep watch. Nothing and no one will approach."

Tears spilled from the woman's eyes. "Thank you, Keelie."

Cameron removed Moon from the birdcage. The owl slowly opened her eyes. Keelie couldn't see any wounds, but she sensed a purpose around the owl, like an invisible blanket of mean intent surrounding her. Whoever had harmed her had done so maliciously.

Cameron placed her on Keelie's arm. Moon's clawed feet pressed against the stiff leather covering her arm, and Keelie put her other hand up to balance the light bird. Moon leaned into Keelie's hand, and she drew her arm toward her chest so that the bird could lean into her body—even though she was wary of the wickedly sharp beak so close to her skin. Ariel trusted Keelie, but she hadn't handled Moon before. Maybe a sick bird, like a sick dog, might lash out in fear.

Keelie swallowed hard. "Okay. What next?"

"You'll need to touch that aspen and let the energy from the tree flow through you to Moon." Cameron pointed at the tree, then stood back.

Touch the tree? Keelie shivered. On the other side of the meadow, the drumming had intensified, punctuated now with excited yells and ululating calls. The dancing had begun.

The tree looked healthy and green, a living version of the broken log in her father's shop. She walked up to the aspen, hands shaking, then jumped back when she saw the face of a young man looking out at her from the bark. This was no allergy.

"Please, Keelie," Cameron said behind her.

Keelie shut her eyes to block the weird hallucination and placed her free hand on the tree. Warmth spread from the rough bark to her fingers, then up her arm. Through her closed eyes, the movement seemed green, like living sap. She wasn't scared any more. It was okay. Or at least, it didn't hurt.

What do you seek, Tree Shepherd's daughter?

Keelie opened her eyes. The tree had spoken to her in her mind. His words seemed green, too, and parts of them sprouted, taking root in her mind.

Moon gave a weak hoot. Time was running out for the owl. Keelie closed her eyes and pressed her hand more firmly against the bark. It was time for her to trust, too.

She pictured herself opening the locked box where she kept her feelings. The box opened, revealing the dark emptiness inside.

If you can heal this owl, please. She needs your help, she thought. *I don't know what to do.*

Tree Shepherd's daughter, you answered my call when fire struck from the clouds. My power is yours to wield. The green light that had crept up her arm now flowed from the tree, through Keelie, filling the box in her mind. She pushed it into and around the sick owl.

Keelie formed an image of a healthy Moon and held it in her mind. As the aspen's skin-tingling energy flowed into her, Keelie kept the image of the green light dissolving the darkness that infected the bird.

She stood still, holding the owl in the aspen's healing magic, until she felt weak and her knees grew rubbery. She locked her right knee and leaned against the tree, and the contact opened the power between them even more.

After a few minutes, Keelie slumped to the ground. Moon's lightweight body had become a leaden burden.

"I'm sorry," she whispered. She couldn't hold her any more.

She felt a final green caress from the tree and a faraway whisper, *Tree Shepherd's daughter*, then heard Cameron say, "You did it, Keelie. You've saved her."

Keelie opened her eyes and she saw Cameron cradling the snowy owl against her chest. Exhaustion filled Keelie's body, but happiness, too. She'd saved Moon with the tree's help.

Zeke leaned down, his face looming in front of her. "Are you all right?"

She nodded, then put one hand behind her to caress the bark. "Thank you," she whispered.

You are a friend to trees, the voice whispered back.

A buzzing filled her ears, as if a mosquito was flying too close. She'd heard the sound before, when it chased Knot.

She turned her head to follow the noise and saw an insect clinging to the aspen's smooth bark. It turned bright, intelligent eyes to her and extended its wings.

Keelie kept her eyes on it, not trusting that it would go away if she closed them. Too much had happened, and she couldn't disbelieve anymore.

"Keelie, don't." Her father's tone seemed urgent.

"Are you a fairy?" She moved her face closer to the oversized bug, and it skittered back a little. She held out her hand, and it moved closer and put a leg onto her finger.

Then it backed up, and a fine spray hit her face. The particles seemed to come alive. In moments they had flown right into her eyes, seeming to pick up speed the closer they got.

Keelie heard herself cough, and then everything went black.

twelve

If this was what a hangover felt like, then she was never, ever going to touch alcohol, Keelie thought miserably. Her head pounded in time with her heartbeat. She pulled the covers higher on her chest, then grimaced at the loud sound the sheets made as they rubbed on her skin.

Raven held up a green dress with about a billion yards of fabric in the trailing sleeves. "How about this one?"

Ribbons of green flowed straight up from the dress. That couldn't be right. Keelie wished she'd taken the willow-bark tea that Janice had sent along. Stupid fairy dust.

When she caught up with the tiny terrorist, she'd feed him to Knot. But how to tell a fairy bug from a real bug?

"Keelie? This dress?" Raven looked at her, eyebrows raised.

Keelie lowered the covers. "Too much," she whispered, and wished Raven would, too. "It's too tempting for Knot. Of course, he might suffocate in it, which would be a plus." He was the one who'd gotten the fairies riled in the first place.

Fairies. She groaned and put her palm against her forehead.

"Raven, could you leave me alone, please? I need to die."

"No way." Raven grinned. Her teeth were so, so—bright.

Raven smiled and put the dress back on the wooden rack that she and Janice had brought in, loaded with costumes for her to try on. She took down the next one.

Keelie groaned. That morning she'd bolted upright, her heart racing, remembering Moon, the aspen tree, the little stick creature, and the poisonous bug. Her awful headache lingered, as if someone was hitting the back of her head while squeezing her temples, like the bellows the blacksmith used over at the sword-making booth.

Angry fairies, Zeke had said. She'd lost the whole evening, put under by fairy dust. He'd also said that the little creature might be mad at her for healing Moon. If she hadn't seen it herself, she would have thought it was more of her father's weirdness. Of course, the whole event in the field made her father look less weird by the second.

"You need that headache tea," Raven said.

"Bring it on. Make it a double." Keelie looked around, in case the creepy little flying thing was around somewhere. "Why did the fairies put a hit on me?"

Raven patted her shoulder. "Your dad's looking into it." She rummaged through the dresses on the rack. "You can lie down a little while longer, but it's better for you to move around."

Her father had already left for his shop when she'd come out of the fairy-induced sleep and discovered her right hand was Crayola green. Janice had been sitting by her bed, a cup of soothing, honey-sweetened tea ready for her. It was cold now. Raven had taken over after an hour, when she'd gone back to finish her shop's bookkeeping.

Keelie reached for the cup that Raven offered. "So you believe in fairies, too? Have you seen them?" The tea was cool, but it smelled good.

"I've never seen them. Mom calls them the *bhata*." She pronounced it "watta." Raven sounded wistful. "But this Red Cap everyone's worried about? I've seen what he can do. Two guys almost killed each other over a missing MP3 player at the Shire, and neither of them is the fighting kind. It was bad vibes, and very weird. Scary weird."

"Scary weird? Coming from She-Who-Likes-Slasher-Movies?"

"Hey, I don't like to live them." Raven tipped up the bottom of the cup with her finger. "Drink up, small fry, and then we'll get your blood moving."

Keelie did as she was told, draining the cup. She felt better already, though the room still shifted to the left if she turned her head too fast. "What do you mean, get my blood moving?"

Raven looked mysteriously at her, then reached toward the floor and pulled out a long black scarf covered in jingling gold coins. She stood up, swishing her hips as she wrapped the scarf around them and knotted it in front. "Time for your lesson."

"Now? Raven, I'm dying. This is not a good time."

"Get up, slacker. Dancing will make you feel better, promise." Raven grabbed the covers and yanked them to the floor, exposing Keelie's poor, dying body to the chill.

"Oh, that's cruel. Now I'll die of pneumonia, too."

Beneath the bed, Knot purred.

Keelie rolled over and bent her head over the side of the bed, anchoring herself with her hands clutching the sides of the mattress. Under the bed, Knot was chewing on one of her socks, drooling over the shredded fabric.

"I took a fairy bullet for you last night, fuzz ball. Let's have a little gratitude." Hanging upside down was a bad idea. Her head was pounding even more.

Knot stared at her with huge green eyes, then darted a paw and swatted at her. As he moved, she saw her cell phone protruding from under his pudgy side.

"Hey, my phone." She reached in and grabbed it, avoiding his claws. She tried to straighten up but slid off the bed, landing in a heap on the wooden floor.

Raven snatched the phone from her hand. "Yuck, it's all covered in dried mud." She scraped at the crusty shell with a fingernail. "I think it's had it."

Keelie lay on the floor, looking up. Any minute the

crime-scene guys would show up to draw a chalk line around her.

"But you never can tell. Maybe if you cleaned it out carefully and dried it fast it might work again."

Keelie closed her eyes. "I need it to work. It's my only connection to my friends in L.A." She thought she heard Raven snort, but she was probably wrong. "Yesterday was so strange. It was like a dream. The day started normal, but then it went out of control. I think I saw Knot wearing boots and fighting those stick fairies with a sword."

"I wouldn't be surprised," she heard Raven answer. "Knot is an interesting creature. Sort of a mystery, like the Bermuda Triangle."

"A mystery? Misery's more like it. I can think of other words to describe him, too."

That one made Raven laugh.

Knot purred as he rubbed up against Raven's legs. She stepped back. "Oh, nasty. I have kitty slime on me. He's drooled all over my custom-made boots."

Something heavy landed on the bed above her head. Keelie didn't need to look to know it was the hairball. He purred.

"Can I look at the dresses later? I think I need to get back in bed." She picked up the sunglasses that she'd dropped on the nightstand the day she arrived and put them on. Darker, but better.

"Do those help? You're still a little green."

Keelie opened her eyes. "At least I'm not seeing green streamers shooting out of your head."

Raven felt the top of her black hair. "Thank goodness.

Green is so not my color. " She gestured at the rack full of dresses. "You've got two underdresses, those are the white ones—they can double as nightgowns. We've got three gowns for you too, including the green one, and Mom measured your shoes for medieval boots. They're sort of a mix between bedroom slippers and boots. Super comfy, mud repellent. You should have those in a few days."

In a few days, Keelie hoped to be gone. She felt guilty accepting the costumes, but she still needed garb to wear until then, and she could always wear them when she came back to visit her dad. It's not like they'd go out of style or anything, being four hundred years past their expiration date already.

"You and your mom are so nice. It sure is different from that Muck and Mire Show outfit." She was sure Elia would find something snarky to say about her new clothes, as well as remind everyone about the tacky handprints on her old Muck and Mire Show skirt. She wondered how much Elia knew about the fairies. Could she see all this weird stuff, too, or was it just a family thing? She remembered how the rain had not touched Elia even when everyone else was soaked.

Keelie rubbed her right hand against her nightdress. The skin on her hand and fingers were still stained green but didn't feel sunburned any more.

Raven couldn't see the fairies nor the faces in the trees. What if she ended up having more in common with Elia than with Raven? She shuddered. No way.

"Sir Davey dropped off some coffee for you. It's in the kitchen. He said to sip it every few minutes."

"Thanks." Coffee as medicine. Gotta love it. Sir Davey was another one she needed to talk to. He'd mentioned Earth magic. Maybe that was what she'd done yesterday.

"I promise I'll be back later. I have to check out what's going on in the meadow."

"In the meadow? What?" Keelie sat up, then clutched her head. Jeez. Like it hadn't been pounding for hours. She remembered that creepy manic midget in the red hat and the thing living in the stream. "What's happening in the meadow? Is it Moon? Is she okay?"

Raven helped Keelie get up. "Moon's on the mend. Remember I told you? Don't worry about what's going on. It's a Shire thing. Our party last night kind of got out of control. I'll be back, I promise. Skins and I are going to go and investigate some stuff. Aviva, one of my belly-dancing friends, lost a silver ring carved with rowan leaves. It's a family heirloom. Maybe we'll find the missing MP3 player, too."

"Okay. If you promise to come back and tell me everything." The Shire partied, and Keelie turned green. If she didn't feel so bad, she'd make a joke about it. "Can I take a rain check on that dancing?"

"Yeah. Get some rest, and when you feel better, I'll show you how to do some hip lifts." Raven helped her get into bed.

"Hip what?" Keelie rose up on her elbows.

Raven lifted her hip and then it dropped in a smooth, fluid movement. Then she did it several times, the coins on her scarf jingling like a tambourine. Knot's head moved up and down like a fuzzy kitty yo-yo as he watched Raven's moves, and Keelie became dizzy. Raven stopped. Keelie plopped back down on her pillow. "I'll never be able to do that."

"Probably not. You're so California. See ya, kid."

Raven left the room, then stuck her head back in, grinning. "By the way, you missed a great party, but I understand. It was for a good cause." She ducked out of sight again, and Keelie heard the door and Raven's voice say, "Hi, Zeke. She's doing a lot better."

Footsteps sounded loudly on the wooden floorboards, making her wince, and then her father appeared in the curtained doorway. "Glad to see you sitting up." He held a tray, and on it there was a silver carafe with a glass lid sparkling with different jewels. She inhaled the aroma of coffee.

"I thought I would bring you some of Sir Davey's 'clear away anything giving you a headache' coffee."

She nodded. "Coffee. Great. I'm still alive. Freaked out, but living."

"Want to hear some good news?" He placed the tray on the bedside table and poured the coffee into a green clay mug embossed with a gold leaf.

"About?"

He handed her the mug, and she gripped it with both hands. The warmth soaked into her skin, then she sipped the strong but delicious brew. Immediately, the throbbing in her head eased.

"It seems your luggage has made it to London." He was smiling, but his eyes held a look of concern. He didn't believe she was all right.

"London. As in England. As in Great Britain." Her head pulsed. She shouldn't have nodded. She sipped more of Sir Davey's coffee.

"It's getting closer. It'll be in New York City in a couple of days. That's New York, as in New York State. As in the United States." He smiled. "Why don't you lay down and rest?"

"I'm fine. I want to change into my new clothes. I'm feeling better. I think I can move now." Her head whirled, but not as much.

Despite her headache, she was happy about the good news. Things were looking up. Her luggage, including Mom's pictures and Boo Boo Bunny, were on their way back to her. She needed to see Mom's pictures. She needed to make sure she remembered her face the way it had been. And she could use a stuffed bunny hug about now.

"If you're up to it, I'd like to have some folks over to talk about Faire business tonight. Just Janice and Sir Davey. They're worried about you, too, and I didn't want to leave you alone. We'll move the meeting if we bother you."

He looked at his hands, his soft voice deepened with remorse. "I feel badly about what happened, Keelie, and that you had to deal with it unprepared."

Keelie wrapped her arms around herself. Had Dad carried her back from the field? She didn't remember anything after the bug bite, or whatever it was.

"You keep saying that we need to talk," she said. "Just tell me now."

He shrugged and looked as if he was about to say

something, then changed his mind. After thinking for a moment, he lifted his head and looked at her. "Remember the tree I was working on yesterday?"

"How could I forget?"

"You said something about an allergy, and then the fairies attacked Knot and we didn't talk again. What did you mean?"

"Mom said I was allergic to wood, ever since the trees talked to me in the park when I was five and I told her about it. She said it was allergen-induced psychosis."

His expression grew grim. "Your mother wanted to protect you, and she did, the best way she knew how. But you don't have any allergies, Keelie."

"I figured. It's been worse since I moved here, but I wasn't itchy or sneezing. I was hearing the trees. I can feel them in my skin. Can you do that, too?"

"Yes." His leaf-green eyes looked directly into hers.

"And that sad face in the oak in your shop was real. I know that now, because I saw a face in the aspen in the meadow, too. He talked to me." Keelie held her breath, wondering if he would trust her with the truth.

He nodded thoughtfully. "I saw the power interchange. Have you ever done that before?"

She shook her head.

"Could you feel the tree spirits in California?"

"Yes. Well, a little. There weren't too many trees where we lived. But here—Dad, just touching wood I know what it is, where it came from. What's that about? Can you do that, too?"

"I do. We're more attuned to nature than other crea

tures, Keelie. All trees have spirits, and their roots drink deep of the Earth's healing magic. There are those who aid the trees, keep malevolent forces from harming them, and in turn, the trees allow them to draw from their magic."

"The aspen called me Tree Shepherd's daughter," Keelie said.

"I'm one of the shepherds." Her father sounded weary. "Seems you're one, too. I was expecting it."

She lowered her sunglasses. "Right. They didn't cover this in Career Day at school. My dream job is not wandering through the woods, watering trees and chatting with them about squirrels and angry fairies."

Dad gave a short laugh. "That's not exactly what it's about, and the teachers at your old school have no idea, but you need to learn to control your gift."

"How about I ignore the gift? So far it's just been a big headache." Literally.

"You can't ignore it. Not in a forest. Keelie, I am so proud of you. What you did was very brave. Cameron can't stop talking about what you did for Moon."

Tears burned Keelie's eyes again. Thank goodness she was wearing dark shades, she was turning into a swamp. This time her tears were not grief. Her father was proud of her.

"I'll come down in a bit and show you my new garb. Janice and Raven picked them out."

Her father smiled and touched her cheek. "I'm sure you'll dazzle everyone. You even look beautiful in Muck and Mire Show clothes. But stay away from the pirates!"

What did he know? "Are they magic, too?"

"No. Most of them are just hormonal college boys looking for pretty girls."

After three cups of Sir Davey's coffee, Keelie's headache had almost completely disappeared, but she really had to go to the bathroom. She sat up carefully, then dropped her legs over the side of the bed. So far, so good.

"Do you need help?" Dad asked.

"No. I'm fine. Raven said I needed to move."

"Are you sure?"

"Yes."

"I need to tend to something in the shop really quick. I want to make sure Scott is handling the crowds and sales. Sometimes he can get overwhelmed."

"I'm better. Go down to the shop."

When Dad left, Knot opened his eyes and yawned. He hopped down onto the hardwood floor in front of the garb that Raven had brought.

Keelie said, "Don't even look at them. If you pee on them, I'm going to have a new kitty muff."

As she returned to her bed a few minutes later, Keelie realized her headache had totally disappeared. She wasn't green either, to her delight. She was happy she wasn't going to go around looking like Kermit the Frog's human cousin.

Crowds walked outside the shop, and from the near distance, cheers resounded as the joust took place. Was Sean riding today? Probably. She glanced at the rack, the dress colors glowing like jewels. Watch out Elia, Keelie was going to be dressed to kick butt.

“I wonder how Moon is doing.” Keelie said to Knot, but he’d disappeared.

After everything she’d been through to heal the owl, Keelie wanted to make sure she was recovering. The path to the mews just happened to go by the jousting ring. Maybe she’d run into Sean on the way, and he’d notice her new look. Goodbye, Mud Girl.

Outside, thunder rumbled from faraway. Did it ever stop raining here? You’d think it was Seattle, not Colorado. Keelie was glad Janice and Raven had gotten her a good thick wool cloak. The Irish cloak’s large hood with the ruffled rim let her see everything without being claustrophobic.

Keelie dressed, happy that the big sleeves were comfortable. She had to watch it around doors, though. Leaving the apartment, she’d gotten a sleeve caught in the door and had been brought up short, landing on her butt on the landing.

“Dad, going for a walk,” she called as she passed the shop.

He was busy showing a chair to a woman with overflowing cleavage. Another hovered nearby, anxious for his attention. Of course.

He looked up and waved at her, then did a double take when he noticed her garb.

“Looks like Sir Davey’s brew did the trick.” He bowed to her with a flourish, and she did what she thought was a curtsey, then took the path to the jousting ring.

She recognized the silver and green, black and gold of Sean’s colors as he galloped around the ring before going into the lists. She paused at the crowd's rim to watch as a page tossed a tall spear into his hand. He caught it lightly, even though Keelie knew they were heavy and awkward. Inside her cloak, she whispered, "Go, my brave knight, go."

"Ah, what lovely is this before me?"

Keelie knew that voice. Donald Satterfield, a.k.a. Captain Randy Dandy, her amorous pirate. She turned, dropping her hood.

He staggered back a little, "Whoa. You." He recovered, putting his hands over his heart. "Ah, lass. You've made my heart stop beating. There's only one medicine for that. A kiss, sweeting, from your lips." He leaned against the tree, blocking her view of the jousting ring, and held out his arms, making kissy noises.

She backed away as he leaned toward her, lips pursed, smelling like mead. "Go away. Not interested."

"But lass, it seems Lady Love conspires to bring us together."

"You're drunk." She made a face and turned to leave but stopped when she heard him laughing behind her.

He'd stopped weaving and stood still. "Keelie, my sweet. Do you think the Faire admin would really let me be drunk around the mundanes? I'd get my pirate ass fired. I just take a sip before speaking to make it real for the guests." He bowed and made a farewell gesture, with his hat in his left hand, the right held over his heart.

She felt her face get red. Of course. She should've known.

Captain Randy Dandy winked and put on his big pirate hat again. "I'll catch you later, sweeting. And believe me, I will. Captain Randy always wins his battles."

Cheering erupted behind her. Keelie spun around to face a large crowd of people, some in garb, some in their ordinary everyday clothes. They clapped and whistled. Keelie whipped back around to see Captain Randy taking a sweeping bow.

"Curtsey," he hissed.

She bobbed down, holding her skirts.

"Pirates." How dare he use her for material for one of his improv performances? What kind of place was this, where your private life became part of the ticket price?

More thunder rumbled, and the crowd started breaking apart. One man herded his kids away, saying, "Time to get home."

The wind raced through the trees, and a branch from a large oak crashed to the ground. She felt the tree shake itself. The branch had been half-dead.

A strong smell of ozone filled Keelie's nostrils, then her hair prickled. A flash of lightning hit the ground nearby. People started to run for shelter in nearby booths, waved in by merchants.

Keelie lifted her face. The clouds swirled wildly above her like vengeful spirits. Rain pelted her face, cascading from the sky. Little muddy streams formed along the paths in the ground, carrying away sticks and little bits of pine bark. Keelie picked up her skirts and ran for the mews. She wanted to check on Ariel and Moon before she went back to Heartwood. Once she reached Ironmonger's Way, though, running was out of the question. The rain had turned the dirt path into a treacherous mud slick. At least she didn't have to worry about mudslides like she did in

California. As she ran, the sodden hem of her skirt slapped around her ankles. She could've sworn she heard that nasty little Red Cap's voice in the wind.

Keelie raised her head again. The sky was a funky green. Green sky? This couldn't be good. She remembered the previous tornado warnings, and the sky had been this same pea soup color. She longed for the sun. It had been days since she'd felt its warmth on her face. The trees swayed as the wind whipped around them. They agreed. It had been too long since the sun had touched their treetops, their roots craved the nurturing energy that fed them.

Everywhere the shops were crowded with mundanes trying to stay dry. The mews were ahead, and she hurried to get into the shelter of the tarps that covered the cages. The musky smell of birds surrounded her.

Cameron's helpers were running back and forth, unlatching raptor cages from their stands.

"What are you doing here?" Cameron looked frantic.

"I came to see how Moon was. What's going on?" Everyone worked quickly and precisely, but there was a thread of fear in their movements.

"Haven't you seen the Weather Channel? Cold front moving through, hitting a warm front that just appeared out of nowhere. Tornado warnings posted everywhere. Security's getting the visitors out."

The wind lifted a tarp off of a vulture's cage. It squawked. A great horned owl banged its wings frantically against its cage. Ariel called when Keelie ran to her. "Cameron, do I need to get her out?"

Gently removing Moon from her cage, Cameron said, "Yes. Find a carrier for her."

Cameron placed Moon inside a carrier that reminded Keelie of the one that Laurie's mom used for their mean Himalayan cat, Pickles.

Once Keelie wrestled Ariel into the carrier, the hawk pecked at her hand. It drew blood, but Keelie hung onto the handle for fear of dropping Ariel. "Where are we taking the birds?" She shouted to be heard over the increasing shrill of the wind.

"Across to Sir Davey's. It's the strongest shelter. Hurry." Cameron raced ahead.

Keelie wondered where her father was, worried for him. Wrapping her cloak around Ariel's cage to try to calm the frantic hawk, she followed Cameron. James ran with efficient and urgent speed as they gathered the other birds. They loaded them into the back of a Jeep, stacking the cages precariously.

Keelie raced toward Sir Davey's shop, more concerned for Ariel's safety than her comfort. Her skirts wrapped around her legs. Hail pummeled her as she crossed the little clearing toward Ironmonger's Way and the Dragon Horde Shop. She had to stay focused, deflecting the trees' fear of the approaching storm. If she left herself open to them, their panic would paralyze her.

Sir Davey barked out orders. "Move them birdies to the back. They'll be safer there." His gray eyebrows rose like little hairy caterpillars when he saw Keelie. "Lass, what are you doing up and about after that episode last night? Does your father know you're here?"

"Your really great coffee fixed me right up." Keelie pushed her cloak back and revealed Ariel's cage. The hawk was bobbing back and forth on her perch. Her shrill calls made Keelie's ears hurt. The pounding of rain on the metal roof didn't help.

Sir Davey nodded. "I see how it is. There's a bond betwixt you and the hawk. Now move her and yourself to the back. And stay there."

Something hard plunked onto the metal roof of Sir Davey's shop, followed by more. The hail was getting bigger. Keelie huddled down next to Ariel and whispered to her. "It's going to be okay. I'm here." Ridiculous thought. If a tornado hit the building, they would both die.

There were more shouts from the front of the shop. Cameron yelled something to James. The howling wind drowned out his reply. The weather radio beeped, and the announcer in a dull, robotic voice said, "Tornado Warning for the greater Fort Collins area, including the High Mountain region."

Sir Davey waddled back into the small room of the shop, muttering to himself as he carried a cage almost as large as himself. Inside, the turkey vulture flapped its wings and squawked.

Plopping the cage next to Ariel, Sir Davey said, "Keep an eye on this buzzard; he's a trouble maker."

He whirled around. "When I find out who or what is behind this storm, I'll be whipping up a spell to teach him a lesson."

Shivering, Keelie looked up. "You think this storm was caused on purpose? Who could do that?" Maybe the singing she thought she'd heard in the wind really had been the Red Cap. Her heart raced. Was that little creep magically that strong?

The buzzard flapped his wings, causing his feathers to brush against her arm through the cage bars. She wanted to move away from the ugly bird, but he stopped squawking and tilted his bald head as if he was studying Keelie, trying to figure her out. He calmly folded his wings. The verdict was in: he liked her. She didn't know if that was a good thing or not.

Twenty minutes after they took shelter, the storm passed. As Cameron's helpers left to assess the damage, Sir Davey walked Keelie back to Heartwood. "Cameron's quite pleased with you. Your help made all the difference today."

Keelie blushed. She'd been glad to help Ariel, but it was nice to be appreciated. "Sir Davey, you said you thought something or someone had caused this storm. Do you think it was the Red Cap?"

He eyed her from under his hat brim. "Don't mention him aloud in the forest. The poor trees have just been through a storm. They're traumatized enough."

Keelie looked up at the tall trunks around them. Solid and unmoving. Silent as ever. But she could feel the nervous energy that ran through their sap. It flowed up and down her skin like a million ants. She rubbed her arms through her big sleeves.

"How can we get rid of him if we don't talk about him?"

Sir Davey gripped her arm in his strong hand. "Leave

it to the adults, lass. This is too dangerous for you. You're new to the magic, and though you're strong, you don't know what you're getting into."

Pounding steps squelched through the mud behind them. It was James. "All the cages were turned over and the tarps are gone. Cameron wants to know if the birds can stay where they are."

"Yes." Sir Davey looked stunned. "All those birds in my shop? The Dragon's Horde has been turned into a veritable roost."

His warning about the Red Cap was sobering, but she'd seen the nasty decaying mushrooms on both sides of the path and all around the shop.

"It's a good thing we're having our meeting. In fact, I may be staying over and sleeping on your dad's couch. Those birds smell."

At the shop there was no sign of Knot, thank goodness.

"Zeke's waiting for you upstairs, Sir Davey," Scott said. He looked at her. "You're all wet."

"Thank you, Lord Obvious." She needed to change into dry clothes and hang up these wet ones to keep them out of Knot's reach. Upstairs, Janice sat on the couch drinking from a green mug decorated with gilded trees. Steam rose from the rim, and the aroma of mint lingered in the air. Her father stood by the stove, pouring boiling water into the pot.

He stopped what he was doing and hugged her, releasing her quickly before she could protest. "I was so worried for you during that storm, but I learned you were with Sir Davey. Is everything okay at the mews?"

"Messed up, but the birds are okay." Keelie lowered her voice. "Zeke, the trees were afraid. I felt them telling me when the storm came."

Zeke sighed. "I did, too. Dark magic has upset the balance of energy in the forest."

"We found the mushrooms, Zeke, and it isn't good." Janice had risen from the couch and walked to the kitchen. She placed her mug on the kitchen table, bracelets jangling. Keelie noticed that Janice wore a purple sweater and jeans, normal clothes for a change. She looked nice.

"I saw the mushrooms too. They were all around the Dragon's Horde."

"You can smell them before you see them." Sir Davey's caterpillar eyebrows vibrated. "Those birds will be staying in my shop until the mews can be repaired. Mind if I bunk with you, Zeke?"

"Good idea. There's another front moving through and the weather might get rough again." Dad handed Keelie a cup of tea. "I can make coffee for you two. I've got some left."

"You have coffee?" Janice's eyes were wide.

Zeke shrugged. "Some of Sir Davey's blend. He brought it up for Keelie this morning. Keelie was feeling a little queasy after the excitement of saving Moon."

"I'll have orange juice, if it's all the same to you." Keelie craved sunshine, even if it was the liquid variety.

"No coffee?" Zeke pretended to be shocked.

Sir Davey took her hand and turned it over. A green

tinge lingered in her palm. "Too much acidity will off-balance the photosynthesis her body is trying to counteract. No orange juice."

"Coffee, then." Keelie sat down on the sofa, hugging a green pillow to her chest. "I'm tired." She leaned forward to examine the weather maps spread across the coffee table. Strange runic symbols were drawn over the Rocky Mountains. There were dots of green outlining forests. Some of the forests were labeled "Sentient." And there were dots of dark brown labeled "Earth."

Keelie asked, "What's this mean?"

"Those are the magical centers over the mountains," Zeke said.

Sir Davey sat down next to Keelie. "The Earth magic centers are fewer, but they are deep and very ancient. Forests come and go, but the Earth is there forever."

"How does Earth magic work?"

"Thought you'd never ask." Sir Davey beamed at her. "Hold out your hand. Don't be afraid." She raised her palm upward, and he placed a cold, round ball of raw, unbaked clay in her hands. It was hard and squishy at the same time, but thankfully not like mud. Where did he get it? She pictured him walking around with mud balls in his pockets.

"Remember, Keelie. Remember mud pies, remember sandboxes, remember splashing in puddles on a warm summer's night."

Keelie closed her eyes and wrapped her fingers around the cool clay. It was soothing, like a balm to her fractured heart. Her fatigue eased.

The memory of splashing with Laurie in her pink wading pool was suddenly clear. She had forgotten about the pool, and how they'd made mud pies next to it and had underwater tea parties and played with their dolls for hours while Mom sat in her lounge chair reading *Glamour* magazine.

Keelie giggled, remembering the warm sun and playing hide-and-seek with Laurie in the flower garden. Mom had complained about the tall lilies that their neighbor had planted and that now grew inside their fence, too. And suddenly, another memory surfaced. She felt her jaw drop as she remembered the little insect-like people that joined in their games.

She could almost feel the warmth of a California night, alive with fireflies that sang to her. Keelie danced with the little lights, and the stars seemed as bright as the blinking fireflies, and her skin tingled with the caress of their magic.

When Mom called, "Time to come in," Keelie wouldn't want to, and Mom would turn on the floodlights. She knew they were more than bugs, because they always disappeared when the lights went on. After the incident in the woods, she never mentioned the fairies to Mom.

Mom. Mom wearing blue jean shorts and a cool white blouse with embroidered roses on the pocket. Keelie squeezed the clay harder. She wanted to slip back into that memory and be that little girl again and have her mom tuck her into bed. She wouldn't play with the fairies if she could have her mommy back.

The memory began to fade. "No! Mommy, come

back." Keelie tightened her grip on the clay. Nausea and fatigue washed over her. She opened her eyes and let the mutilated clay drop from her fingers onto the floor.

Sir Davey watched her, his gray eyes grave. Keelie closed her eyes again and saw the images of Moon, the face of the man in the aspen tree, and the stick man flying in front of her. Finally her mother's face appeared, exactly as she remembered her. She hadn't forgotten her at all. Keelie opened her eyes and noticed that Sir Davey's eyes were misty. He held her hand.

Tears slipped down her face, too. She couldn't stop them. She tried to push all the sadness back into the box she'd created for her feelings, but the lock had been broken. The overwhelming sadness wouldn't fit anymore. It had grown too big for her to hide, and she had no choice but to let some of it out.

"More," she whispered.

Davey shook his head. "I didn't do anything, Keelie. You summoned that memory on your own. Your quartz works the same way as the clay. Things of Earth ground you and help you to focus your energies without distraction."

Keelie barely paid attention to Sir Davey. She stood up, releasing his hand. She didn't want clay or crystals to ground her. She wanted Mom. Keelie wobbled and would have fallen if Zeke hadn't caught her. He held her in his arms, and she relaxed. Just this once she would hold onto him. Just this once she would let him comfort her until the sadness shrank enough for her to stuff it back into its box and build another strong brick wall around it.

Her dad held her, and she held him back and cried into his shoulder. He kissed the top of her head. "I miss her, too. Keelie. I miss my Katy."

Keelie excused herself to wash her face. When she walked into the bedroom, Knot was on her bed, his weird green eyes focused on her. She saw herself reflected in the window against the growing darkness outside. It was too early for night. Another storm was approaching. As she looked, lightning flashed silently beyond the forest.

She heard her cell phone ring, the subtle chirp her mother had insisted on. The sound was coming from the bedside table. She picked up the mud-encrusted phone and checked its screen, but it was blank. She would have to call Pacific Bell for a replacement. Wonder what service they had in the Dread Forest?

"Stupid mud."

A tiny voice came from the phone. Surprised, she held it to her ear.

"Hey, you answered." Laurie's voice!

"You wouldn't believe it. This phone is destroyed. I haven't been able to get it to work at all," said Keelie. "How are you? How's everyone at school?"

"Okay." Laurie sounded impatient. "Cousin Addie is coming through for us. She'll be at the Faire on Sunday evening, and she's springing you then."

"Sunday." She should have been happy, but she felt flat.

"Yeah, that's all the time you've got left to suffer at the Freak Faire."

Hearing footsteps outside the bedroom, she whispered, "I've got to go, Laurie. Call me tomorrow."

Quickly, Keelie shoved the cell phone under her pillow as Dad poked his head through the bedroom curtain. "Aren't you coming back out?"

Knot watched her. When she made eye contact with him, his gaze dropped to her pillow, then back to her, as if he knew what she was planning.

"Yeah. I was just looking at my new clothes." That was lame.

Her father's face faded. A cold fear clamped around Keelie. Hrok's voice was in her head, *Tree Shepherd's daughter, help her.*

She shrieked as she dropped to the floor. Her arms felt as if they were being torn out of their sockets as the wind tugged on her body like an evil zephyr, demanding her to dance with it. The branches of the oak tree outside the shop slapped and scratched the glass window panes. Hrok's voice echoed in her head. *Tree Shepherd, stop the storm.*

Stop it? How could her dad stop a storm? She felt as if her arms and legs were being pulled, her hair yanked by the roots.

Then she lost her connection to Hrok, hearing instead sadistic laughter in the howl of the wind. The Red Cap. Panic swelled inside Keelie, bursting out of her in a scream.

In the dark and cold was the green panic of the trees as they thrummed their danger call deep underground, root to root.

Sudden warmth drew her attention, and then she heard the weather radio beep its storm warning. Hands. Hands were clutching at her.

"Open your eyes, Keelie," Janice said.

"We're right here, lass. Open your eyes." It was Sir Davey's voice.

She did, and saw Sir Davey and Janice were kneeling on either side of her. "Dad." Her voice came out in a croak.

"He'll be all right. Are you with us now?" Sir Davey's voice was like an anchor, a strong rock that would hold her down, keep her safe.

Keelie closed her eyes again as a cry for help rose in her mind once more. She saw a tall, regal aspen growing in the forest on the other side of the mountain. She sensed that the aspen was a queen, and the smaller aspens surrounding her were her handmaidens and members of her woodland court. The trees were in danger, surrounded by debris whirling counterclockwise. Lightning sizzled and hit the aspen. Fire consumed her papery bark. In that moment, Keelie felt the tree's life force fading away.

"Keelie." She heard her father's voice, but it was in her mind, a warm green haze that wrapped around her. She struggled to find her voice. "Tornado."

Fear and pain flooded through her. Hot pain seared her ankles. It felt as if rough fingers had grabbed hold of them and were pulling. The aspen's roots were being torn from the Earth. The last of the tree's consciousness filled Keelie. *Protect the magic, Tree Shepherd's daughter.*

The green blanket that resonated with her father's

magic enfolded her as the tree crashed to the forest floor. Its spirit disappeared from her mind, but she was left with the image of the tornado plowing through the woods like an angry titan of air.

thirteen

Keelie felt arms lift her. She opened her eyes to see Dad's concerned face as he put her on her bed.

"It's over, Keelie."

"Oh, Dad, she's dead, and something killed her. That wasn't a real storm. That was magic. Did you hear it laughing? She died, and it laughed."

Janice gasped. She stood at the foot of the bed, her hand over her shocked face.

Sir Davey was at her side, face grim. "The Red Cap, sure enough."

Zeke nodded. "I think you're right. Tomorrow we'll

find her and hold the Tree Lorem. Keelie will take part, of course. The Queen Aspen spoke directly to her."

Sir Davey's eyebrows rose. "Surprising."

"What's a Tree Lorem? Some kind of funeral?"

"You could call it that. It's a ceremony of farewell and respect, and the tree's magic will be harvested and given back to the Earth."

Something warm and furry snuggled against her head. A soft hypnotic purring lulled her into drowsiness, but she overheard Sir Davey and Dad speaking in hushed tones.

"Dare we hope she's the one?"

"Don't be ridiculous. This is my daughter."

"Only in legends can a tree hepherd have the connection your daughter has. She's new to the magic, and yet the aspens speak to her, call to her from the other side of the mountain."

Keelie didn't want this connection. She didn't want to feel trees dying. It was hard enough to grieve for Mom. She couldn't handle a whole forest.

"It scares me, Jadwyn. She's only now come back into my life, and I don't want to lose her. But what if she is the one? There are those who will not accept it. My mother, for one."

"Will you two be quiet?" Janice said in a scolding whisper. "Keelie's been through enough the past two days; let the poor child rest."

Keelie wanted to sit up, but the purring was getting louder, and she was getting sleepier. So, her grandmother wouldn't accept her? It hurt a little, although it shouldn't.

She'd never even known the woman existed before this month. Two could play that game.

■ ■ ■

"Not a morning person, are you?" Keelie said.

Sir Davey glared at Keelie from across the kitchen table. The hair on his wooly eyebrows stuck out in several different directions.

"Mmph. Can't believe Zeke doesn't have coffee in this place."

"We drank it all yesterday. I need a Starbucks fix."

"I need sleep. Trees tapping on the window, Zeke coming in and out all night long, and that cat. You need to trim his claws."

She leaned against the table. So she had Sir Davey as an ally against Knot. Ha! "What did he do?"

"Besides snoring, he kept me awake with the racket he made sharpening his claws on my backside."

"He uses me as a scratching post, too." She showed him her wounded ankle.

Sir Davey shook his head, "Never heard a beast so loud before in my life. You'd have thought I was bunking down with a mammoth with a head cold."

"Where's Dad now?"

"He went out around dawn, hasn't returned. He did say if he wasn't back for us to go and help Cameron with the birds. And though I'm beholden to Zeke for letting me rest here last night, I'm looking forward to getting back to my own home. Bird-free home," he amended.

On the way to the mews, Keelie was surprised at the varying degrees of damage to the shops. A metal roof had been blown off the music store where they sold penny-whistles, harps, and dulcimers. Rotten mushrooms encircled the overturned fairy-wing stand in the children's area. The fairy wings were caked with mud, but in the pale morning sunlight, they glittered, looking sad with their little bits of sparkle.

Across the street, Janice was outside hanging a blue tarp over the doorway into the herb shop. She glanced up at them but continued working.

"Let's go and say hello. She looks upset."

Keelie hurried after him.

"Good morning. Looks like you suffered some damage, though not as bad as some." Sir Davey said.

Janice sighed wearily. "With a little help from Zeke, I can have the wind damage repaired."

Raven pushed aside the overhanging tarp. "Move!" she shouted. She had a black bandana over her hair, and she wore a black Wildewood Faire, New York top and low, hip-riding jeans. She scowled as she held a dustpan loaded with a pile of decaying mushrooms out in front of her. "Oh, this is so nasty. I never will eat a portabella again."

Keelie covered her nose. "Gross. It smells like Knot's litterbox."

Raven said, "I'll talk to you later, Keelie. I've got to get this putrid mess over to the compost pile." She ran, the dustpan held before her like an evil offering.

Sir Davey's forehead wrinkled. "Is that the extent of the damage inside? Mushrooms?"

"Oh, no. I've only just started checking things out. Most of my dried herbs are caked with mold and mushrooms. I can't sell them."

Janice came closer and lowered her voice. "It's the Red Cap. Dark magic. This has got to stop, Davey. Skins and Raven drove a couple of the college kids to the emergency room last night. The storm hit the Shire pretty hard."

Janice suddenly became quiet as Tania walked by with a companion. She had a sneer on her face as she passed them. "I'm surprised you had damage here; we didn't have any at all."

Janice turned away. Apparently, she had nothing good to say in reply.

Keelie recognized Tania's friend as one of the pub owners. He stopped and bowed his head. "Good morrow, gentles."

Tania continued on her way, not even acknowledging Sir Davey or Keelie.

Keelie stared after her. What a witch!

"How goes it, Al?" Janice asked.

He said, "Not good. I see you've had some damage, too. Some of the kegs in the pub were opened, and I had a lake of Guinness on my floor. Going to cost me a fortune to replace it all. I don't know if I can absorb the loss."

Sir Davey said, "I'll be back later. I have to check on my shop, and I promised Keelie we'd go to the mews." He nodded to the pub dude. "It pains my heart to hear about the Guinness on the floor."

"Ah, I'd have a sticky mess to clean up, but Heartwood's cat's been lapping it up all morning. Didn't know a cat could hold his ale like that. He could drink a Viking under the table."

Keelie made a mental note to store her new garb and the La Jolie Rouge clothes in the Swiss Chalet—far, far away from that cat. Beer had well-known bathroom side effects.

In the Dragon Horde shop, Dad was helping James load a Great Horned Owl into a crate. The bird seemed calm. James latched the cage door. "That'll do it. Thanks, Zeke. Don't know how I would've done it if you hadn't been here to help."

"Any time, James. We're family here."

"Not everyone feels as you do. We're grateful." James picked up the crate and made his way out of the shop.

"Watch it. Owl coming through." They couldn't see whoever was behind the giant crate. The owl hooted.

"Good morning, Keelie, Davey," Dad said. For someone who had been up half the night, he didn't have any dark circles under his eyes. Of course, Keelie was the same way; she could stay up all night studying and next morning, she wouldn't have to use a cover stick like most of her friends at Baywood Academy.

From the back of shop, Keelie heard a familiar shrill cry, followed by squawking. It sounded like two avian toddlers throwing tantrums. She quickly made her way past Sir Davey's rock displays.

There were two girls and a cute guy in green hospital scrubs writing notes on clipboards. They looked like college kids.

"Make sure you have them strapped down. I don't

want them to get jarred on their trip." Cameron said, waving a thin package. "I've got their medical records in this folder."

Ariel flapped her wings against the cage. "What's going on?" Keelie asked as she kneeled down to soothe the hawk. Immediately, she settled down, as did the vulture in the next cage.

"I'm sending some of the birds to the raptor center at the university. Most of the mews were destroyed last night during the storm, and the weather forecast says that this same pattern will hit us for the rest of the week. We're still going to try to hold the Birds of Prey show on the weekend, but I'll feel better knowing that the others have shelter."

"What? What about Ariel?" Keelie didn't want the hawk to be sent away the way she had, to live among strangers. "She belongs here."

The vulture beaked the cage wires as the really cute guy tried to grab the handle. He cursed and pulled his hand back. "Ma'am, no one can get near this vulture."

Keelie leaned over the cage, and the bird folded its wings and tried to snuggle closer to her.

"Wow. That's amazing," the vet guy with the curly blond hair said. "You've got a way with birds."

"Thanks." Keelie blushed as he winked at her. Cute as he was, Ariel wasn't going to some university.

"Cameron, I can help with Ariel. Please don't send her away."

Dad leaned against the doorframe. "I'll help her with the hawk."

Cameron said, "Well, I can't ask for a better reassurance than that." She turned to the guy. "Tell the others I'll be right there."

"Yes, ma'am." He wrote something on the clipboard and walked away.

Keelie looked down at the vulture, and he blinked its beady eyes at her, as if he was asking, can I stay with you, too? She felt sorry for him.

Sir Davey said, "The ugly one can stay with me."

"What?" several voices asked at once.

"It can stay with me." Sir Davey sounded out each word in a loud voice.

"Somebody needs his coffee," Keelie replied.

"I'll have a pot brewing soon, but I'm not caffeine deprived. I can take care of the vulture." Sir Davey looked down at the caged predator.

"I never took you for a bird lover, Davey. You complained so much yesterday when we brought them here." Cameron smiled broadly. "I guess Louie can bunk with you."

Zeke laughed. "Think it'll improve business, Davey?"

"Better than that cat of yours. We heard it was drinking spilled stout at the pub."

"Not again. I guess I'll find him with the pirates." Zeke shook his head. "I hope he hasn't run up a bar tab."

"Tell me you're kidding," Keelie said.

"Wish I could stay, but I have to run to the raptor center in Fort Collins." Cameron picked up a cage with a small kestrel in it. "I learned something interesting from the clerk down at the convenience store. Rumor has it that the Faire lands will be sold for a strip plaza. I wouldn't be surprised if Admin tries to pull something like closing down the Faire early because of the damage. Possibly condemn some of the buildings right away."

Dad's eyebrows narrowed. "You heard this strip plaza rumor from the store clerk?"

Cameron nodded. "It's the station near the exit."

"I'll need to check this out," he said.

Ariel rubbed her feathery head against Keelie's fingertips. She smiled at the hawk. At least they still had some time together.

"I left my list of repairs on Davey's desk in the back." Cameron walked toward the front door, holding the cage high and clear of all the merchandise.

"I'll start on them when I get back. Keelie and I have plans for this afternoon." Zeke put a hand on Keelie's shoulder.

Dad's to-do list was getting longer and longer. He was going to need a BlackBerry to keep up with it all. She wondered if he'd be opposed to one, since he didn't find a need for microwaves or cellphones.

"What about Ariel?" Keelie asked. She didn't want to leave her in the teeny, tiny carrier.

"Bring her with you. We're going into the forest. Ariel will be fine."

Excited, Keelie slipped on the heavy glove and put her arm into the cage for Ariel to hop on.

As they walked down Ironmonger's Way, Ariel perched on Keelie's arm, tenting her wings for balance. Once they cleared the bridge, Keelie peeked over to see if she could see the mysterious creature that lived in the water and had saved her from the Red Cap. Maybe the storm had washed the creature away.

Dad turned to Keelie. "We're going into the forest, and I want you to only observe. Don't speak, even if what happens is strange. I will answer all of your questions later. We must hurry, the time draws near."

That sounded so fairy tale Grimm. *Time draws near.* Okay. Dad was getting all tree-mystical on her. As long as he didn't carry a staff with a big crystal on it, Keelie was prepared not to freak out. After everything she'd seen and experienced, she didn't think there was anything that would freak her out.

Knot ran ahead of Keelie, as if he wanted to be the leader of the expedition. Couldn't she do anything without the hairball showing up?

Deeper into the woods, the claustrophobic feeling began to envelop her. Sweat dripped down her back, and she found it hard to breathe. It had been like this when she'd been lost and met Elianard.

Ariel called out and turned her feathery head toward Dad.

Keelie stopped. What if she couldn't find her way out? What if she ran into those bug and stick things? What if the Red Cap showed up?

Dad turned around.

"I can't go."

Her father looked puzzled, then his eyebrows rose. "Oh, that's right. I'm so sorry. I forgot about it."

"Forgot about what?"

Dad placed his hand on Keelie, and soothing warmth spread through his fingers. Is this what trees felt like when he touched them? She felt her anxiety slip away, dissipating like fog in the morning sun. She inhaled, then took several cleansing breaths the way she did in yoga class at school.

"Better?"

"Yeah. I don't know why I get claustrophobic in these woods. I never did before."

"It's a spell to keep interlopers out."

"The Dread."

"How did you know that?"

Before she could answer, Ariel flapped her wings and rose to the upper branches of a tall cedar tree.

"Ariel, get back here."

"Let her go. She'll be fine. She's beginning her journey."

"Journey. Not what I want her to do. What if she gets away?"

"The trees will watch her. Now follow me."

Yep, tree mystic.

As they walked along, Ariel zipped ahead of them and waited on a tree branch. When they caught up to her, she would fly to another perch and wait. Other than the beating of Ariel's wings and the crunching of their feet on the sticks, there was complete and total silence. Knot flitted silently from one side of the path to the other.

A gentle breeze tousled her hair, bringing a hint of decay in the air. Mushrooms again. Ariel flew to her. Keelie extended her arm, and the hawk landed precariously. She turned her head, and her golden eye glinted. Ariel rubbed her feathery head against Keelie's cheek.

Keelie held still until Ariel spread her wings to regain her balance.

"Come along, Keelie."

A silver glimmer in the center of a circle of mushrooms caught Keelie's attention. "Hold on, Dad."

Keelie walked over to it and knelt, careful not to dislodge Ariel. It was a silver ring. She picked it up and examined it. Raised leaves danced around the bright, slender circle. Raven said her belly-dancer friend Aviva had lost a ring like this one.

Ariel called and turned her head toward the large oak tree. Something shimmered, but she saw no one. Shoving the ring into her jeans pocket, Keelie sensed something was there.

The hair on her neck stood up. The air shimmered again. She smelled cinnamon. This was creepy. Was this the Red Cap?

She held very still and tapped into the inner sense that let her talk to Hrok. The remaining chlorophyll in her blood sang as the trees responded. And there, in front of the tree, stood Elianard, dressed in richly embroidered robes, clutching his staff. Their eyes met, and he glared at her as he realized he was visible.

He walked toward her, and she backed up.

"How is it that you wield so much power, Keelie Heartwood? Hawks are lucky, they say, and this one in particular protects you. Why is that? How is it that you, a half-human brat, can tame the wild, call on the trees, and defeat my spells? What charm are you wearing? I feel its power."

"I wear no charm. And what are you, exactly, some sort

of overgrown leprechaun like the little nasty dude in the red hat?"

Keelie toed one of the gross mushrooms on the ground. It deflated, and its putrid odor wafted up.

Elianard looked startled. "The Red Cap?" He searched around nervously. "Is he here?"

Keelie hoped not. She'd barely survived her last encounter with the manic midget. But if Elianard thought she sensed him, it would be like bug repellant. She lifted her chin and sniffed. Ariel called, turning her head this way and that, glaring at Elianard with her good eye.

"He's close."

Elianard swirled his robe, turning watchfully.

"Elianard. You walked so silently I didn't notice you." Zeke walked toward them, eyeing the richly dressed man warily. So, Dad didn't care for Elianard, either.

Ariel launched herself from Keelie's arm skimming Dad's head with her wing tip.

"Come, Keelie, it's time for the ceremony. What you're about to witness is a very important ritual, one of the most important that a tree shepherd must do." Dad's face and voice were filled with sadness.

Keelie nodded, glancing at Elianard.

He stiffened, then must have realized that Keelie wasn't going to mention the invisibility spell. With a slight bow, he walked ahead of them.

To her surprise, Sean and several other jousters stood solemnly by a wooden wagon, surrounded by others she'd seen at the Faire. The Equus Island horses were hitched to it. Everyone was dressed like Elianard in dark green robes embroidered with trees. To her surprise, Elia was with them, looking sad, too.

Dad clasped Keelie's hand in his. Calmness flowed through her.

Dad dropped her hand and raised his, palms up, toward the assembled group. "You stand in the forest of Reinanlon. Before you lies the Aspen Queen Reina."

As if on cue, a shaft of sunlight broke through the clouds and illumined a slender fallen tree, its trunk charred. Without touching it, Keelie knew it was the aspen that had communicated to her at the moment of its death last night.

Goosebumps dotted her skin.

"We have come to honor her magic and to send it forth into the world to heal, and we ask the forest and all those that loved her permission to do so," Dad said.

Everyone bowed heads. Keelie did likewise. Ariel was perched on a small aspen nearby.

A gentle wind blew through the trees. A fall of green leaves that smelled like cherry blossoms cascaded down onto the fallen aspen, a tribute from her sisters. Ariel flew up through the cascade, a blur of wings in the flickering green. Keelie looked up and gasped when she saw another hawk flying through the branches toward Ariel.

The two hawks circled one another. Then Ariel called out and dove. Keelie thrust her gloved hand up and Ariel made a perfect landing. The other hawk soared higher and higher, and Keelie's heart ached for Ariel because she would never be able to fly that high and free. The bird gazed at her with her good eye, as if saying, I will.

Sean and the other jousters walked forward and lifted the log as if they were pall bearers at a funeral and reverently placed the log in the wagon, its branches dangling behind, scraping the ground with its quickly withering leaves.

"Come, Keelie," Dad said.

She picked her way through the debris-strewn forest with the others, dodging dangling branches. A sadness clung to the trees like dew in the morning, and it wrapped itself around her Irish cloak. She inhaled, and deep grief surged through her, from the trees and from the green-robed people around her. She had to push it away. Keelie reached out and steadied herself by touching a tree. Aspen. It was an aspen, too. Raw pain coursed through its trunk. She could hear its heart beating with a slow, steady rhythm, reminding her of Skins playing his drum back at the Shire.

Our queen.

Root mother.

Keelie hadn't said she loved her mother that morning she died. They'd argued over the belly button ring. Mom had been late for her flight. She'd said, "We'll talk about this later. Love you, Keelie." Mom had kissed her cheek.

She slowly sank to the ground and let the tears flow. She would never again have the chance to tell Mom she loved her.

How will we leaf without our queen? How will we flower?

How would Keelie live without Mom?

Dad touched her shoulder, and some of the grief dissipated, sinking, like her tears, into the leaves on the ground.

The small aspens and other trees that made up the woodland court of the Aspen Queen were in pain. Their grief was intense, and she tried to block it, but couldn't. Her heart was so heavy, she didn't know if she could move. She just wanted to curl on the forest floor and close her eyes and wish herself back to that morning before Mom died.

One by one, the mourners came forward to lay a hand on the fallen tree, whisper a word, and step away. What were they saying? Would she do it wrong?

"Come, Keelie, say farewell."

Standing next to the wagon, she spread her hand over the tree. As she touched it there was a loud crack. The tree split right down the middle, revealing a center piece, a small charred heart.

Murmurs of amazement broke out from the crowd.

"A gift. The tree gave her its heart."

Dad reached for it, then placed it in her hand. She clasped her fingers over it, feeling the warm roughness of the charred wood. Black flakes rubbed off on her skin, revealing the smoothness of ebony inside.

"Not fair. She's not even one of us." Elia's strident voice killed the silence.

Dad pulled Keelie to his shoulder, ignoring the girl's complaint. He's the rock she needed, Keelie thought, not a tree. She felt his love brimming full, overflowing from deep within his soul. She let the tears fall unbidden down her cheeks. For the aspen, for the forest, for Mom.

■ ■ ■

Knot rode in the wagon beside the aspen log, sitting like a kitty guard. He was behaving himself, not at all like a cat with a hangover from lapping up a keg of spilled Guinness. Walking alongside the wagon, Keelie kept looking through her lashes at Sean. He stared straight ahead like the other jousters as they escorted the wagon to the Faire.

She wondered what he thought of Elia's outburst. Others had been shocked, and they still discussed it as they walked. Elianard and his daughter had vanished soon after the incident.

This all seemed so *Lord of the Rings,* except for Knot. She pressed her hand around the heart of the tree. She wondered what Sean thought of her now. She wasn't sure what it meant, other than she knew she'd been given a very precious gift from the Aspen Queen.

The wagon came to a complete stop outside Heartwood. Dad, Sean, and the others carried the log inside the shop.

Sir Davey bowed his head as the log passed. The turkey vulture was on the ground next to him, like a really ugly pet chicken.

"Dad?" Keelie said.

"It's okay. You can stay with Sir Davey."

"New friend?" She watched the turkey vulture rub its bald head up and down against Sir Davey's pants leg like a devoted dog. Ariel skimmed over him, her talons touching Sir Davey's head before landing on the oak outside the shop. "Birds. I'm going to be bird-brained before this Faire is over and done with." The coffee in his hand hadn't done anything to improve his disposition.

Knot hopped down from the wagon and sauntered up to the shop entrance. The turkey vulture hissed as the cat walked by. Knot ignored him, then ducked under a table as the jousters filed out of the shop.

They moved silently and fluidly. Sean was last. He stopped, smiling, and winked at her. "May the blessings of trees be with you, Tree Shepherd's daughter." He lowered his voice to a whisper. "You'll have to tell me what you did to get that tree's heart."

Tongue-tied by his nearness, she realized that she'd let the moment pass and he was on his way out of the shop. She watched him climb gracefully into the wagon with the other jousters. They were probably going back to Equus Island. Keelie was going to have to sneak over there one night. Their parties might be just as good as the Shire's. They had to be. Sean was there, not to mention all the other jousters.

That evening after her shower, Keelie noticed the lights through the floorboards. Dad was in the workshop. She pulled on her shoes and slipped her cloak over her underdress and went down to the workshop.

Dad was preparing the Queen Aspen, his tools nearby, like a surgeon's.

"What are you going to do?"

"We're going to make a rocking chair. The magic of the

tree will be transformed into healing energy." She clutched the small wooden heart in her hand. This part of the tree would always be hers.

It was so sad to look at the log and to know that a sentient spirit once lived inside it. As Dad bent down to remove a small handsaw from his toolbox, Keelie saw the pointed ear tip. She remembered Elianard's words.

"Dad."

"What, Keelie?"

"Remember when Elianard showed up when we were walking toward the Tree Lorem?"

"Yes."

"Didn't you think it was strange that he just appeared like that?"

"Not really." He was preoccupied with the wood, running his hands down the charred sides of the trunk.

"I saw him appear. He had a spell that made him invisible."

Zeke looked up at that. "What?"

"He wanted to know what charm I had, why I had so much power. He called me a half-human."

The handsaw clattered onto the floor.

Keelie stared at Dad over the tree. "Elia's called me that, too."

With his hands, Dad moved his hair behind his ears to show their pointed tips. She pulled her hair back, revealing her own. One round, one pointed.

"Keelie. I wanted to tell you when the time was right. I should have done it years ago." Her father looked remorseful.

She thought of Sean's ears, and Elia's. Every other person at the Faire couldn't have the same weird birth defect.

"No need, Dad. You're an elf. I'm...what am I? Some sort of half-breed?" Keelie touched her right ear. It was round. With a trembling hand, she fingered her left ear, which she knew wasn't exactly round or pointed, it had its own unique shape—a smooth tip.

Walking over to her, Dad reached out a hand and gently tilted her head up to him. She couldn't look away. "Keelie, I know you've found life at the Faire shockingly different from your old life. I know life with me has challenged what you understand as reality. The world is full of different creatures, and of the ones that think and reason, humans are only one small part."

He pointed at the aspen. "You've met the tree folk, and the *bhata* and *feithid daoine*. You must be aware that Knot is more than a cat."

Kitty claws snagged her pants, and as she moved her leg, the hairball clung to her leg.

Dad smiled wistfully. "He adored your mother, too."

"Oh, and I bet she returned the love. But, I want to know more about the elves."

"Many of us here at the Faire, and around the world, are elves," he continued. "We are more than human, and we are nature's guardians. I am a tree shepherd, and you seem to have inherited my gift."

"That's why I have this unnatural bond with furniture," she said. He seemed pleased that she hadn't fainted from shock, or screamed and ran away.

She didn't know what it meant to be an elf, exactly,

but deep within her understanding flowed, as if the dam that had kept it back was gone. Strange things that had happened suddenly made sense. She wasn't crazy, and she wasn't a freak. She had Ariel to thank for teaching her to open her heart.

"Did Mom know you were an elf when she married you?"

"Yes. There were no secrets between us."

Relief warmed her. She was glad Mom had known, although it raised fresh questions about why Mom had taken Keelie to California.

"The magic is real with very real consequences," her father said. "You need to master it, or it can control you. Or worse, others could use it through you."

She shuddered, thinking of the Red Cap. Then a thought occurred to her.

"Does that mean Mom left to get away from the elves?"

He sighed. "Yes. To get you away from them. You were so small, so helpless. And she knew that one day you would face what she faced from small-minded individuals." He grasped her firmly by the shoulders. "Understand this, Keelie, and never doubt for a moment that your Mom and I loved each other. What we had was special. And it makes you special, too."

Tears formed in Keelie's eyes. Unspoken words choked her. Dad moved a stray curl off her forehead. "You are what is best about both of us, my daughter," he said.

"Why didn't you tell me sooner?"

"Because I didn't know how you'd take it, Keelie. No,

that's not true. I knew exactly how you'd take it. You wouldn't have believed me.

"I just got you back in my life. We're both grieving for your Mom. I didn't want to lose you, as I feared would happen if I told you the truth. Would you have believed me if I had told you?"

She shook her head miserably.

Dad put an arm around her shoulders. "Leaving California was hard for you, but you would have come to me soon, anyway, Keelie. Your magic matures between puberty and adulthood. Your mother would have brought you back." He kissed her hair. "I just wish you didn't have to come because your mother was gone."

"Would you have been together?" She couldn't believe that her mother would have been comfortable as a Rennie.

"Time worked against us, I'm afraid," Zeke said. "And after a while we found that the only common ground we shared was you. I'm not going to lose you again, Keelie. We'll work it out."

The aspen's charred heart tingled. She opened her hand and looked at the heart resting on her palm. Would she break Dad's heart by returning to L.A.?

fourteen

Keelie's back ached, and she smelled like cedar wood shavings and sweat. After working all night with Dad on the aspen, she'd been up at seven in the morning to work with Cameron in the mews. A girl finds out she's an elf, and the next day, she's putting together cages.

The aspen's wooden heart hung on a silver chain beneath her shirt. Dad had turned it into a pendant, wrapping it with silver wires instead of drilling a hole in it. It gave her a sense of security. Ariel flew overhead, and every now and then, another call answered from nearby. The other hawk lurked nearby. Did Ariel have a boyfriend?

Sir Davey had buried protection stones around the cages, hoping to ward off the Red Cap. Keelie had been curious, but she was not ready to learn more about Earth magic. Mud magic. She was trying to cope with the trees.

Dad had been summoned to a meeting of the elves in their secret part of the woods. He was going to mention the Red Cap. Some elves had been denying its existence, but it was time to do something about it. Enough harm had been caused, including the two college students still hospitalized.

A meeting of all the Faire folk had been called for later this afternoon. Keelie would need to shower before she attended. She hoped to see Raven, who had been busy cleaning up the herb shop.

"Well, well. She does one good thing, and she's her daddy's darling." The sweet voice had a spiteful edge. Elia.

"I was having a wonderful morning until I saw you," said Keelie. "You're like a thunderstorm on a picnic. You show up when you're not wanted."

"Boom. Boom. Boom," said Elia. Her green eyes held a murderous glint.

"Oh, was that your imitation of thunder? Or was that your brain firing off some neurons?"

"Funny, human," Elia sneered.

"Human? And you're not? At last we agree on something. I know about the elves, Elia."

She flinched but quickly regained her composure. "Listen, just because Sean is singing your praises now—don't get comfortable in your newfound glory. You may be enjoying a momentary glimmer of sunshine, but remember you're the mud girl, and eventually it must rain. You'll have to go back to the slimy mud hole you crawled out of." She smiled and played with a silver ribbon on her frothy pink dress.

"Oh. Mud girl, am I? I may have my feet firmly planted in the soil, but I don't play dirty, as certain nasty people do." Ariel winged toward Keelie, then landed on a cedar tree.

Keelie held out her gloved arm. Ariel came to her, her talons digging into the leather. Keelie thought she saw a small stick person watching her from a nearby holly bush. When she looked again, it was still there. Keelie smiled, but it disappeared into the camouflage of the woods.

"Lass, is everything okay?" Sir Davey came to stand beside Keelie. Louie, the vulture, waddled after him.

Elia frowned when she saw Sir Davey. "I should've known that Keliel Heartwood would take up with your kind, dwarf."

Keelie wanted to smack Elia or make one of the silver doodads on her candy-colored dress fall off for being rude to Sir Davey. "Where do you get off being so nasty to everybody?"

"I'm not, as you say, nasty to everyone. In fact, I'm often praised by my own kind for my ability to socialize with the tourists and still retain a sense of nobility about me." Elia lifted a handful of golden ringlets in one pale hand and tossed them over her delicate shoulder.

Keelie made barfing motions, jabbing her finger into her open mouth.

Sir Davey laughed. "Crude, Mistress Keelie. Your father would disapprove."

She rolled her eyes. "Then don't laugh."

He winked at her, then tilted his nose in the air. Louie hissed and shook his bald head as he stared at Elia.

"Why don't you go and be with your own kind and let the rest of us have a nice day and finish our work," Sir Davey said.

Elia's eyes blazed with anger. "You dare insult me?"

"It's not an insult; it's a suggestion." Sir Davey crossed his arms on his chest.

"A hint," Keelie added.

Elia tucked a long strand of hair behind her ear, and that's when Keelie clearly saw the pointed tip. It was like Sean's and like Dad's. She was reminded that Elia, like her father, was an elf, and Keelie was half-elf. Were they related? What a repugnant thought. And if a half-elf could do the things Keelie could, what was Elia capable of?

Right now Keelie had more important things to do than stand in the middle of Ironmonger's Way and trade insults with Elia.

"Be careful, mud girl. You never know when the wild part of your hawk will take over. She might fly away and never come back," said Elia.

A cold chill of foreboding traveled down Keelie's spine. She walked over to Elia until they were face-to-face, nose tip to nose tip. "Is that a threat?"

Ariel flapped her wings as if saying, I'll take her on.

"No. Just a warning."

"Don't ever threaten Ariel." The wooden heart warmed against her skin.

"Or you'll do what?"

"Step away, Keelie!" shouted Sir Davey.

She did. She could feel small tremors beneath her feet. Colorado didn't have earthquakes, did it? The San Andreas fault couldn't have followed her here.

With a devilish grin on his face, Sir Davey held out his hand and wiggled his fingers. Mounds of dirt erupted in a circle around Elia as earthworms writhed to the surface.

She screamed as she tiptoed around the growing heap of wriggling worms. Wherever her feet touched the ground, a new fountain of worms spewed forth. Sir Davey continued to wiggle his fingers, emitting a wicked chuckle as he did so.

Elia shrieked, lifted her long dress, and ran. Keelie clamped her hands over her ears. Eventually, Elia's screams became less and less piercing as she made her way back to wherever she stayed during the day.

"I guess she's going back to her kind," said Sir Davey.

Keelie laughed.

Sir Davey's happy expression quickly turned serious. "Be wary of her and some of the jousters, and be extra vigilant with Ariel. I didn't like the words that fell from that foul mouth of hers. That one is planning something."

"Yeah, well, I can handle her."

"I think you're right. You may be only half-Elven, but you can do things that she cannot."

"Like what?"

"The tree magic. Her skills are different."

"And scary. Would you walk me back to the shop?"

He bowed. "Milady, 'tis my honor."

Keelie was curious about what she'd just witnessed. As she walked beside the dwarf, she wondered if he would be insulted or if he'd lecture her if she asked. Finally, curiosity won. She blurted, "How did you make the earthworms come out of the ground like that?"

The dwarf studied her with steel gray eyes. "Are you ready to know about such things?"

She studied him for a moment. It would take forever to learn the truth about all the freaky things going on around her.

In the woods, she saw another stick person moving among the cedar tree trunks. This one looked bigger, almost the size of a small dog. The forest folk were getting braver.

How could she live with the truth when she returned to the real world? She'd remembered chasing the fairies when she'd been a small girl. And now she was seeing them again.

"Ah, you're thinking that if you do give voice to all the oddities you've seen and done, it will make them real everywhere you go," Sir Davey said.

Keelie stopped walking. "Okay, I admit it." She placed her hands on her hips. "Because from where I'm from, these things aren't part of the real world."

"What happens to you if you believe they're real?"

Her chest tightened at having to actually speak it out loud. "If I believe that fairies are real, that my dad's cat wears boots and wields a sword, and if I truly believe that

I can feel and see a tree's spirit in the bark of a tree, that makes me not a part of my mom's world. Believing what I thought was imaginary and only possible in children's books takes part of me from my mom and part of her from me."

"Keelie, you'll never lose your mother," Sir Davey said. "She may be gone from this existence. But she lives on in you. She'll be with you every day of your life. As far as believing in magic and fairies and boot-wearing cats, and seeing faces in the trees, you'll have to accept that those things are part of your world, just a part you didn't know about before."

Sir Davey took her hand and patted it reassuringly. "When you face the challenges of this world, be they real or what you claim to be imaginary, then face them with your heart. For everyone who loves you is in your heart. From within your heart comes the magic that makes you who you are."

Keelie realized that she and Sir Davey had arrived at Heartwood. She knew that because she'd opened herself to the magic, she'd made a difference to the forest on the night of the storm. She'd taken a chance. There was room in her heart for Ariel, her mom, and maybe her dad, too. Still, Keelie feared that if she loved anyone else as much as she loved her mom, she would lose her mom bit by bit.

"Don't overdo it, young lady. It takes energy to talk to trees."

Keelie laughed. "And to make earthworms wiggle out of the ground."

"Quite right. Time for me to go and rest up for the day."

"Thank you, Sir Davey."

"Whenever you need help accepting the magic, Keelie, make sure you come talk it over with me. Especially if someone says or does something that might turn your world upside down."

Keelie couldn't imagine what could be more disturbing than seeing faces in trees, touching trees and feeling their spirits, and seeing fairies flying through the air. "I promise."

The dwarf turned around to walk away.

"Sir Davey?"

He stopped and looked at Keelie.

"Are dragons real?"

"The ones I know are all busy posing for illustrators of fairy tales." He waved goodbye.

An owl hooted and distracted Keelie. "What kind of answer is . . . ?"

Keelie turned around. Where was Sir Davey? She looked down the lane. He had disappeared.

Weird. And she thought nothing about the Faire could surprise her any more.

Keelie dragged her body up the flight of stairs to the rooms above her dad's shop. She was exhausted, stinking from bird poop, and grossed out after watching Ariel eat her rat. Cameron said she'd watch her while Keelie attended the meeting. She opened the door, and the yummy smell of pizza greeted her. Dad sat at the kitchen table reading a newspaper. He gazed over it, then lowered it. "Hungry, Keelie?"

She nodded.

He rose from his chair and motioned with his hand. "Sit. You look exhausted."

"I am exhausted." Keelie plopped into the chair. She lowered her head to see if Knot was underneath, waiting to ambush her. He wasn't there. In a perverse way, she was disappointed. She liked scooting him out and watching him glide across the hardwood floor on his butt.

"Right." Her stomach rumbled, reminding her she hadn't eaten since breakfast. She sniffed. "Do I smell pizza?"

"Yes. Cheese. I've been trying to keep it warm till you got home."

"You know, if you had a microwave, you could warm it up if it got cold," she said. "This fast," she added, snapping her fingers.

"No microwave. Messes up the tree vibes. Speaking of which, when you finish eating and before we have to go to the meeting, let's work on the rocking chair."

Downstairs, Keelie watched him work, knowing that he was receiving the strange knowledge that crept through her whenever she touched wood.

She reached out to touch the yellowish cream board Dad held out to her. It smelled faintly of turpentine. Her fingers tingled as she stroked it, and in her mind came the image of a grove of tall pines growing in the hot sun. Bees seemed to buzz around her, but she knew they weren't real, just part of the wood's sleepy memories. "It's pine, from a coast. I can smell the sea."

Dad's face lit up with a smile. "Wondrous. It's Georgia pine, from a forest near Savannah."

He dragged a large branch out from underneath the counter and placed it on top. "Try this one. What can you tell me about it?"

Rubbing the tip of her index finger along the smooth joints of the tree branch, Keelie smiled. "This fell off during a storm from the tiptop of an oak, along with some mistletoe. It used to be a perch for eagles."

Dad grinned. "Amazing. It comes to you as if you'd studied the lore your entire life. Keelie, this is fantastic."

"I think it's creepy."

He laughed. "I guess it could seem so to an outsider. You can imagine why we keep this knowledge to ourselves. In older times, it was cause to be burned at the stake."

Keelie wondered what it would be like to burn at the stake, knowing as you died about the trunk you were tied to and the logs your feet rested on.

Her father's comment pleased and frightened her. Generation to generation in his family. Was she so much a part of him? Would her mother's side fade away under his influence?

"Missing her, aren't you?"

"Yes. A lot." She wasn't surprised that he knew her thoughts. Any weird look on her face could be correctly interpreted the same way.

"I know." Dad swung his body around so Keelie couldn't see his face. Crouching down, he ran his hands along some branches and other pieces of wood on the floor.

"Whenever I need to think things through, I make something. Kind of a Zen-Green thing happens."

"Really. Well, let's get to work." Keelie said.

Dad smoothed sandpaper over the wood of the chair they'd made together. Tall and slender, with a gently dished seat and sturdy legs, it reminded her of her mother. The smooth ash was the color Mom's hair had been, and she'd been just as slim and graceful.

Dad had vetoed the legs Keelie wanted—lithe ones like Mom's—but these made the chair strong, and they were a powerful foundation. The chair was like Mom, but it was a part of her and Dad—their creation.

He looked up from his work. "A final sanding, then an oil finish. What do you think?"

"Beautiful."

He nodded, pleased. "We do good work, daughter."

The phone rang.

Dad answered it. "Hello? Yes, this is Zekeliel Heartwood…You've got to be kidding. You folks said that it would be routed to New York, then on to Colorado…This is absolutely ridiculous. Just get my daughter's luggage to LaGuardia, and I'll have a friend pick it up there."

Keelie's heart plummeted to her feet. Where was her luggage now? Where was her Boo Boo Bunny? Where were the photographs of Mom? She pictured it at the bottom of the Atlantic Ocean alongside the remains of the Titanic.

On the other hand, since when did her sandals-and-whole-grain dad know someone in New York? She was amazed he even knew the word "LaGuardia."

Dad hung up the phone. "It seems your luggage has been routed to Greenland."

"Greenland. As in the Arctic Circle? As in the North Pole?"

"We'll get your things, eventually. Don't worry."

"I'll try not to. I'm going to get a quick shower before the meeting."

Keelie dressed in her bedroom, brushing cat hair from her clothes. She hadn't had time to take her clothes to the Swiss Miss Chalet. Somehow Knot had slipped inside the wardrobe and was asleep on her handbag.

Her cell phone rang. Keelie's heart thumped against her chest. It would be Laurie calling to firm up plans for the Great Escape. She reached for the bag. Knot hissed, ears flattened against his head, and he swatted at Keelie.

"Bad Knot. Give me back my bag." He swished his tail. "I still haven't forgiven you for stinking up my underwear."

He glared at her. The phone stopped ringing. "Fine. Be that way."

The cat licked his bottom.

Keelie pulled the bag out from underneath Knot, and he tumbled to the floor. He landed on all fours. His purring thrummed through the room. "What is with you? Every time I'm mean to you, you like it. Sicko kitty."

The cat rubbed up against her leg. She moved him out of the way with her foot. He went sliding across the floor on his belly.

"I've got to go. By the way, when you squat like that, you look like a furry-headed toad."

The cat's eyes dilated to dark moon orbs. His purring increased.

"Get over it, you grody cat."

She opened the door, and Knot shot past her. He thumped his way down the steps, stopped, and sat on the bottom step as if waiting for her. She looked down at him; he swished his tail back and forth.

She walked down the steps past him and into the shop.

"Dad, make your cat go away. He's leering at me."

"Knot. Behave."

Knot walked over to the oak tree in front of the shop and began sharpening his claws.

The Poacher's Inn was fast filling with the Faire folk. Keelie settled next to Dad, leaning against the wooden fence. Cedar.

Elianard glared at her as Elia primped, looking bored. Tania prattled on and on about Admin's threat to close down the Faire permanently if repairs weren't made to the booths immediately. Even though there was only two weeks left of the High Mountain Renaissance Faire, a lot of merchants and craftsmen depended on the income earned in those remaining two weeks to carry them over to the next Faire.

Keelie pressed her back against the fence, watching Knot, who had perched on top of the old-fashioned bar that wrapped around the building's exterior. He had his head stuck out, doing a vulture impersonation, eyes glued to Sir Davey's new companion, Louie the turkey vulture. Louie didn't realize he was being made fun of.

Raven represented the herb shop while Janice cleaned up the mess back home. Raven had no idea how lucky she was to have her mom.

Elia fanned herself with her hand and sneered at Keelie. Behind her, Elianard seemed to be muttering.

Ha! Keelie remembered that according to Sir Davey, she was much more powerful than Elia.

A whiff of rot came with the breeze that blew through the porch of the Poacher's Inn. The heart pendant became warm and tingled against her skin. Something pushed against the sole of Keelie's shoe, and she moved her foot, stepping aside and sweeping her skirts up. A small sapling was pushing up from the board. Keelie watched, shocked, as it sprouted limbs and green needles popped out and unfurled along each edge. The smell of fresh cedar filled the air.

Keelie quickly covered the growing tree with her skirts and looked around to see if anyone had noticed. Elianard was staring at the tip of her shoe, which was peeping out from her skirt. He looked as if he thought a grizzly bear was about to jump out from her petticoat. Or a Red Cap.

Her alarm was going off.

Something poked her in the back. She smelled cedar and groaned, not daring to turn around. She tapped Zeke on the arm.

"Dad, we have a problem." She moved her skirts. His mouth dropped open as he looked at the cedar branch growing from the floor. "That's not all." She moved her shoulder to show him the branch that had sprouted from the fence.

"How?"

Keelie lifted her hands up in an I-don't-know-what-I-did gesture.

Raven came over to stand beside Keelie. Her friend stared at the tree branch with a perplexed look on her face. "That's new."

Then she motioned nonchalantly with her hand. "Listen, everyone is going to go on and on about Admin. Been here, done this. Meet me at the herb shop in about an hour. They're having a sale at the Shimmy Shack, and we can snap up the bargains before the mundanes snatch them up this weekend."

"Cool. That'll give me time to go and check on Ariel."

Keelie whispered to her dad. "Do you mind if I go and check on Ariel and then go with Raven to a sale at the Shimmy Shack?"

Dad looked up from the branch, and he nodded absentmindedly. "That sounds like a good idea."

As the two girls walked away from the deck, they could hear the next speaker's droning voice.

"You've saved my life, Raven. I think I would have died of boredom."

"The bodies will be thick in there. As a survivor of previous Faire meetings, let me warn you—run, do not walk, next time one is announced."

At the mews, Keelie said goodbye to Raven, who headed toward her mother's shop to get her money. Keelie had put hers in her belt pouch that morning. Cameron was walking around with Moon on her shoulder. She'd stayed behind to monitor the repairs in progress.

"Hey, Cameron."

"Hi, Keelie."

"I thought I'd let Ariel fly while I went over to the Shimmy Shack. I think she's got a boyfriend around because there's another hawk flying nearby."

Cameron stopped and looked up. "That's not good."

"Why not? I think it's cute."

"Keelie, Ariel is half-blind. She cannot hunt for herself, let alone defend herself from another hawk if it attacked her."

"What do you mean?"

"Mate or kill. If this hawk is territorial, it's not after making friends. It'll want Ariel gone or dead. Keelie, Ariel can never be free."

Never be free. Keelie looked at the half-blind hawk and thought of her plans to escape to California. She could take Ariel with her. She thought of the hawk living among the palm trees and malls, or her old neighborhood, where flowering shrubs were the tallest vegetation.

She'd be miserable, just as Keelie was here. But was she? She'd made friends, she had her father, and the trees were counting on her to protect them from the dark magic. Zeke couldn't do it alone.

When had she stopped being miserable?

fifteen

Confused, Keelie hurried to Janice's shop to find Raven. She could talk to Raven, who had one foot in both worlds, too.

Knot stalked her as she walked. He snuck from tree trunk to tree trunk, then disappeared. Tarl walked down the path, arms full of stained and bedraggled fairy wings. Another Muck and Mire denizen followed with a similar load.

Tarl grinned. "Good morrow, Keelie."

"What are you doing with those?" Keelie had heard

that the poor girl who ran the fairy wing cart was devastated because all of her stock was ruined in the storm.

"I bought 'em all for the Muck and Mire Show. Dirt cheap."

"Dirt cheap. I get it. Ha."

"We can give you a part in our new show: Midsummer Night's Mud. You can be Slime Mudfairy."

"Pass, but thanks for the invite."

"If you ever change your mind, you know where to find us." The two squelched on down the path.

If you liked mud, this place was heaven. The sky had darkened again, guaranteeing even more puddles and goo.

Raven was standing in the door of the herb shop, which was partially covered with a blue tarp. She waved at Keelie. "Hey, can you give me a second? I've got to run an errand for Mom."

"Sure." Keelie welcomed the chance to go into the fragrant shop. She spotted an orange tail dangling from a tree branch by the door, swinging back and forth like a pendulum. The rest of the psycho kitty was concealed in the leaves. She remembered the Cheshire Cat from *Alice in Wonderland*, whose grin was the last thing to disappear.

It would have been a shorter book if the cat had peed in Alice's luggage.

Keelie ignored him. Why couldn't she have a normal cat? No, wait. It wasn't her cat. He belonged to Dad. If she were to get a pet, it would be a normal animal. Of course, a wildebeest would be normal, compared to Knot.

The herb shop door was propped open, and Keelie stepped inside. "Janice? It's me, Keelie," she called.

She rubbed her fingers on her skirt to make them stop tingling. The shop door was made from pine. She sniffed deeply, eager for the scent and healing energy of the herbs. She coughed. The shop smelled like bleach and rotten mushrooms. The storm had destroyed the atmosphere.

Janice appeared with a large lit candle embedded with herbs. She walked slowly so as not to disturb the flame. "What a mess, huh? We had to throw everything out, and it still smells." She placed the lit candle on a table.

"Can I do something to help you?" Keelie asked.

"There are more candles in the back. Bring them up, and we'll light them here."

The back of the shop still had a roof. Plastic bags full of herbs lined shelves, and a row of china dishes held fat pillar candles. Keelie stacked three on top of each other, grabbed a box of matches that was on the table next to them, and walked back to the front room.

Lighting the candles reminded her of her mother, who enjoyed eating by candlelight. She remembered her mother's face, glowing across the table in the golden light. She knew that Mom had a stressful day if she served dinner on the little table for two under the windchimes on the patio. The candle flames would flicker and dance, an echo of the fireflies that hovered around the flowers at the back fence.

She wondered now if those fireflies had really been bugs. Her mother certainly would have wanted her to think so.

Janice interrupted her thoughts. "It looks like Knot followed you. He's sitting on my back porch washing himself. What did you do to deserve such an escort?"

Keelie hurried to the front door of the shop and glanced across the lane, but the orange tail had disappeared. "I don't know. I keep telling him he's gross, but he just purrs and purrs."

A big smile flowed across Janice's face. "That's because you're an animal lover. I heard that you helped save Cameron's birds."

Keelie's smile faded. "Yes. Have you heard how the guys who went to the hospital are doing?"

"Their injuries are healing well, but they're under psychiatric observation. They told their doctors that they were chased and bitten by the Red Cap." Janice rolled her eyes.

Keelie stopped breathing for a moment. "Were they?"

"They had bite marks on their arms and legs." Janice sighed. "They're seasonal employees, you know. College students. They don't know any better. But I told your father earlier that this is worrisome because the Red Cap allowed itself to be seen. Those boys are so lucky to be alive."

"You think the Red Cap was going to kill them?" Keelie remembered the evil laughter and the hands pushing her under water. It was going to kill her too, but Knot stopped it.

"The Red Cap is very dangerous. And no one knows why it's here. Another mystery is why it came into my shop, of all places."

"It was here?" Of course. The rotten mushrooms that Raven had shoveled out were a sure sign. "Are you guys in danger?"

Janice bit her lip. "Raven will be going back to school soon, and I'll be leaving, too. There's no way I can get my herbs back up or the smell out of here in the two weeks left.

So I'm leaving in a few days. I have to make sure the shop is repaired and winterized before I go. But we'll see each other again. I'll be in New York, and you and your dad will be there in about three weeks." Janice's smile was maternal. Keelie stepped toward her, sinking into her embrace.

Janice smelled of herbs and comfort, canceling the bleach and rot. A rush of warmth coursed through Keelie before guilt hit her like a cement truck. What would Janice think of her when she left? There would be no New York.

"Hey, almost forgot. I've got something for you." She hurried to the back of the shop and returned with a cobalt blue bottle with a dropper lid.

"Here's a tincture for your chlorophyll poisoning. Three drops in the morning whenever you feel like you've had too much tree loving."

She had to ask something before her heart grew any bigger and shoved Mom out.

"Janice, remember when you mentioned that your mother died when you were young? Have you forgotten her over the years?"

Janice's bracelets jangled as she reached to touch Keelie's shoulder. "Oh, baby. No. I never, ever forgot my mother. I think about her every day. I miss her even though I'm forty-five years old. I will always be her daughter. She will always be my mother. Nobody can replace her. Just like no one can replace your mom. It takes time to heal from the pain of losing someone, but when the pain fades, the good memories stay."

"What if I change? What if I become so different from

the girl that Mom loved that she wouldn't love the new me that I become?"

Janice brushed a curl from Keelie's forehead. "Your mother would know you if she were to walk in right now. She would love you even if you allow yourself to love your father. Even in your new garb, looking like a fairy tale princess from the Renaissance, she'd love you."

"Would she love me even if I were to believe that magic is real, and that I can see the stick fairies? Would she love me if I can feel the spirit in a tree? Would she love me if I saw Knot wearing boots and waving a sword?"

Janice hugged Keelie. "Oh yes, she would. She would love you just because you are her daughter. She loved your father, and you're part of your father. There is nothing you could do to stop that love."

Those words broke the lock on the box that contained Keelie's pain. The words spilled out fast, as if she were afraid if she stopped she'd never say them. "I yelled at Mom the morning she flew away. She didn't want me to have my belly button pierced. I told her I didn't love her, that she was mean. She was late for her flight, and she said we would talk about it when she came home. She told me she loved me, but I didn't answer her."

Janice hugged her. "Let it go, baby. Let it go. Your mother knows that you love her. Moms always know that their daughters love them, even when they argue. Understand this: if your life turns out differently from the one your mother envisioned for you, it's still your life, not hers. Don't live her life. Her gift to you, and your father's gift to you, is your own life. She would want you to be happy."

Rubbing a tear away from her cheek, Keelie wished she was having this talk with her father. Would he understand?

"How did you know what I'm thinking?"

"I didn't. I guessed. My mother wanted me to be a doctor because of all of my experience with cancer. I didn't want to do the Western-medical route. I had an intuitive gift for herbs. Therefore, I followed my heart, and I am doing what my mother wanted—but my way."

"Mom was pretty tough about school and becoming a lawyer."

"Maybe you can find a way to blend some of what your mom wanted with what you want."

Raven stuck her head in the door. "Ready for Shimmy shopping? Are you guys having an Oprah moment? What did I miss?"

Keelie laughed, embarrassed, and wiped her tears away. "Not cool, am I?"

Raven grinned. "Muck and Mire clothes are uncool. You ditched them."

"You should see the fairy wings Tarl got for his troupe."

"No way." Raven laughed. She put a hand to her forehead. "Let's go shopping. I've got to get that image out of my mind."

"Keelie, you can come talk to me anytime about your mom or about anything." Janice patted her arm.

"I think I'll be taking you up on that offer."

Unless she was gone on Sunday.

Exotic incense filled the air around the Shimmy Shack, and as Raven opened the door a wave of hypnotic drumbeats rolled out. Raven snapped her fingers and circled her hips as she walked into a room filled with the chatter of many voices.

Keelie froze on the doorstep, struck by the colors that filled the room. It was like being inside a rainbow, like Aladdin's cave, like another world.

The single open room was heated by a wood stove, making the inside toasty warm and dry. Incense filled the air, drifting up in thin plumes from burners throughout the large room. Rugs and large pillows covered the floor, occupied by girls who leafed through magazines, painted designs on each other's hands, and in general made noise.

The space behind a richly painted screen in a corner served as a dressing room. A furry orange tail stuck out from underneath it. The pervo cat was watching people undress. She made a note not to dress around him anymore.

The walls held pegs covered in colorful silk scarves arranged by hue. Mirrored and jeweled skirts, spangled bras, and fringed costumes were on one side of the store, while the other one held the tribal costumes in dark shades. Reds, blues, and greens accented black. A counter was stacked with henna kits for painting faces and hands.

Keelie examined everything, fascinated.

A tall woman with wavy, dark hair, wearing a sparkly coin-embellished top and low-slung red skirt, jingled toward them on bare feet. "Raven, your veil came in."

"I was hoping it had." Raven followed the woman, who ducked behind a wooden counter and pulled out a folded square. Keelie watched as Raven unfurled the cloth with a flick of her wrist, then held it in the fingertips of both hands and swirled it gracefully around her body.

"Wow." Keelie wondered how much practice it took to move so perfectly.

"Keelie, this is Aviva. She owns this fabulous place."

Keelie smiled, thinking a handshake somehow didn't fit the tone of this store.

Aviva grinned at her. "So you're Heartwood's heir. I've heard good things about you, Keliel."

"Thanks." Did everyone know her weird name? Aviva. This was the person Raven said had lost the ring. Keelie fished the silver circle from the leather pouch slung around her waist. "Is this yours?"

Raven stared it at, eyes wide. "That's your ring."

"It sure is." Aviva held her hand out for it. Keelie dropped it onto her palm.

"I found it in the woods yesterday."

"I never go into the woods." Aviva eyed her suspiciously. "You wouldn't happen to know where Zak's MP3 player is, would you?"

"Aviva, shut up. You lost the ring in the Shire. Keelie's only been there once, the first night she was here. Whoever found it—"

"—stole it."

"—or could have dropped it in the woods."

Aviva dropped her gaze from Raven's furious eyes. "You're right. I'm sorry, Keelie. Thanks for finding my ring."

"Yeah, any time."

"Hey, stop!"

Heads turned at the yell from behind the screen. Knot had squeezed out from under it, a gold tassel in his mouth. He looked around, wild-eyed, then ran for the door, ducking through it just as it banged shut behind the newcomer, a startled woman who dropped the bundle she was carrying.

"Knot, come back." Keelie ran to the doorway, leaping over the bundle and pushing aside the woman in her haste to catch up with the cat. She saw his orange tail above the tall grass on the other side of the path, like a flag.

"Stop, you moron cat. That's not yours." She ran through the grass and back onto the path on the other side of the little meadow. She passed the destroyed fairy-wing cart, empty of its ruined and now-reincarnated merchandise, the archery stand, a couple of food stands that were busy with the sounds of electric saws and the smell of cut wood, then up past the kiddie area and the smell of sheep at the petting zoo. Knot bounded ahead, the tassel flying behind him as he raced up the path.

What was he planning to do with it? He just wanted her to chase him, stupid furball. Sir Davey stared, astonished, as they shot past, and then they went beyond the herb shop and the bookseller, and up Wood Row to the clearing.

She knew where he was headed now. And she waved at Scott as she ran through Heartwood, trying to cut Knot off at the stairs. But he was too fast for her, and he was at the top of the outside staircase and through the kitty door before she set a foot on the second step.

That tassel had better be in good shape, because she

sure wasn't paying for it. She banged the door shut behind her and yelled for the cat.

"You'd better give it up, klepto kitty. You've embarrassed me for the last time." She looked under her bed and behind the sofa. Not in the bathroom, nor the kitchen. A wet spot on the floor drew her eye. A pawprint. And then she saw others, headed to her dad's room. The wet ground had given him away.

She pulled the curtain aside softly, and then screamed, "No!"

Knot was squatting in the opened bottom drawer of her father's nightstand, about to do his worst.

sixteen

"Get out of there, Knot." Keelie spoke sternly, using her mother's lawyer voice. "You are so dead if you pee in Dad's drawer. And I won't be doing the killing, either."

He blinked at her, green eyes half-closed, tassel dangling from the side of his mouth like a drooping gold cigar.

She reached for him, and he leaped past her, dropping the tassel. She picked it up with her fingertips to avoid the drool he'd left on it.

It seemed to be okay. She turned to close the drawer in case Knot decided to return, and stopped. A book of photographs lay on top of a white folded blanket. It looked old, but smelled familiar. So familiar that tears came to her eyes. It smelled like Mom.

Keelie sat on the floor, resting her back against the side of her father's bed. She put the photograph book on her lap and reached for the white blanket, except that it wasn't a blanket, it was a finely crotcheted shawl. She wrapped herself in it, pulling it up around her shoulders and to her cheeks, as if Mom was hugging her again. She closed her eyes and let herself go—let herself cry for the face she'd never see again.

When she could think again, she opened the book randomly. It was a photographic chronicle of her life. She turned the pages, amazed at the pictures. How did Dad get all of these? Each photo was neatly labeled in her mother's precise handwriting. Mom had assembled this book. Mom had made this for him.

She turned back to the beginning. The first photograph was of a very young version of Mom with long golden hair down her back. She wore a lacy, medieval-looking wedding dress with a long jeweled belt. Whoa, was that a garland of flowers in Mom's hair? Keelie smiled. Mom would be so embarrassed to know she was seeing this early version of her.

Dad stood next to her in the photo, his long dark hair pulled back into a ponytail. Weird, but he seemed exactly the same today. He hadn't aged at all. To Mom's left was Grandmother Josephine in a dark suit with her usual fluffy white blouse, and by Dad's side was a woman with long, rippling gray and silver hair tucked behind obviously pointed ears. Her hair was held by a thin crown of silver wire. Her beautiful green chiffon dress was embroidered in a scrolling silver design. Keelie looked closely. Leaves. What else?

She stared at the picture, a slice of time long ago. Mom looked so happy. She had her arms through Dad's and gazed up at him, a smile on her face. It was obvious that she really loved him, at least early on. What had changed?

Keelie stroked the slick paper of the photograph as if she could really touch her mother. *Mom, why did you take me away from him? Why did you break up our family?*

She'd never know. Her dad knew his version of the truth, and Mom's was gone forever.

In the second photo, Mom sat cross-legged on the floor beside a baby with a riot of dark curls. Smiling, Keelie touched the baby's hair. Dang, her hair had been doing the wild puffy 'do even then. On the other side of the curly-haired baby, Dad waved a stuffed dog, trying to get her attention, a goofy smile on his face. The baby was focused on her blocks, ignoring both parents.

Keelie brought the picture closer. Her baby blocks seemed to have been made from cherry wood. She slapped her hand against her forehead. She was becoming wood obsessed. Was she going to I.D. every piece of wood everywhere for the rest of her life?

Another photo showed Keelie, a little older, sitting in Dad's lap, holding a baby doll. Keelie smiled. The baby doll had pointed ears. Where had it come from? Dad's smile was just as goofy as the one in the other pictures. This was a guy in love: in love with his wife, in love with his baby.

It occurred to her that sometimes when he thought she wasn't watching him watch her, he still got that goofy smile on his face.

She looked up toward the ceiling. If Mom was hanging out on a cloud with the other angels, Keelie wanted her to come down and talk to her. To answer her questions. She closed her eyes. When she opened them, she was still alone in her father's bedroom.

She shivered, although the cool mountain morning was no colder than usual. The shawl had come loose while she looked at the photos and she wrapped it tighter. Maybe it was just psychological, but she felt warmer, safer.

She had a few more days to decide if she belonged in Dad's world or whether she would return to the world her mother had given her. A third choice came to her. Dad could come to California. Not L.A., but maybe the wooded hills of the north. They could be a family again, and Ariel could live with them.

She'd still be close to her friends, and to all the memories she'd made with her mom and Grandmother Josephine, but she wasn't sure anymore whether she belonged there. She'd been certain of the answer when she'd arrived at the Faire, but not anymore.

The thought made Keelie restless. Maybe she needed a walk to clear her head. She had decisions to make about her life. And she wanted to know more about being an elf. It was a big step to go from preppy California kid to finding out she wasn't all the way human, talking to trees and fighting evil forces in the forest. It sounded like the plot of a video game, but it was her life.

If she did go with Addie to California, Keelie knew she would break Dad's heart. They had gotten so close after all these years of being apart.

But hadn't *he* left Keelie with Mom all those years ago? Sporadic letters from Renaissance festivals across the country, toys shipped for Christmas via UPS. That wasn't parenting. He hadn't been there for the really hard stuff. For when her tooth got knocked out rollerblading, or when the boy she had a crush on had asked her to a dance, then didn't show up to take her. Mom had been there. She'd understood.

A faraway voice in her head asked, *What about the time you saw the thing in the forest, and Mom told you it wasn't there?* But it was. And Mom had seen it too. And it was not a white horse, either, not with that giant horn.

Keelie felt a sudden urge to be outside among the trees. She wrapped the shawl tighter around her shoulders. Feeling very different from the Keelie Heartwood who had tried to catch up with Ms. Talbot only the week before, she stepped out onto the landing of the outside stairs.

What had changed her? Dad? Ariel? Certainly not that hateful cat. She'd also developed an obsession for wood and craved to be around living trees. If she went back to Los Angeles, she would have the beach, but only foreign transplants, palm trees, and scrub to talk to. She wondered what kinds of faces they had. Maybe she could grow an herb garden to satisfy her need for greenery, or buy a sapling.

Keelie wiggled her bare toes, smiling. Sir Davey had said that working in the mud would make the magic bypass her mind and tap into her heart. Maybe walking barefoot on dirt would do the same thing. Maybe she should go to the meadow to talk to the aspen. She remembered the pulse of energy it had sent through her when she'd touched Moon.

Right about now, Keelie could use some of that healing energy for herself.

Her phone rang inside. She followed the sound to where her bag was on the floor by her bed, and of course, Knot had shed his fur all over it.

"Hello," she answered.

"Hey. All plans are in place for the Great Escape."

Keelie didn't want to think about the Great Escape, not when she was planning the Great Compromise.

"Can we talk tomorrow? Dad's calling me."

"Dad? I thought he was Father, the troll, the old man, the sperm donor."

"Tomorrow. We'll finalize the plans."

"Okay, Keelie. Tomorrow." Laurie sounded mad at her.

Keelie shoved the phone under her pillow, then wrapped the shawl tighter around her, feeling guilty. Knot was on the bed, glaring at her with his weird green swamp-gas eyes. He hissed.

"Shut up, you old masochist. I'm not paying for that tassel, either. Wait till I tell Dad."

Zeke called her from outside.

Knot's fur rose in a lion's ruff.

"Chill, furball. I'm not going anywhere."

Knot hissed again, unmollified, and backed up a step as if readying for an attack.

"Shut up, psycho kitty."

His purr cranked up.

"Hey, didn't you hear me calling you?" Dad stood by her curtained doorway. He stared at the shawl.

"Dad, I can explain."

"Please do." His gaze shifted to Knot, who'd fallen flat to the bed and was pretending to be asleep.

"It's his fault." Keelie jabbed a finger at the cat. "He stole a tassel from the Shimmy Shack, and I chased him to get it back, and then he was in your room, and I thought he was going to pee in your drawer, so I was just protecting your stuff."

"I see."

"And when Knot left, I saw the book of pictures and the shawl. And it smelled so much like Mom. . ."

His voice softened. "I see." He turned away for a second, then looked back at her. His eyes seemed brighter, as if he was holding back tears. "Keep it. I was going to give it to you anyway."

"Thanks. Why were you calling me?"

"You got a box from my mother. Your grandmother. Let's open it and see what she sent."

Keelie followed him to the living room, remembering what Dad had told Sir Davey about her being "the one." And whatever that was, her grandmother wouldn't accept it. She thought of Elia's taunt about half-humans, and Elianard calling her a half-breed. Was her grandmother like that, too?

"Let's open the box." Dad cut the brown wrapping paper, and a strong smell like cinnamon drifted around the room. Keelie recoiled. It smelled like Elianard. She picked up the paper wrapper and smoothed it out. The return address read "Dread Forest, Oregon." Could she live in a place called the Dread Forest?

She watched Dad open the box and looked inside. "Wow. You want to see what your grandmother sent you?"

"There's nothing in there that might bite?" No telling, around here.

"No." He laughed and ruffled her curls with his hand, as if she was a little kid. She smoothed them back down and leaned over to look in the box.

"Dad, what if instead of living in the Dread Forest we lived in northern California, you know, where the big redwoods are?"

"Our home is the Dread Forest." He looked at her curiously. "Why are you asking?"

"If we lived in California, I'd be near my friends, and we could still live in a forest. I could even take care of Ariel. We could be a family."

"We're already a family, Keelie. And your grandmother lives in Oregon. We have a lot of family there, actually."

"Maybe you do, but I don't. I haven't had a single birthday card, or phone call, or *damn, you're still alive* from her since—um, let me think—oh yeah, my entire life." She was yelling, and she hadn't meant to.

Dad stared at her. "Where did that come from?"

"You are so clueless. We are not a family. Mom was my family. We're starting out, but that doesn't mean you can tuck me into your little woodland world like a chipmunk or something. I'm not a tree. You are not *my* shepherd."

"I never said I was. I'm your father." He was yelling now, too.

"Quit yelling."

"I didn't start it, you did."

"Oh grow up. You are such a Peter Pan with your groupies and your elfie ways. All granola and oatmeal and ceremonies with the trees. I need to get out of here. I need to touch some concrete. See you later."

"Where are you going? Come back here. We're not finished."

"Oh, we so are." She slammed the door on her way out, but it clicked shut so she opened it and slammed it harder.

As she stormed down the stairs, she saw Knot in her window, his mouth hanging open in kitty shock. And that made her feel great. She stuck her tongue out at him and headed for the Shire.

She needed human companionship. If there wasn't a party on, she'd get one started.

Scott started to say something to her, then turned around and walked the other way. She glanced at the mirror over a table in the shop. Blotchy and swollen around the eyes. Fabulous. Sean would fall to his knees when he saw her—and throw up.

The sky was roiling again, a perfect reflection of her feelings. She needed some thunder, some lightning. At the bottom of the hill she saw the bridge and slowed, remembering the Red Cap. Maybe she shouldn't be alone out here. And she should have brought her cloak.

She stepped onto the bridge, expecting to hear the

voice beneath it, but she heard only the water gurgling through the rocks. The grass was slick and muddy all the way up to the bridge, and mushrooms dotted the banks.

Keelie shuddered. The Red Cap had been here, probably after the storm that had flooded the stream. Where was the creature that had saved her? And what was it?

The logical conclusion, since this was Water Sprite Lane, was that it was the sprite herself.

"Hello? Sprite? I wanted to thank you for the other day. You saved my life." No answer.

She stepped off the path and walked downstream, looking at the water going around the trees that bent over the creek. The bank was higher here, and below she could see sandy areas, little beaches that marked sediment deposits.

She would have loved to play here when she was a little girl. At the next bend in the creek, she saw a movement near the water. A big fish was gasping, beached on the sandy shore.

"Poor thing. I'll save you." It might have been too late, but she jumped down, holding on to roots as she went.

The fish turned large brown eyes to her and gasped her name.

Keelie backed up, banging her head on a tree root. Aspen. Something crawled onto her shoulder from the ferns that hung over the bank. She froze, hoping it wasn't a snake or a big bug. The mossy face that looked at her from an inch away seemed familiar now.

"Bhata."

The stick seemed pleased. An arm like pine needles scratched gently at her cheek, the other pointing at the fish.

Keelie knelt by the fish. It blinked up at her, long whiskers at either side of a wide, lipless mouth, and held up a thin, bony arm with three webbed fingers on a small hand. "Keeliel."

"Sprite?"

It closed its eyes, then opened them again.

"It is you. Are you hurt? Can I put you back in the water? What can I do to help you?"

At the edges of her sight she saw that other stick fairies had come, as well as some of the buggy ones, the ones her dad had called by another name. The banks were filling with them.

She hesitated, then put a hand out and pushed at the sprite, grimacing at its cold, clammy fishiness. *Ew.*

The sprite cried out, and the little arms wrapped around her wrist, its sticky fingers grasping at her skin. Keelie was torn between screaming, running, and helping the poor thing.

Sympathy won. She looked around for something she could use like a back board, and she saw the aspen above her, its slender trunk rising toward the tree canopy, its roots partially exposed by erosion.

Keelie pulled off her charred heart pendant and wrapped it around the sprite. Nothing happened. Her eyes on the sprite, she reached behind her and grasped a thick root.

The world turned green. In the meadow yards away, she saw Hrok, and beyond him, on the large rock, was

Sir Davey, surrounded by scientific equipment, busily working.

She looked down at the sprite. "Heal."

Nothing happened. She thought of the night in the meadow when she had healed Moon. Did it have to be a particular tree?

Hrok, help me.

Let go of your shields, Keliel Tree Talker. Let the magic flow through you. Release your fear.

What fear? The sprite was kind of gross, but she wasn't afraid of it. What was she afraid of? The Red Cap. Her father's anger. Herself. Her plans. Her future. What she had become.

No, what she had always been. It was the truth she feared. And what was that? That she wasn't totally human. But that her parents had acted all too humanly. They'd loved each other and had given up that love for her. And now she was planning to leave her father.

She couldn't go back to California. She wasn't the same Keelie anymore. She was Keliel Tree Talker, the Tree Shepherd's daughter. She had to discover what that meant. That would be her life from now on.

A rush of green energy pulsed through the root, burning her muscles as it scorched its way to her other arm and down, down, filling the sprite. Keelie tried to release it, afraid so much energy would hurt the little being, but it held her tight in its grip, getting stronger, taking in the magic like an oxygen-starved swimmer.

Around her the air buzzed and clicked with excited

fairies. Finally, the strange, sticky fingers released their hold on her, and she let go of the root.

The sprite vanished, leaving the charred heart pendant on the sand.

Keelie picked it up and wiped the grit off of it. The sprite was nowhere to be seen. "Ingrate," she muttered.

And then the *bhata* attacked her.

seventeen

Keelie climbed the roots, her long dress bunched over her arms, thanking the aspen as she went and keeping her face in the crook of her elbow so that the *bhata* couldn't scratch her face or get at her eyes.

When she had her feet back on the ground, she ran, skirts lifted, grateful for the big sleeves that kept the clicking stick things from getting on her arms. Before she reached the path, a swarm of bugs came from the bridge and she veered, heading toward the meadow. The bugs caught up with her quickly, and they clung to her hair, digging at her scalp and pinching her neck.

Her skin buzzed with their magic, and she felt queasy from the chlorophyll she channeled to save the sprite. She quickened her pace, and then the queasiness turned into fear as she hit the outer edge of the Dread. Her chest felt tight, and she felt as if the woods were closing in on her.

The *bhata* clicked and pinched their way into her clothes. Keelie screamed and yanked the hem of her gown up and over her head. The *bhata* that had covered it were enfolded in the discarded gown, but others took their place.

"Sir Davey," she cried. "Help."

He turned, his mouth sagging open as he saw what pursued her. "Up here, lass. Hurry."

Hurry? Was she strolling? She leaped the last few feet and grabbed the rock, her feet scrabbling for purchase on its lichen encrusted sides.

Sir Davey pulled her up to the top of the rock. The *bhata* that had been all over her had gone, but the buggy ones still hovered. Davey stared at them. "The *feithid daoine*. You don't see them often."

"I'd rather not see them at all. I don't know what I did to piss them off, but they swarmed me like I'd attacked their honey or something."

"Where?"

Keelie told him about the sprite and about calling on Hrok and the aspen to save it.

"And the sprite vanished, you say?"

"Yes." The wind had picked up, bringing the scent of rain.

Davey noticed, too. "This rock isn't the safest place to be in a lightning storm. We'd better get you back home."

"What is all this stuff?" The rock was covered with boxes, huge chunks of crystals with wires attached to them, and a metal disk that swirled around atop a wooden pole staked into a pitted hole in the rock. It looked like an elementary school science experiment.

"There's bad magic right here somewhere. It's elusive, and I'm trying to track it down."

"Bad magic? You need equipment to find bad magic? It chased me all the way from the creek."

Sir Davey looked up from his equipment, caterpillar eyebrows wiggling. "That's not bad magic, lass. That's just the *feithid daoine*."

"*Feta* what? I can never remember that. The stick people are the *bhata*, right?"

"Right."

"They started it. They hate me."

"They were probably trying to tell you something."

"Yeah, like that they hate me. Message received, loud and clear," she yelled across the meadow.

The metal disk at the top of the pole started spinning around, and the crystals started to glow. Sir Davey looked at them. "Uh-oh."

"What does it mean?"

"Incoming. Duck." He pushed her down just as lightning flashed overhead.

Keelie heard the Red Cap's maniacal song. "Do you hear that?"

"No, what?" Sir Davey was adjusting dials. "You'd better get back home, Keelie."

Keelie thought of her angry father and the awful things she'd said to him. Dad or the Red Cap? Either way, she was toast. She clutched the charred heart.

The air turned green, but it was thick, like syrup. She closed her eyes and pushed at it with her mind, and felt Hrok nearby, but nothing else. Hrok cried out a warning.

She opened her eyes and saw that the wind had whipped up forest debris, which hung in the air. Moss near her opened a mouth to cry. The *bhata* were being whirled around the meadow like a tornado of sticks and leaves.

Movement on the ground drew her gaze. It was Elianard, she could have sworn, but he was hurrying away through the trees. And then another movement, faster, toward her, and that smell! Cinnamon and mushrooms, two smells guaranteed to make her gag for the rest of her life. The horrid combination clogged her nose.

The Red Cap attacked Sir Davey, and they rolled off the rock and onto the ground. The Red Cap's mouth opened impossibly wide, like a giant toad's but lined with cruel teeth. Its eyes were on Keelie, laughing, as it started to suck Sir Davey's aura from him. Fog-like tendrils the color of bronze shimmered as the creature pulled.

Keelie crawled off of the rock, grabbing a crystal to bash the Red Cap with. But the Red Cap had grown powerful on his feast of Davey's life force. The *bhata* fell from the sky around her as their energy was sucked into the Red Cap, creating a vortex of death around him.

She fell, and a finger of lightning struck the ground

nearby. The electricity made her hair prickle, and it danced on her skin. Pellets of rain beat down on her, and thunder rumbled, the sound increasing until it was deafening.

Her mouth was full of dirt. She spat, thinking of Earth magic, and her chest burned. She reached up to push away whatever was burning her, but it wasn't an ember. It was her necklace. The charred heart was glowing green, and it beat with the rhythm of forest sap, the bright glow of summer.

Keelie crawled forward and pushed the heart into the Red Cap's mouth. It screamed, gnashing its teeth, and backed away. She dragged herself toward it, surrounded by a green glow as she passed the *bhata*, revived and flying upwards.

She could feel the trees around her, a solid company that covered the meadow and the hills. All the trees were with her, and she grabbed Sir Davey and pushed his remaining energy into the greenness. Perhaps he would die. Perhaps he was dead already.

Beneath her, the ground trembled. She felt it ripple beneath her. What had she done?

The Red Cap snapped its teeth and stood, then with fiery eyes locked on hers, it began to sing. Keelie caught a glint of silver in its teeth. The necklace!

Behind the Red Cap, the earth bubbled, the way it had when Sir Davey had called upon the worms to frighten Elia.

The bubbling widened, and roots shot out of the earth, wriggling into the air as if something deep underground was seeking purchase in the storm.

Keelie held tight to Sir Davey as the Red Cap drew nearer. One of the roots lashed out, knocking him down. The charred heart rolled free, and Keelie reached for it. The Red Cap's jagged teeth snapped at her, snagging her sleeve and scratching her. She caught the chain and pulled it free, her arm burning from the creature's bite. Was he poisonous?

He turned, growling, and stopped as a great book appeared on the heaving earth's surface. Caked mud crumbled from the binding that glowed bright with silver, even in the gloom of the storm, revealing a design of thorns surrounded by rays. In her head, she felt her father's energy joining the trees. He channeled even more energy, drawing tree power from the surrounding mountain.

The Red Cap screamed and dove for the book. Another root slashed at him. He bit it in two.

Behind her, Keelie heard a cry and, thinking her father had come, turned to warn him. But it was Elianard, and his eyes were fixed on the book.

Keelie clutched the charred heart. No way could she reach the Red Cap before he got the book.

Throw it, Keelie. Her father's voice echoed in her head.

I can't. Sir Davey is hurt. He's dying, Dad.

You have to do this. Throw the heart. Try to hit the book.

She let go of Sir Davey and struggled to her feet, staggering from the Dread and the dark magic. She pulled her right arm back and threw the charred heart as hard as she could, her eyes on the bright thorns of the book cover. The green-glowing heart arced over the Red Cap's head and landed on the dirt by the book, then rolled backwards onto it. Silver shone green just as the Red Cap reached out and touched it.

Lightning forked to the ground, blinding Keelie. She cried in pain and flew backwards, hurled by the explosion of the bolt. Trees screamed as their roots burned, and she hit, hard. Then all was black.

Keelie came awake to grayness. She opened her eyes. The darkness was punctuated by flashes of red. Fire trucks. A crowd had gathered. Dad's face appeared above her.

"You're awake." He looked concerned and overjoyed. A weird mix.

"What happened?" She couldn't smell smoke, so the forest wasn't on fire. "Sir Davey?"

"His eyebrows are scorched, but he's okay."

"The Red Cap?" She wished she could speak in complete sentences, but her throat hurt so much she could barely croak out the words.

"Gone. Scorched. All that's left is a crater with a book cover and a red cap. We, ah, removed them before the fire department got here."

"My head hurts."

"You got knocked down pretty hard. How does your left arm feel?"

She moved it. "Sore. Okay, I guess."

Her dad picked up her arm and held it up so that she could see. A crisscross of deep scars covered her forearm. It looked like a long-healed wound.

"The Red Cap bit me. But it's healed." She stared at her forearm, amazed.

"The trees did it. It's why Sir Davey survived."

"The Red Cap was sucking his life force. Like the sprite."

"Yes, the sprite. You've made a lot of friends, daughter. The sprite called on the *bhata* and the *feithid daoine* to warn you."

"I thought they were attacking me."

"I have something for you." Dad opened her hand and dropped something into it. Something rough and rounded.

She looked into her cupped hand. A little lump of silver—all that remained of her melted chain—and the charred heart. The Queen Aspen had saved them all.

eighteen

Standing atop the Heartwood steps, Keelie gazed up at the starlit sky as fireflies flickered around her. She wrapped Mom's shawl tighter around her shoulders. The leaves of the trees sang a rustling song of peace. From above, a purr thrummed an accompaniment. Keelie glanced up at the hunched feline shape silhouetted against the sky.

She glanced into the apartment where Dad slept on the couch, a green pillow with silver trees covering his face. He'd had several mugs of mead with Sir Davey, claiming it soothed his ragged fatherly nerves. And the pirates had been there, too, outdrinking everyone at the Poacher's Inn.

A gentle breeze lifted her hair. The scent of flowers mingled with cinnamon. Keelie looked around. Elf smell. Was it Elia? Someone stood in the overhang of Dad's shop and then stepped forward until he stood in the glow of the indoor lights. Sean. He placed his finger against his lips and motioned with his hand for her to come down. Keelie's heart fluttered. What was he doing here?

Dad's snores still puffed out from underneath the pillow. She shouldn't wake him up. He deserved his rest.

Fireflies lit her way. Restraining herself from running down the wide wooden steps, she took slow, precise steps. Mom had advised her not to seem too eager when she met her dates. Keep an air of mystery about you, she'd said. Keelie rubbed her palms against her pants legs, just in case they were sweaty.

Sean held out his hand, and she put her hand in his, gracefully, as she'd seen Elia do.

"What brings you here?"

He wore an embroidered shirt, very Elven-looking, over jeans. His fashion combined the human and Elven world. Just like she did.

"I came to see you, fair maiden."

Delight tingled up her spine.

"Walk with me to the jousting ring." He clasped her hand inside his.

Was there a party there? "Okay. We'll stay on the path, right?"

A knowing smile spread across his narrow, handsome face. "Of course."

Neither spoke as they walked, but it was comfortable, and Keelie enjoyed feeling his skin against hers. After a while the silence had become like a sound. She racked her brain to think of something clever to say. She wanted to be witty, to impress Sean with her intellect, because after dating Elia, a smart girl would be a refreshing change.

Keelie had drawn down lightning, bested a Red Cap, and saved the Faire, but she couldn't think of anything to say.

"Everyone's talking about what you did today. You were very brave. You saved a lot of lives."

She smiled, partly at his compliment and partly because he'd been the first to speak. "Thank you." She wanted him to kiss her. She really, really liked him, and she might never get another chance. And then, of course, if Elia found out that Sean had kissed Keelie, it would send the snarky elf girl into a tailspin of mega proportions.

More silence. Fireflies flickered, and the wind danced through the trees. Keelie could feel their green humming as they rejoiced in the disappearance of the dark magic. She couldn't see them, but she knew the *bhata* and the *feithid daione* were in the woods celebrating, too. Her skin vibrated in tune with their magic.

They passed the armory. It was dark and quiet now, unlike the weekends when the blacksmith's hammer clanged against steel as he made swords, expensive souvenirs for mundanes to buy.

Sean stopped and turned to her. It was dark, but a soft glow from a safety light atop a pole illumined his face.

Something warm and furry rubbed up against Keelie's leg. Knot had followed them. Sean rubbed the tip of his finger against her cheek. She leaned forward, waiting for the kiss that was sure to follow. Being this close to him was exciting.

She remembered the night at the Shire when Captain Randy had sat so close to her, touching her breast, and how she hadn't wanted him to stop. It'd felt so good to feel his body pressed against hers, and Keelie wanted to feel that with Sean. More, because Sean was someone she could actually date.

He lowered his face to hers. He was really going to kiss her. She lifted her head, anticipating the feel of his lips on hers.

Knot snagged his claws into her pants leg, making her gasp and pull back. A sharp kitty shiv scraped her skin. She forced herself to ignore the pain. She wanted to stay in this moment with Sean. She wiggled her leg in attempt to dislodge the demonic feline. He wasn't budging.

"Are you okay?" Sean looked concerned.

Her cheeks were hot with embarrassment. She pointed down. "Knot." The cat's eyes glowed as he glared up at Sean.

She whispered, "You are going to be an orange kitty-fur muff." Knot arched his back and hissed, but backed away.

Sean smiled and leaned closer to her, then his lips gently pressed against hers. A shiver fluttered down her back, and her heart beat faster. When Sean pulled away, his forehead wrinkled and he forced a smile on his face. Keelie felt her stomach butterflies turn to nausea. He was disappointed in her kiss. She'd done something wrong.

Crestfallen, Keelie leaned against the fence railing for support. Oak from North Dakota. "Is something wrong?"

He lifted his knee to reveal Knot attached to his leg. Knot's tail swished back and forth, and he was doing a weird psycho cat growl. Keelie bopped him on the head. "Get down."

He purred.

"He was your mother's guardian." Sean said it as if it explained the weird behavior. "He's protecting you now."

"What kind of a guardian?"

Sean shook his leg in an attempt to dislodge the mental-case cat. "I remember when he'd attack anyone he thought was a threat to her. He's mellowed out quite a bit since then."

Keelie said, "Wow. You must have been five when Mom married Dad. What a memory."

"No, that was only fifteen years ago." Sean smiled down at her. "I was seventy," he added casually.

Keelie reeled and was glad she was leaning against the rail. Otherwise, she would've fallen down with shock. She mentally added seventy and fifteen, and blurted out the answer. "You're eighty-five years old!" The image of a pruny, wrinkled old man formed in her mind.

Sean nodded. Knot de-snagged himself from Sean's pants leg, jumped to the ground, and sauntered off with his tail at full mast. Sean appeared relieved. "I'm one of the youngest elves to be permitted to work with the horses.

And I think when I ask your father for permission to court you, he'll be impressed." He noticed her expression and frowned. "I said something wrong."

"No. Everything's fine." Keelie wondered if he was joking, but he wasn't the kind of person to play a trick like that.

An awkward silence hung between them, like an invisible curtain.

"May I still court you?"

"I have no idea what that means. I'm so confused." She rubbed her hand across her forehead. Sean didn't look eighty-five. He looked hunky and nineteen, and her body was getting a delightful tingle looking at him, except for the number eighty-five that kept flashing across her mind. She envisioned wrinkled hands covered in brown spots, sparse hair, halting steps. None of those were here. What did it mean about her aging process? She was a human-elf hybrid. Would she live half an elf lifetime? A normal human lifetime? Did anyone know?

Dad had a lot of questions to answer.

"Sean, would you walk me back to Heartwood? I've got to talk to my father."

"Your father did not tell you." It wasn't a question. Sean's eyes widened as he read the answer on her face. "I think he's in for a long night."

They walked back up the path, and Sean's fingers touched her hand, as if asking permission to do more. She let his fingers curl around hers, then pressed his hand lightly.

A curious thought came to Keelie, and she had to ask it. "Sean, if you're eighty-five, how old is Elia?"

He grinned, as if he'd been expecting the question. "She's only sixty. But be wary of her. I think she plans to do something to you. She has not taken kindly to the respect that some of the elves now have toward you."

"What does that mean?"

He sighed. "There are those who consider you an abomination because of your human blood, but others have reconsidered their opinion."

Stunned, Keelie said, "How generous of them." An abomination? She was beginning to dislike her father's side of the family more and more. No wonder Mom hightailed it out of the woods. Keelie wrapped the shawl more tightly around her with her free hand.

As Sean and Keelie walked, holding hands, the only sound around was the crunching of their feet on gravelly sand. Fireflies danced around them, and she wondered now if they were really bugs.

Sean's revelation about his age hadn't disturbed her as much as the thought that the elves didn't like her, and all because of her heritage. She wanted to calm down and enjoy the moment with Sean. It had been hard enough to accept the fact that he was an elf, and she supposed the age thing just went with it. She wondered what other surprises awaited her. Like, if Sean was eighty-five, how old was her father?

If this was Keelie's new reality, she wanted all the facts. Power to talk to trees—check. Targeted by mean red-capped gnomes—check. Not quite human—check. What hadn't they told her? At school they taught her that information was power, and she needed information now.

They stopped at the base of the stairs, and Knot ran between them. He stopped midway up the stairs, his tail slashing back and forth as if to hurry them up. Great, she was learning cat-tail language.

Sean towered over her. She wondered if he was going to kiss her again, and went up one step to make it easier for him. Just in case. So far, this might have been the best night of her life. She couldn't wait to tell Laurie everything. Everything but the elf part.

Sean held her chin lightly in his fingers so that she couldn't look away. "When we first met, I tried to convince myself that the feelings I had toward you were brotherly, but it wasn't true. It hasn't been for a while. I want to be more to you than a brother."

She shivered, wondering why Knot growled menacingly. "Knot, shut up." The cat was wrecking her moment. She grabbed the handrail, seeking reassurance in the familiar wood.

Sean placed his hand atop hers. "After this night, I'll be watching over you, too. When the Faire ends, our paths will part, but we'll meet again in the Dread Forest. I'll be thinking of you, Keliel Heartwood. Hopefully you'll allow me to steal more kisses before the Faire ends."

Knot hissed. Keelie put a hand behind her back, made a fist, and shook it at him.

"You don't have to steal them. They're yours, Sean." She pulled her hand out from under his and put it on his chest, leaning forward to kiss him.

Sean put his arms around her, and she closed her eyes, feeling the warm softness of his lips on hers, the strength of his arms around her. She didn't have any experience, but he sure did. Eighty-five years' worth. The thought must have made her move back, because he kissed her cheek.

"Good night, Keelie."

She opened her eyes to see Sean walking away into the darkness. Eighty-five years old. What was she getting into?

An orange blur followed him. Things wouldn't be so dreadful in the Dread Forest. She just had to get over this age thing.

Upstairs, Keelie lifted the green pillow from her father's face and smacked him on the legs with it. He bolted up. "What? Keelie, are you all right?"

She placed her hands on her hips. "We need to talk. Now!"

■ ■ ■

Keelie liked her new look. The mirror reflected a curly-haired brunette with fashionable flair. Maybe Mom would have enjoyed the way Keelie had redone Renaissance flair with contemporary touches.

Her cool new boots were an old pair of her mother's that Dad had saved for all these years. They fit her perfectly.

She thought she looked great, except for the dirt under her nails. She could almost hear Mom's voice saying, "Keelie, what were you thinking? You need a manicure."

Keelie put a hand over her heart. "You're here, Mom; I'll love you forever."

Keelie and Dad had talked for hours. He'd answered some of her questions, although she was still confused.

"Keelie, wait up." Raven jogged toward her, wearing some of her new clothes, too. "I heard you were out with Sean last night. Elia is so mad she can't stand it."

"Yeah?" Keelie felt a mixture of fear and joy. She was afraid of what Elia would do, but it was great that she was suffering. She tried to dredge up a little pity for the elf girl, but none came.

Keelie was grateful that Raven didn't bring up Keelie's abrupt departure from the belly dance shop. "So she's really mad?"

"Sure enough. So far today, she's pulled her best friend's hair, slapped one of the members of the Royal Court, and pitched a fit in front of the Rose Arbor." Raven laughed. "Everyone is enjoying it so much. We've never seen her this angry before."

"I wonder how she found out." She either had a spy in the woods or Sean had told her. Or Elia herself had followed them. That last one didn't seem likely.

She thought of sixty-year-old Elia. She didn't know how much Raven knew, but she was pretty sure that some aspects of the elves' lives, including maybe that they were elves, weren't shared with humans. Zeke had told her that she would age a lot slower than most humans, but she wasn't going to live to be five hundred years old, like her grandmother.

Her dad sure didn't look 327 years old. He looked good.

And Dad said the plus side was that as Keelie aged, she wouldn't get wrinkles. So she'd never have a Botox face.

Raven headed back to her mom's shop, and Keelie went on to the mews, still thinking about the elves. Now that their problems were over, the trees weren't talking. They might know something that she could do to help Ariel. Maybe the oak in the meadow would let her know, although she wasn't excited about returning to the meadow.

At the mews, Keelie slipped her hand into the leather gauntlet and opened Ariel's cage. Ariel called out and flapped her wings. Keelie could not accept that Ariel would never be free. If there wasn't a medical way to heal her, maybe some form of magic would.

Ariel hopped onto Keelie's wrist.

Cameron popped up from behind the cages. "Hey. Just cleaning cages." She smiled when she saw the hawk on Keelie's wrist. "You work wonders with her. She knows when you're coming."

Ariel rubbed her feathery head against Keelie's cheek. Her golden eye glinted and her head bobbed up and down, as if sensing something different about her human best friend. Keelie wished she could talk to hawks, too.

Cameron chattered on. "And who would've thought that Sir Davey and Louie would've bonded the way they have."

Keelie said, "I'm going to look in on Sir Davey. I'll check on Louie, too."

"Thanks."

Outside the mews, Keelie released Ariel, who winged to the aspen trees near the Dragon Horde Shop. Her right wing brushed a tree and she careened toward the ground, then recovered and flapped back up onto a branch.

Arms pressed her shoulders. Keelie didn't turn. Her tear-filled eyes were on the hawk.

"We'll have to decide soon, Keelie. Is it fair to keep her in a cage for the rest of her life?"

Keelie didn't want to hear Cameron's sympathy. "There has to be a way to help her." She closed her eyes and tapped into the trees. "Watch her."

The leaves in the tree rustled in reply.

Ariel followed her, flying from tree to tree until she got to the Dragon Horde. "Don't go too far," she cautioned.

The shop windows glittered with crystals. She sniffed. Coffee. Sir Davey had brewed his headache-eradicating blend. She heard a moan from the back of the shop and hurried toward the location of the sound.

Sir Davey sat on his little couch with a huge chunk of hematite pressed against his forehead. Louie perched on the sofa's edge with his beady eyes fixed on Sir Davey.

He opened his eyes. "I'm dying, lass. My head won't stop pounding, and whenever I look up, I see this harbinger of death looming above me. He's waiting for me to die."

Keelie said, "You need to get up and move around. Get the bloodstream going. It worked for me."

Sir Davey moaned. "You were touched by magic. I brought this on myself."

She went to the kitchen. She poured coffee, thick and strong, into an earthenware mug and took it to him.

Louie spread his wings as Sir Davey sat up and accepted it. "The room won't stop spinning."

"Drink your coffee. It helps. Trust me. I know."

"I guess you do, lass. No side effects from last night?"

"No. I'm fine."

"You look different. I think it's your eyes. They seem more Elven than human. As if you know things that others don't."

"I had a long talk with my dad. By the way, how old are you?"

Sir Davey chuckled into his coffee mug just as he was about to take a sip. He winced as he swallowed. "Aye, learned about the age thing, did you?"

"Yes. So, how old are you?"

"Old enough to know better and young enough not to stop." He put a finger in the air as if testing the wind.

"You're not going to tell me."

"No. I have to have some secrets. Keep an air of mystery about me. Ladies like that." He waggled his steel gray caterpillar eyebrows up and down, then winced again.

Keelie stood. "You're not off the hook about this, but get some sleep."

Louie settled back down on the edge of the sofa. Sir Davey closed his eyes and pulled the coverlet up to his chin. "You did good, Keelie."

She turned out the light. "I know."

Outside, the early afternoon sun was bright, and the air was crisp and clean. She raised her face, allowing the soothing warmth to cover her. It was the comfort of a hot bath, as opposed to the feel of Sean's lips on hers.

Sean had said he'd wanted more than friendship, and she was ready to explore that avenue, too, regardless of his age.

Keelie climbed Ironmonger's Way to the herb shop, where she noticed that the blue tarp had been replaced with a brand-new door. The scent of lavender wafted from the shop.

Aviva was walking around the building. She blushed when she saw Keelie and hurried past her. Try and be nice, and some people have to be mean about it.

She knocked on the front door. "You guys open for business yet?"

Raven opened the door. It was unlocked. "How's Sir Davey?"

"Hung over. He'll live. You want to come up to Heartwood?"

"I can't. We've got more cleaning to do. And Mom keeps burning candles. The shop's going to violate anti-smoking ordinances pretty soon. I'll be heading down to the Shimmy Shack later if you want to join me."

Keelie dug into her pocket and pulled out a five-dollar bill. "Will you pay for Knot's tassel? I feel really bad about it. And I hope Aviva doesn't think I took her ring. I saw her just now, and she didn't exactly look friendly."

Raven waved her hand. "Forget her. I was so mad at her, and I let her know in no uncertain terms that's no way to treat a really good frend of mine. Besides, you returned the ring. What planet is she from?"

"She could be like Elia, an el—"

"An elf like Elia? No, Aviva's been smoking and partying too much at the Shire. And I know all about the elf thing, kid."

Keelie grinned. "Raven, you know everything."

"Hold on. I've got something for you." Raven ran into the back and returned with a small box. "Open it."

"What is it?"

"It's a present, doofus."

Keelie removed the lid and pulled out a string of gold tassels. She laughed. "Thanks, I think."

Raven shrugged. "Didn't seem fair for Knot to get one, especially after you chased him. I figured you really wanted that tassel."

"*Knot* so." Keelie tried to keep her face straight.

Raven swatted her arm. "Stop it, or I'll have to kill you. Hey, there's a really big party down at the Shire tonight. Word is out that the pirates have set up their own tent in celebration of Captain Dandy Randy. Seems our Don Satterfield sold a software game he created to one of the big companies."

"So, all that time he spent in his mother's basement playing video games paid off? Good for him."

"Want to go? I'll be your personal security guard if you do. The pirates won't mess with you. Unless you want them to, of course."

"I'd love to go. I knew there was more to Captain Donald than his cute booty."

Raven rolled her eyes. "When we get to the New York Faire, I'll show you around. They really know how to throw a party at Rivendell."

"Rivendell? Is that the name of the town?"

"It's from *The Lord of the Rings*, California girl."

Everything seemed to be from *The Lord of the Rings*. She'd have to read that book.

"See you tonight around nine."

"See ya."

Ariel skimmed over Keelie's head as she walked up King's Way. The stained-glass shop was closed, and Ariel landed in the cedar trees between it and the front gate. The hairs on the back of Keelie's neck prickled. She looked around, but she didn't see anything unusual. She'd gotten the same feeling from the Red Cap, but he was definitely gone.

Ariel perched on a tall cedar branch and watched her.

Keelie stared at the pay phones. She needed to do this. Laurie would need to know that the Great Escape was off. There was no going back to California for Keelie now. Her life was with Dad and Ariel. She was no longer the same person who had walked through the gates, although Mom's girl was still there, inside of her.

Keelie pulled some quarters from her pouch and dropped them into the pay phone's coin slot. She dialed Laurie's number.

"Hello?" Her friend's voice seemed so normal, and brought back memories of what normal had been for her in California.

"Laurie, it's me, Keelie."

Keelie had to hold the phone away from her ear to protect her hearing from Laurie's loud shriek.

"Oh. My. God. I thought you were never going to call. I mean like I've been trying to call you for ages and ages and ages."

"What are you talking about? I've been talking to you every other day about the Great Escape. You need to call your cousin Addie and tell her that Sunday is off."

"What cousin Addie? What are you taking about? I haven't talked to you since you called that night from some pay phone. I mean, that's so desperate. Calling collect on the pay phone."

The hairs on the back of Keelie's neck were at full alert. She sensed a tinge of the dark magic she'd experienced with the Red Cap.

"Hey, Keelie, are you there?" Laurie's voice asked, but she sounded faraway.

Elia stood underneath the cedar trees. She put her thumb and index finger against her ear and mimicked a phone call, then smiled broadly.

Keelie swallowed. She'd been had. Elf girl was toast.

"Laurie, I'll call you later. I've got to go."

"Okay, but call me back really soon. I have to tell you all about Constance's new boyfriend, and the really cool shirt she bought at La Jolie Rouge. It's to die for."

"Bye, Laurie." Keelie hung up, and the receiver clunked back into place.

A beating of wings alerted Keelie in time to thrust her leather-covered arm into the air. Ariel landed on her wrist.

Keelie's skin crawled with the green tree energy. "*Beware.*"

Elia stood much closer, eyes small and slitted, staring at Keelie and Ariel. How had she done that? Keelie didn't see her move. "You should've left when you had the chance," Elia said.

Keelie lifted Ariel closer. The hawk shifted uneasily. She stroked the bird's smooth, feathered back, comforting her. "I'm not leaving, Elia. I belong with my father."

"You are a mistake. Half human. Like your stupid bird. We Elves know what to do with mistakes. We fix them." The air around them shimmered. Keelie shivered. It felt like magic, but not like the warm tree magic. This was more like fingernails scratching inside her skin.

Ariel cried out and tried to flap her wings, then fell to one side. Keelie grabbed her and pulled her close. The hawk hung limply in her arms.

"What did you do to her?" Keelie asked, frightened.

"She's not dead. I cursed her, that's all."

"Cursed her how? Take it off."

"Make me." Elia backed away, smiling. "That's right, you can't—human. Now this will prove to everyone that you're not so special. You're a half-breed mongrel."

Suddenly, Ariel was awake, her head whipping back and forth. Her beak scratched Keelie, drawing blood.

Keelie cried out, but not because of the pain. As the hawk turned her head, she'd noticed the reason for her distress. Both of the hawk's eyes were now milky white. She was completely blind.

Elia shrieked when a fuzzy orange ball yowled and leapt from the gabled roof of the stained-glass shop onto her golden curls; it seemed as if Knot had fused himself to her head. She ran down King's Way screaming and swatting at Knot, who clung to her head as if he were a rodeo bronco buster.

Keelie watched as Janice removed the poultice from Ariel's eye. After twenty-four hours of Janice's, Cameron's, and Sir Davey's careful nursing, the hawk was still blind.

Raven had hovered near Keelie off and on, encouraging Keelie to go to the pirate party. But she'd stayed with Ariel. Elia was so going to pay for what she did.

"Honey, we've tried everything," Janice said. "I've made every recipe for eye injuries that I know."

Sir Davey said in a very solemn voice. "I've used every healing spell I know, lass, but I can't break an Elven curse."

She lifted the hawk onto her leather-covered forearm. Keelie leaned against the mew's wooden partition fence. She brought Ariel close to her face, and the hawk rubbed her head against Keelie's cheek. The downy softness reminded her of Mom's goodnight kisses. Being near Keelie was the only thing that calmed Ariel, and she'd stopped eating.

Janice seemed about to say something else, but she was suddenly quiet. Keelie looked up. Cameron was walking toward them, and her dad was with her. Keelie's throat tightened.

Cameron looked at her, and Ariel. "Keelie, we need to talk."

Keelie couldn't answer. Her heart beat faster. She knew where this was going.

Ariel opened her wings, and Keelie forced herself to relax her clenched fists.

Zeke reached out to take Keelie's free hand.

"Dad, Elia did this."

Dad lowered his voice. "I know, and she'll have to face

the Elven council for her actions. Elianard has reassured them that he will see to Elia's punishment."

Keelie wanted to barf. "Elianard isn't going to punish her. I think I saw him racing the Red Cap for that book, and when Elia zapped me, I felt a tinge of dark magic."

Dad said, "All the more reason to wait it out. I think this goes deeper than Elianard, and for whatever reason, your destiny is tied up with it. We have to be careful. You have to promise me you will not go near Elia and confront her about Ariel. It's not the Elven way. The council will resume discussions in New York. Elianard and Elia will be there, too. When we go to New York, we'll take Ariel with us and take care of her. I promise you I'll do what I can to find a cure to restore the hawk's sight. There are ancient Elven texts in the Dread Forest that could hold the answer."

Keelie sighed. "Dad, I won't go near Elia, but if she comes near Ariel in New York, then I will use whatever magic I can wield to protect her. That's the human way."

epilogue

Where was her luggage? Keelie stood in front of the Swiss Miss Chalet. She'd accepted the fact that Dad was an Elf with magical powers, and that she herself was half-Elven, but the stylish California girl in Keelie balked at the curlicue-decorated wooden house on the back of the rusted pickup truck.

Stuff was bulging out of every window, and her father was using what must have been some pretty awful Elven words as he worked to store it all.

"You're going to have to get a bigger camper," she yelled to him.

He leaned out a window and looked down at her. "This will expand. I've just got to add more space over the cab."

"Dad. No. It's going to look like something from a *Mother Goose* book. You know, the crooked house down the crooked lane? Except this one will be the crooked house on wheels."

"I think you're going to have to share Knot's bunk."

She thought of his reindeer-embellished, fleece-lined kitty bed. Where was he?

A horn honked, and driving up in a plume of dirt was a small pickup truck loaded down with pirates in full costume. The truck stopped in front of Keelie. All of the pirates in the bed of the truck raised up their mugs of ale and *argghed* in unison.

Captain Dandy Randy was driving. He stared straight at her with a lusty glint in his eyes, then he made smoochie kisses at her. Keelie placed her hands on her hips and made smoochie lips back at him. She could play the part of a pirate wench. He placed his pirate hat on top of his head and opened the truck door. His booted feet crunched on the parking lot gravel.

He swaggered up to Keelie. The other pirates whooped and hollered in the back of the pickup and held up their mugs of ale. Several hearty "hail, maties" were issued.

Captain Dandy Randy winked at Keelie. "I've returned a fellow pirate to ye, seeing as you're about to set sail."

He opened the passenger door. A furry orange lump on four legs stepped out. He had a red bandana tied around his ears, and he purred as he walked past Keelie. His tail was at full mast. "Knot?" Keelie asked.

Captain Dandy Randy nodded. "True pirate at heart. Drank several tankards of mead with me and the crew. We'll miss him. We're here to send him off."

Knot hopped into the cab of Dad's pickup. She spun around. "Hey, *I'm* riding shotgun, furball."

She turned and smiled at Captain Randy. "Congratulations on your program."

"Thank you." She saw a shy young man under the pirate personae. He lifted his head and smiled at her.

"Are you going to New York?"

He shook his head. "Maybe. Lady Raven will be working on the marketing for me new program."

Keelie smiled. "Cool. Well, if I don't see you in New York, I guess I'll see you next year." He saluted and turned around, then stopped and gazed at Keelie with those lusty pirate eyes. He said, "What the hell?"

He walked over to Keelie, wrapped his arms around her, lowered her back, and planted a kiss on the lips—a deep kiss, with swirly tongue and all. There were more whoops and whistles coming from his fellow pirates.

He hoisted her back up. She stood, stunned. "Remember me, lass," and he swaggered back. All the pirates cheered him. Captain Randy cranked his truck and drove away in a plume of dust.

Keelie said, "Wild."

Dad was beside her. "What was that all about?"

She shrugged. "Pirates. You never know with them."

She strolled away, humming "Yo, ho, ho."

Dad yelled out, "Well, stay away from them."

In the truck cab, Knot sat on the passenger-side seat

next to the window, as if he was ready to travel to New York. The kitty kerchief was gone.

Keelie walked over to him. "Take your spot in the new food chain, kitty. I'm going to ride next to the window. If I don't, I'll get carsick, and I might throw up all over your fur."

The cat lowered his body onto the seat, tucked his front legs beneath him, and began purring. It sounded like a challenge.

A California Airlines truck drove up and came to an abrupt halt. Keelie felt a shiver of anticipation trill up her spine. Her luggage. It had to be. She wanted to jump up and down, but instead leaned against the truck's cab. No telling if Sean might walk up.

The delivery man sprang out, and Keelie knew from his open-mouthed reaction that he'd never seen anything like the camper.

He looked at her, then back at the wooden house on the back of Dad's truck. "That looks like a ski lodge on wheels."

"I know," said Keelie. "Go ahead and yodel if you want to."

If Raven was here, they could break into a song from *The Sound of Music*, the musical she and Laurie had performed with the drama club last year.

"I've got a delivery for Keelie Heartwood."

"That's me," Keelie said. She wanted to scream "Yes!" and pump her fist in victory. Her luggage was here.

Her dad stuck his head out of the camper window. "Is that what I think it is?"

The delivery man unloaded several large boxes with

stickers of different ports of call, then asked her to sign his electronic clipboard.

Keelie signed, but her eyes were on her father, who surveyed the number and size of the boxes. His face turned pasty pale. Ha! He might have to trade in his house on wheels for a Winnebago. She envisioned one like the rock stars traveled in, with a shower and a television. She wondered if they were hard to drive.

The delivery man pointed toward the camper. "Man, that's a work of art. I've never seen such detail in wood."

Dad's color returned to normal. He stood up straighter. "Thank you, good sir," he said, bowing courteously. The delivery man gave him a weird look.

Visions of satellite television and rock-star tour bus luxuries faded away as her dad commandeered space in other campers for the boxes.

After the delivery man left, Janice, Sir Davey, and Scott all arrived with their campers and trailers to pick up boxes before hitting the road. Sir Davey did drive a Winnebago, a nice new one. She pointed it out to her dad.

"That's what I'm talking about. Modern comforts."

His answer was a disdainful eyebrow lift.

Janice drove up in a Jeep Wagoneer. Raven had a pissed-off expression. Plus, it was early in the morning. She exited the Wagoneer.

"What's wrong with you?" Keelie asked.

"Mom. We're going to some forest to pick some wild herb. Oh boy, a week in the woods stooped over, digging up some pungent green plant to make some stinky tincture."

Keelie tried not to laugh. It was hard to envision Raven out in the woods.

"Look," Keelie said. "There's Cameron. She has Ariel and Louie. She's got all the permits and stuff to carry them across the states."

Cameron was driving a huge RV a lot like Sir Davey's, except hers had flying raptors airbrushed on the sides. She stopped. Keelie stood on tiptoes, peeking, hoping to get a glimpse of the hawk. "How's Ariel?"

"Missing you, but she'll be fine. Okay, kiddo, we'll see you in New York," Cameron said.

Dad stepped up. "Cameron, we'll rendezvous with you at the Wildewood Festival."

"I'll see you two there," Cameron said.

Keelie and Dad backed up. "Bye, Cameron. Bye, Ariel. Bye, Louie," shouted Keelie as the raptor bus disappeared in a cloud of dust. Keelie tried not to be sad; she would see Ariel in a couple of days.

Dad had quickly loaded most of the boxes, except for the smallest, which he put in the Swiss Miss Chalet. Keelie couldn't wait to dig out Mom's pictures and Boo Boo Bunny.

Sir Davey contemplated the back of the overflowing Swiss Miss Chalet. He rubbed his goatee with his index finger and thumb.

"You know, Zeke, you may need to talk to that friend that I bought my Winnebago from when you arrive in New York. You've got to remember that Keelie is going to need lots of room."

Keelie bent down and hugged Sir Davey. "Oh, thank

you. I sure don't want to share a bunk with Knot. He sheds. Worse, he drools."

"Sure. And nobody wants to share anything with Knot." Sir Davey wiggled his gray eyebrows up and down. "And Knot's not big on sharing."

Dad rolled his eyes heavenward. "I can expand the camper to increase the room inside."

Janice placed her arm around Keelie. "Zeke. At least consider talking to Dave's friend in New York." She squeezed her, then whispered, "We'll see you soon."

Raven rolled her eyes heavenward. "Think of me in nature. We're definitely going shopping when I return to the real world."

Keelie nodded.

Janice sighed. "Get in the car, Raven."

"I don't want a cavern on wheels," Dad said.

Keelie stopped. She had to consider that last comment. Did Dad literally mean that? Dwarves liked the Earth. Did the inside of Sir Davey's Winnebago look like a cavern? She looked at the big Winnebago, dying for a peek inside.

"He's got deals on Forest Glades with all the modern comforts," Davey said.

Dad threw his hands up in surrender and then glanced at Keelie. "We'll talk about it on our way there."

Keelie skipped over to him and kissed him on the cheek. "Thanks, Dad."

Janice honked her horn, and Raven leaned out the window and waved as her mom drove away.

Keelie waved back.

Sir Davey loaded up three of Keelie's boxes, and she saw that he was a little misty-eyed.

"I'll see you at the Faire," she said. She bent down and kissed him on the cheek.

He smiled. "Take care of yourself and Zeke. He's mourning the loss of your mom, too. He loved her, and don't let anyone tell you different—like some high-minded elves we know."

"Sir Davey, is this the camper my mom and dad lived in when I was a baby?"

He nodded. "That's why your dad is having a hard time letting go of it. Your mom loved the gingerbread trim."

He hopped into his Winnebago, cranked it, and drove away.

Keelie looked at Dad's weird camper. She watched her dad lock the back door and smiled. She'd lived in this camper with her mom and dad as a family. She could live in it a little longer.

"Hey Dad, so what can you do to expand this ski chalet?"

Her reward was an answering smile and a look of relief. *I could have gotten that Winnebago*, she thought, watching him. *I was this close.*

Dad came to Keelie. "I have something for you. You remembered when you asked me to save it?" He pulled an aspen branch from the back of the ski chalet. "I found it when Scott was packing up. It was leftover after we made the chair."

She said, "Thanks." The slender stick was dry and worthless, but Keelie had something in mind. It was perfect for the experiment she was thinking of. "Dad, I need a few minutes."

He nodded. "I'll be here."

She hurried to the meadow. The crater left by the lightning blast had been backfilled by Admin, leaving a big raw patch in the grass. Keelie walked to the middle of the blackish brown area, so alien in the middle of all that green. She felt the trees watching her, and the others, the forest folk. She stuck the twig into the ground, deep enough that it was only thigh-high.

"Hrok, I've brought you a companion. I hope." She grasped the dead twig and with the other hand held the charred heart, which hung around her neck. Sean had given her a new chain when he'd said goodbye. He'd kissed her and told her to hold his kiss in her heart till they met again. She thought of the Queen Aspen's sacrifice. Had she brought the tornado and the lightning down upon herself?

The tree's heart warmed in her hand. She pushed the energy down her arm. It grew easier each time she did it. The hand that held the twig tingled as the life-giving force sizzled down through the twig and into the ground. The dirt around it moved, and hundreds of rounded threads poked up, unfurling into grass.

Keelie was disappointed. She'd wanted the wand to take root and be a companion for Hrok, a piece of the Queen Aspen come back to life. At least she'd greened up the place a little. The dirt patch had been like a scabbed knee, ugly and painful to look at.

She walked away, stopping to run her hand over Hrok's bark. *Goodbye, my friend. See you next year.*

Fare you well, Keliel Tree Talker. May you grow many rings.

She felt him in her mind, the energy in his sap, his branches upheld to the sun, and the tickling of his leaves in the breeze. And around him, the others of the forest. And one more, a new one, though not a baby. She turned, mouth open. A single leaf had unfurled from the tip of the twig.

The Queen Aspen's branch lived.

As they left Colorado, Keelie saw Uncle Harry Mac's Tattoo and Body Piercing Shop, its bright neon lights muted in the sunlight.

Half-Elven she may be, but the California girl that was her mom's daughter hadn't forgotten the belly button ring.

There had to be a tattoo and body piercing parlor somewhere near the Faire site in New York, and she would make it her quest to find it.

About Gillian Summers

A forest dweller, Gillian was raised by gypsies at a Renaissance Faire. She likes knitting, hot soup, costumes, and adores oatmeal—especially in the form of cookies. She loathes concrete, but tolerates it if it means attending a science fiction convention. She's an obsessive collector of beads, recipes, knitting needles, and tarot cards, and admits to reading *InStyle* Magazine. You can find her in her north Georgia cabin, where she lives with her large, friendly dogs and obnoxious cats, and at www.gilliansummers.com

Look for Book II of the Faire Folke Trilogy in Summer 2008.